JIM HANVEY, DETECTIVE

OCTAVUS ROY COHEN

Edited, with an introduction and notes,
by Leslie S. Klinger

LIBRARY LIBRARY OF CONGRESS

Copyright © 1923 by Octavus Roy Cohen
Introduction and notes © 2021 by Leslie S. Klinger
Cover and internal design © 2021 by Sourcebooks and Library of Congress
Cover design by Heather VenHuizen/Sourcebooks
Cover image: *Just One Long Step to Sea Cliff, L.I.* Federal Art Project,
1936–1939. Works Progress Administration Poster Collection, Prints &
Photographs Division, Library of Congress, LC-DIG-ppmsca-04892.

Published by Poisoned Pen Press, an imprint of Sourcebooks,
in association with the Library of Congress
P.O. Box 4410, Naperville, Illinois 60567-4410
(630) 961-3900
sourcebooks.com

This edition of *Jim Hanvey, Detective* is based on the first edition in the Library of
Congress's collection, originally published in 1923 by Dodd, Mead and Company.

Library of Congress Cataloging-in-Publication Data

Names: Cohen, Octavus Roy, author. | Klinger, Leslie S, editor.
Title: Jim Hanvey, Detective / Octavus Roy Cohen; edited,
with an introduction and notes, by Leslie S. Klinger.
Description: Naperville, Illinois : Library of Congress/Poisoned Pen Press, [2021]
| Series: Library of Congress crime classics | Includes bibliographical references.
Identifiers: LCCN 2020053740 (print) | LCCN 2020053741
(ebook) | (trade paperback) | (epub)
Subjects: LCSH: Detective and mystery stories, American. | LCGFT: Short stories.
Classification: LCC PS3505.O2455 J56 2021 (print) | LCC
PS3505.O2455 (ebook) | DDC 813/.52--dc23
LC record available at https://lccn.loc.gov/2020053740
LC ebook record available at https://lccn.loc.gov/2020053741

Printed and bound in the United States of America.
KP 10 9 8 7 6 5 4 3 2 1

CONTENTS

FOREWORD

Crime writing as we know it first appeared in 1841, with the publication of "The Murders in the Rue Morgue." Written by American author Edgar Allan Poe, the short story introduced C. Auguste Dupin, the world's first wholly fictional detective. Other American and British authors had begun working in the genre by the 1860s, and by the 1920s we had officially entered the golden age of detective fiction.

Throughout this short history, many authors who paved the way have been lost or forgotten. Library of Congress Crime Classics bring back into print some of the finest American crime writing from the 1860s to the 1960s, showcasing rare and lesser-known titles that represent a range of genres, from cozies to police procedurals. With cover designs inspired by images from the Library's collections, each book in this series includes the original text, reproduced faithfully from an early edition in the Library's collections and complete with strange spellings and unorthodox punctuation. Also included are a contextual introduction, a brief biography of the author, notes, recommendations for further reading, and suggested discussion questions. Our hope is for these books to start conversations, inspire further research, and bring obscure works to a new generation of readers.

Early American crime fiction is not only entertaining to read, but it also sheds light on the culture of its time. While many of the titles in this series include outmoded language and stereotypes now considered offensive, these books give readers the opportunity to reflect on how our society's perceptions of race, gender, ethnicity, and social standing have evolved over more than a century.

More dark secrets and bloody deeds lurk in the massive collections of the Library of Congress. I encourage you to explore these works for yourself, here in Washington, DC, or online at www.loc.gov.

—Carla D. Hayden, Librarian of Congress

INTRODUCTION

The unlikely detective—usually an amateur sleuth not part of law enforcement—has been part of crime fiction almost since its inception. In early novels like *The Moonstone* (Wilkie Collins, 1868) or *The Dead Letter* (Seeley Regester, 1866), family members or friends of the victim have stepped up to lead the efforts to discover the wrongdoer. Although these early years of American crime fiction produced parodies of Sherlock Holmes, the comic possibilities of the detective trade went largely unexplored. Two of the earliest American examples, *Philo Gubb: Correspondence-School Detective* (Ellis Parker Butler, 1918) and George Barr McCutcheon's *Anderson Crow, Detective* (1920), both featured ridiculous characters, men who thought themselves to be clever sleuths but who ultimately succeeded by dumb luck.

It wasn't until 1922 that one of America's most popular magazine writers, Octavus Roy Cohen, created a detective whose slow and stupid appearance masked a sharp mind and a tenacious character: Jim Hanvey. The great mystery editor-critic Ellery Queen described him admiringly:

[Hanvey was a] gargantuan figure with a huge chin and short fat legs. His chief recreation, when he wasn't just resting with his shoes off, was the movies where, being a supreme sentimentalist, he wept and suffered with the emoting actors on the screen. Fish-eyed, always smoking atrocious black cigars and wearing a golden tooth-pick, this regular-guy gumshoe befriended all criminals who had returned to the strait-and-narrow—the friend and yet "the terror of crooks from coast to coast."*

Hanvey was born in the *Saturday Evening Post*, a magazine for which Cohen wrote frequently, in the May 6, 1922, issue.† The character proved popular, and Cohen wrote three more stories about him for the *Post* in 1922, all collected in this volume, which was first published in 1923. Two of the remaining three tales in this collection appeared in other venues: "Pink Bait" was first published in *Collier's*, and "The Knight's Gambit" appeared in the *Chicago Tribune*, on July 7 and 8, 1923, respectively. "Caveat Emptor" appeared only in the collection.

Cohen didn't abandon Hanvey after publication of the book.‡ He would write an additional dozen short stories about Hanvey that appeared between 1924 and 1957 (the latter after

---

* Ellery Queen [Manfred Lee and Frederick Dannay], *Queen's Quorum: A History of the Detective-Crime Short Story as Revealed by the 106 Most Important Books Published in This Field since 1845*, rev. ed. (Boston: Little, Brown, 1951), 76.

† The story was "Fish Eyes." "Homespun Silk" appeared in the June 17 issue, "Common Stock" in the July 22 issue, and "Helen of Troy, N.Y." in the October 7 issue.

‡ Cohen was profiled effusively for his stories of "darkies" in Charles Baldwin's 1924 edition of *The Men Who Make Our Novels* (New York: Dodd, Mead, 1924) but the four-page profile only notes in passing that Cohen is also "the maker of several hair-raising detective stories" and mentions *Jim Hanvey, Detective* among other books of Cohen's (109). The book apparently did well enough to be consistently mentioned in various *Gold Star Lists of American Fiction* of the era and is favorably mentioned in many overviews of crime fiction, but only briefly.

a twenty-three-year absence), as well as three novels between 1929 and 1932. Hanvey even appeared in two films, *Curtain at Eight* (Majestic Pictures, 1933), starring C. Aubrey Smith as the detective,* and *Jim Hanvey, Detective* (Republic Pictures, 1937) featuring Guy Kibbee in the role.†

Cohen's regard for the skills of his own creation was low—he called Hanvey "the apparent personification of the ultimate in human stupidity."‡ Much of the charm of the stories, however, is the confirmation that appearances can be deceiving. While these tales feature neither murder nor any real detection, time after time, Hanvey's shrewd intervention foils the schemes of con men and women. In that respect, the stories are similar to the "howdun-nit" style of mystery popularized by William Link and Richard Levinson in their very successful television series, *Columbo* (1968, 1971–1978)—the viewer knew full well who committed the crime, and the pleasure was in watching the detective trip up the criminal.

Cohen described Hanvey's "theory of detection" as part of a short biography he wrote for *Sleuths: Twenty-three Great Detectives of Fiction and Their Best Stories*:

Hanvey, James H.: *b. Bayonne, N.J., June 26, 1889; o.s. James H. Hanvey and Mary (Mordan) H. Unmarried. Educ.: Public School No. 6, Bayonne, and Bayonne High School (for one month). Head of identification bureaus of police departments*

---

* Smith was certainly an odd choice: tall, lean, and the quintessential stiff-upper-lip Englishman, Smith plays Hanvey in name only. The film is loosely based on one of Cohen's full-length novels featuring Hanvey, *The Backstage Mystery* (1930).

---

† Kibbee was far better suited to the part than Smith. He usually played the jovial, bumbling character, and he is a delight in the film, playing a detective called out of retirement to recover a missing emerald. The plot thickens when an innocent man is accused of murder. The script is only loosely based on Cohen's stories.

---

‡ Quoted in a "Retro-Review" of *Jim Hanvey, Detective* by Charles Shibuk, in the *Armchair Detective* 11, no. 2 (April 1978): 127.

in several large cities; noted for wide acquaintance among criminal classes; particularly active and expert in cases involving more intelligent criminology, viz: confidence rackets, forgery, embezzlement; employed for several years prior to 1931 as special investigator for numerous organizations, including Bankers' Protective Assn. Theory of detection: *To keep suspect talking, in the belief that a thread of truth will occasionally be found in the warp and woof of lies.* More important cases recorded in "Jim Hanvey, Detective," 1923; "The May Day Mystery," 1929; "The Backstage Mystery," 1930, *and various magazine accounts by Octavus Roy Cohen.* Hobbies: *Detective stories, motion pictures of sentimental type, gaudy pajamas, gold toothpicks, strong cigars and equally strong chop suey.* Residence: *Country at large though maintaining apartment in New York City.*[*]

In addition, Cohen's criminals are often more devious than evil, just regular folks trying to make a living outside the law. Because their victims are foolish rich people or banks or insurance companies, the reader has a certain sympathy with the "villains," whom Hanvey treats with respect. This fresh perspective, together with Cohen's ear for dialogue (and the stories are filled with slang of the day, some indecipherable almost one hundred years later) make the stories of Hanvey's cases vivid and fresh. Ellery Queen ranked the collection as one of the 106 most important ever published in the field of crime fiction.[†] While that may be a little fulsome, Hanvey is a rare commodity in the world of crime fiction: a warm, bighearted, genuinely likable detective.

—Leslie S. Klinger

---

[*] Kenneth MacGowan, ed. (New York: Harcourt, Brace, 1931), 410. The collection includes "Homespun Silk," included in this volume at pp. 34–61.

[†] *Queen's Quorum*, 76.

Fish Eyes

Clifford Wallace was noticeably ill-at-ease. He worked intensively yet mechanically at his post in the Third National Bank, within the narrow confines of a cage bearing the inscription Paying Teller Number One. Horizontal lines of worry creased his forehead and a single lock of white stood out with startling clarity against the deep brown of his hair.

Beside him were piled great stacks of money divided into neat packages. Behind his back the huge doors of the cash vault gaped, disclosing more money. At the right of his cage were the inclosures of the three other—the junior—paying tellers. The marbled lobby of the big bank was a welter of discordant activity, of impatience—the clink of silver, the soft shuffling of new bank notes, the slamming of ledgers, the hum of banking during the rush hours.

Today was the busiest of the month for Paying Teller Number One. Today came due the pay rolls of the three largest corporations in the industrial district of which this city was the metropolis. More than a million and a quarter dollars in cash occupied the cage with Cliff Wallace; a million and a quarter dollars in silver and bills, only a few of the latter in denominations of more than one hundred dollars.* It was Wallace's task to make up these pay rolls and deliver them to the armed men who came with the checks. He was sorting the money now, indifferent to the exasperated stare of the little man outside the window who impatiently rattled his own modest pay-roll check for $208.

Behind the irate little man a line formed slowly—two or three other representatives of small businesses, then a strikingly pretty young woman in a blue coat suit, and behind her, two stalwarts from the Garrison Coal, Iron and Steel Company. Cliff knew the proportions of the check they carried—$278,000. Real work there, work requiring intense concentration. It was so easy to make an error of a few hundred dollars when one dealt casually in single amounts greater than a quarter million. Cliff received the little man's check and counted the money deftly, cramming it into a canvas sack. He was visibly annoyed when the man insisted on opening the sack and counting the money for himself. Cliff's eyes sought those of the pretty girl and a brief glance of understanding passed between them. Both were taut of muscle and tense of nerves; upon the face of each was an unnatural pallor.

The little man completed his count, closed his canvas sack and moved off pompously. The next man in line presented his check and received his money. So, too, did the next. The girl pushed her check through the window—the pay-roll check of the wholesale hardware company for which she worked; $728.56. With it she presented a leather satchel. Cliff Wallace unlocked the barred window of his cage to take the satchel. He placed it on the shelf at his right, the shelf containing the mountains of bills. Again that look of understanding—of apprehension—passed between them. They spoke with simulated casualness.

---

* A payroll of $1,250,000 in 1923 is the equivalent of over $75 million in 2020. Samuel H. Williamson, "Purchasing Power Today of a US Dollar Transaction in the Past," MeasuringWorth, 2020, https://www.measuringworth.com.

"Good morning, Phyllis."

"Good morning, Cliff."

That was all. Yet, save for those first glances, they avoided each other's eyes. The oldish-young paying teller sorted out the amount of her pay-roll. And then working discreetly, swiftly and dexterously, he piled beside it a small stack of new bills. In that stack of bills was a hundred thousand dollars; one thousand one-hundred-dollar bank notes. Once he permitted his eyes to rove restlessly about the lobby. They paused briefly on the gray-coated figure of the bank's special officer, who lounged indifferently near the Notes and Discounts Window. Apparently the bank detective had neither thought nor care in the world. Reassured, yet with no diminution of his nervousness, Cliff Wallace returned to the task in hand.

Into the girl's brown leather satchel he put the amount of her pay-roll check, and then he crammed into it also the one hundred thousand dollars.

His face was ghastly pale as he faced her once more. The hand that held the satchel trembled violently. He conscripted a smile which he intended to be reassuring, and the smile with which she answered him was so obviously an effort that it seemed to shriek her guilt. For a second they remained rigid, staring into each other's eyes, then the envoys of the Garrison Coal, Iron and Steel Company coughed impatiently and the girl moved away. The paying teller fingered the $278,000 check nervously, his eyes remaining focused on the blue coat suit which was moving with horrid slowness toward the whirling doors that opened onto the street. And finally she disappeared and Cliff Wallace breathed a sigh of infinite relief. Thus far nothing had been noticed. He gave his attention to the task of assorting huge stacks of bills for the Garrison company.

Meanwhile the girl in the blue coat suit turned into the swirl of traffic on the city's main thoroughfare. She threaded her way through the crowd, walking with unnecessary swiftness, with the single thought in her mind of putting as much space as possible between herself and the Third National Bank. Her fingers were wrapped tightly about the handle of the brown leather satchel, her face bore a fixed rigidity of expression, her heart was pounding beneath the plain tailored waist she wore. It seemed incomprehensible that the transaction in Cliff Wallace's cage had gone unnoticed. It had been so simple—so absurdly simple.

And now she was making all haste toward the office where she worked. Cliff had warned her that she must return promptly from the bank in order that the inevitable investigation should disclose no suspicious lapse of time.

She turned up a side street and thence into a gaunt, red-brick building labeled Sanford Jones & Co. Biting her lips with a fierce effort at self-control, she entered the building and turned immediately into the women's washroom. Trembling fingers found the door key and turned it. Then making certain that she was alone in the room she took from the shelf a large piece of brown wrapping paper which she had placed there earlier in the morning—that and a bit of twine.

She dropped to her knees, opened the satchel and took from it the one hundred thousand dollars. She felt a vague amazement that so much money should be of such small bulk. She arranged the bills neatly in three stacks of equal height and wrapped them carefully in the brown paper. Then with the package securely tied with twine she closed the satchel, unlocked the washroom door and swung into the office. No one had noticed her brief excursion into the washroom; that much was evident.

Straight toward the cashier's desk she went, and in his hands placed the satchel. His eyes smiled briefly into hers.

"Got back pretty quick this morning, Miss Robinson."

She forced a smile. "Yes. Not much crowd at the bank. I did get back in a hurry."

The bit of dialogue pleased her. The cashier had noticed specifically that her absence from the store had been of briefer duration than usual. He would remember that when the detectives made inquiry.

She seated herself at her typewriter. Beside her, on the battered oak desk, she placed the innocuous-appearing brown paper package, the package containing one hundred thousand dollars. She was horribly nervous, but apparently no one noticed anything unusual in her manner. The wall clock indicated the hour of 10:30. From then until noon she must work.

It was difficult. Her thoughts were focused upon the money before her. Once a clerk stopped by her desk to chat and his hand rested idly upon the package of money. She felt as though she must scream. But he moved away eventually. She breathed more easily.

At five minutes after noon she left the office for her lunch. With her went the package of money. She made her way to the City Trust and Savings Company, an imposing edifice of white marble nearly opposite the Third National. She entered the building and descended the broad stairway to the safety-deposit vaults, noticing with relief that there was an unusually large crowd there. She extended her key to the ancient man in charge.

"Two-thirty-five, please. Mrs. Harriet Dare."

Mrs. Dare, now dead, had been Phyllis' sister. Phyllis had access to the box. Too, she maintained in this bank a box in her own name, so that should official investigation progress to the point of examining the safety-deposit box of Phyllis Robinson, nothing to excite suspicion would be found. That was one of the strongest links in the safety chain that Cliff Wallace had welded.

The man in charge ran through his index and handed her a

card to sign. Her hand trembled as she wrote her name: Phyllis Robinson. The old man took her key and his, unlocked the box and left her. There were a number of persons in the vault: One pompous gentleman ostentatiously clipping coupons from Liberty Bonds* of fifty-dollar denomination; an old lady who had already locked her box and was struggling vainly to assure herself that it was thoroughly locked; a fair-haired clerk from a broker's office assuming the businesslike airs of his employer; a half dozen others, each reassuringly absorbed in his own business. Phyllis took her box—it was a large one—and carried it into one of the private booths which stood just outside the vault door.

She placed the tin box and her package side by side on the mahogany shelf. A quick survey of the place assured her that she was not observed. She wondered vaguely why she was not. It seemed as though someone must know. But apparently no one did. Swiftly she transferred the hundred thousand dollars to the strong box. She was amazed to find herself computing financial possibilities when all the while she was frightened. It was an amount to yield seven thousand dollars a year carefully invested.† Two persons could live comfortably on seven thousand dollars a year. And that meant every year—there'd be no diminution of principal. Nearly one hundred and fifty dollars

---

* Liberty Bonds were bonds first sold by the US government during World War I, and buying them became a patriotic duty for many Americans. The fourth issue of the bonds, in 1918, had an interest rate of 4.25 percent per annum, and the bonds matured in 1938. In 1934, the government called the bonds but defaulted on its obligation to redeem the bonds in gold. Although the bonds were paid in full in US currency, the significant devaluation of the dollar (that is, what a dollar would buy, which, according to statisticians, dropped to less than seventy cents) meant that in real economic terms, millions lost a large part of their investment.

---

† The equivalent of an annual wage of over $400,000 in 2020, clearly a decent living (Williamson, "Purchasing Power," Measuring Worth, 2020). A 7 percent investment return was considered quite reasonable as recently as 2010; in 2020, with incredibly low interest rates, most portfolio managers are satisfied with 4 to 5 percent, well ahead of inflation.

a week. Every comfort and many luxuries assured. Freedom. Independence. Fear.

She returned the box to its compartment and emerged upon the street again. With the money put safely away a load had lifted from her shoulders. She felt a sense of enormous relief. The danger mark had been passed, the scheme appeared to have justified itself. But now her nerves were jangling as they had not been before. She was frightened, not so much for what the immediate future might hold as by the experience through which she had just passed. No longer was she keyed up by action. Retrospection left her weak and afraid. She knew that she couldn't do it again; marveled at the fact that she had committed this act at all.

She ate a tiny meal at the dairy lunch which she patronized regularly. At 12:40 she returned to the office, where she threw herself into the grind of routine work, seeking forgetfulness and ease for her jangling nerves. But her thoughts were not on the letters she typed; they were at the bank with Clifford Wallace, chief paying teller.

Meanwhile Cliff's inscrutable, rather hard face gave no indication of the seethe within him. He did his work with mechanical precision, counting large sums of money with incredible speed, checking and rechecking his payments, attending to his routine work with the deftness and accuracy that had won him this post.

There was in his manner no slightest indication that he had just engineered the theft of one hundred thousand dollars in currency. Never friendly at best, he was perhaps this day a trifle more reserved than usual; but even had his fellow workers noticed the fact they would have ascribed it to the abnormal pressure of work. It was seldom that three big pay rolls became due at one time. And the handling of such huge sums of money is likely to cause temporary irascibility in even the most genial of men.

The hour hand of the big clock on the marble wall crept to the figure two. A gong sounded. Immediately work was suspended at the long rows of windows. Then the little barred doors were dropped, the patrons of the bank drifted out gradually, and the bedlam of a busy day was succeeded by the drone of after-hours work—the clackety-clack of adding machines, the rustle of checks, the slamming of books, the clink of silver and gold.

Pencil in hand, Cliff Wallace checked over the money in his vault. Paying Tellers Numbers Two, Three and Four made their reports first. Then Wallace gave his attention to his own cash. The door of his cage was open, so that the cages of the four paying tellers were temporarily en suite. Behind Wallace's back the door of the cash vault gaped. The vault itself was part of his cage, its contents Wallace's responsibility. He worked swiftly and expertly. And then, a few minutes before 4:30 o'clock, he presented himself before Robert Warren, president of the Third National. He was nervous and ill-at-ease. In his left hand he held a paper covered with figures. His face was expressionless, unless one was sufficiently keen to observe the hunted, haunted look in his cold blue eyes. Here was the crisis. He pulled up a chair and seated himself, after having first closed the door of the president's office.

"Mr. Warren"—his voice was steady and incisive, giving no hint of the emotional strain under which he labored—"I have just checked over the cash. I am precisely one hundred thousand dollars short."

The president's swivel chair creaked. The gentleman strangled on a puff of cigar smoke. His big, spatulate hands came down on the polished mahogany desk surface with a thump. His eyes widened.

"You—you are what?"

"My cash is one hundred thousand dollars short."

The statement appeared to have difficulty in penetrating.

"My dear Mr. Wallace—that is impossible! An exact amount?"

Cliff was more at ease. It was a scene he had rehearsed a hundred times, and it was developing just as anticipated.

"I realize the impossibility, sir. But it is nevertheless a fact."

Robert Warren's face hardened slightly. He regarded his chief paying teller with a critical, speculative glance. Wallace returned look for look. The president spoke:

"Please explain yourself, Mr. Wallace. Am I listening to a statement or a confession?"

"A statement, sir."

"H'm!" Warren was himself again. Only superficially was the man genial. He had cultivated geniality as a business asset. Basically he was utterly emotionless. He realized that the thing to which he gave ear was of vital import, and as that realization hammered home, his demeanor became intransigently frigid. "H'm! A statement?"

"Yes, sir."

"Your cash is—er—an even one hundred thousand dollars short?"

"Yes, sir."

"How does that happen?"

"I'm trying to find out myself."

"You are quite sure?"

"Certainly, sir. I would not have come to you had I not been sure."

Silence. Again that clash of eyes. "This puts you in an exceedingly awkward position, Mr. Wallace. Personally."

"I understand that, sir."

"One hundred thousand dollars is a great deal of money."

"Yes, sir."

"The responsibility is absolutely and exclusively yours."

"I realize that."

"Its loss cannot but be due to carelessness on your part."

"That is probably true."

"Probably?"

"Yes, sir. I am not certain about any phase of this—this—unfortunate situation."

Warren lighted another cigar. "Of course the bank will not lose. You are bonded. I must notify the bonding company immediately."

"Of course."

The younger man's poise seemed to get on the nerves of the bank president. For once in his life he had come into contact with a man more unemotional than himself. His fist pounded the desk suddenly.

"Damn it! Wallace, what does it all mean?"

"That that amount of money has disappeared, sir."

"One hundred thousand even?"

"To the dollar."

"When did you notice the loss?"

"Just a few minutes ago, sir—when I checked over the cash."

"You rechecked?"

"Twice."

"Have you been alone in your cage all day?"

"I believe so, sir."

"You only believe?"

"I can't make a too positive statement. The cages of the other paying tellers open into mine. Almost every day the door between my cage and theirs is open for a little while. It is possible that that was the case at certain times today."

"You are not positive?"

"No, sir."

"But you believe that the door was open—in the regular course of the day's work?"

"Yes, sir."

"And you believe that one of your assistants took that money?"

Wallace's face twitched, ever so slightly. "No, sir."

"No?"

"Even if my door had been open, Mr. Warren, I don't believe they would have had a chance to take that much money."

"But—but, Wallace—there are only four men in this bank who could have taken it—provided it was taken; yourself and your three assistant paying tellers."

"I realize that."

"And you say that you don't believe they could?"

"Yes, sir."

"H'm! Do you realize the inevitable conclusion?"

"That if they didn't, I did?"

"Exactly."

"Yes, sir, I realize that."

"Yet you say that you did not."

"Of course."

Robert Warren showed a flash of irritation. "You seem damned unexcited."

"I don't believe this is any time for me to become excited, sir."

Robert Warren rose. "Come with me, young man. We'll lock the doors of the bank and check every cent of cash we have. There must be some mistake."

"I sincerely hope so, sir."

A careful check-up showed plainly that there was no mistake. One hundred thousand dollars had disappeared from the bank during the course of the day's business. It was gone. The three assistant paying tellers were nervous and excited. The cashier, a nervous, wiry little man, rushed around the bank like a chicken suddenly bereft of its head. The bank's private detective, a portly, unimaginative individual, strutted around the empty lobby trying to look important and succeeding not at all. He believed it incumbent upon him to detect something or somebody, felt that the weight of the world suddenly had descended upon his shoulders. But his brain worked in a single unfortunate channel. His attempts at deduction led invariably into the *cul-de-sac* of "It just couldn't happen."

That was the reaction expressed by every bank employe who knew what had occurred. The thing was impossible. The paying tellers, who had worked in team preparing for the rush of the day, were all reasonably certain that the cash had been correct at the beginning of the day—as certain as they were that it was not now correct. Through it all Clifford Wallace worked with them. Tiny lines of worry corrugated his forehead. And when, at seven o'clock, it became evident that the money was positively gone and had disappeared probably during the course of the day's business, the president, the cashier and Clifford Wallace retired to Warren's office. The president and cashier were smoking. Cliff declined their proffered cigar.

"I never smoke, you know."

"The point now is," spoke Warren, checking off that particular point on his thumb, "that the money has disappeared and we must do something. The question is, what?" He turned his gaze upon Wallace. Cliff met the stare steadily and answered in a matter-of-fact voice:

"The obvious thing is to place me under arrest, Mr. Warren."

"Obvious, of course."

"But Mr. Warren"—it was the nervous little cashier—"you don't believe Cliff stole that money, do you?"

"Certainly not, Mr. Jenkins. Of course I don't. And equally of course I am not going to have Mr. Wallace placed under arrest."

A flicker of triumph crossed Clifford Wallace's face, to be followed instantly by his habitual stoniness of expression.

"I am perfectly willing, Mr. Warren—"

"It isn't a case of willingness, Wallace. If I thought for a moment you were guilty—or even could be guilty—I wouldn't hesitate. Not if you were my brother. But the thing is impossible. You've been negligent—probably; I'm not even sure of that. I understand banks well enough to know that a certain laxity of routine is naturally and excusably developed. It is my personal opinion that the money did not disappear from the bank. It either never was here or it is still here."

"Yes, sir." Cliff was calmly attentive.

"I am going to search every employe* as he or she leaves the bank. That will insure its remaining here tonight. By tomorrow morning the bonding-company detectives and the representatives of the Bankers' Protective Association will be here. Whatever action they care to take, Wallace, will be strictly up to them. Personally, I wish to take occasion to assure you of my confidence in your integrity and to express the belief that this is an explainable mistake of some sort, which will be set right tomorrow."

"And you are not even going to keep me under surveillance tonight?"

"No."

"Pardon me, sir, but I believe you are making a mistake. You will be criticized—"

"They can criticize and be damned to them."

Wallace returned to his cage, where he busied himself arranging the shelves for the following morning. Then quite as usual he closed his vault doors, set the time lock, visited the washroom, and left the building after undergoing a thorough search. Once outside, his shoulders went back unconsciously. He knew that he had won. The very simplicity of his crime had caused it to be crowned with success.

But he did not allow his elation to strangle caution. Every move

---

* Now an uncommon spelling for "employee."

in the game had been thought out meticulously in advance. He did not deviate a hair's breadth from his regular evening routine. He went to a cafeteria and ate a hearty meal, although the food almost choked him. At the desk he telephoned Phyllis Robinson.

"May I come to see you this evening, Phyllis?" He did that four or five evenings a week; they were secretly engaged.

"Yes."

There was a distinct nuance of tremulous inquiry in her voice. It annoyed Clifford. They had threshed out every detail of this sort. She must keep a stiff upper lip, had promised not to betray any untoward interest in his comings and goings immediately following the robbery. But that was just like a woman, making plain in the tone of her voice the vast relief she felt at knowing that he was free. Wallace didn't like that. It was an indication of weakness, and weakness had no place in his elaborate scheme. Besides, he knew well that Robert Warren was no fool, realized that for all Warren's protestations of belief in his integrity, the bank president already had a detective shadowing him. He had anticipated that and a good deal more. He had expected to spend this night in jail, and perhaps several others. Certainly under observation. This freedom caused elation, but brought about no lessening of caution.

At 7:45 he presented himself at the garage where he kept his modest little roadster, filled the tank with gas and drove down the street. This was a nightly ritual. Straight to the home of Phyllis Robinson he went; it was a rambling two-story structure set well back of a high-terraced front yard, its wide veranda blanketed cozily with honeysuckle—a modest place, one which had seen decidedly better days. Phyllis, an orphan, lived there with an aunt. The place was a boarding house. All very discreet and proper.

She greeted him in the hallway. He was irritated by the patent effort of her casualness. He directed their conversation, they chatted about innocuous nothings until they were safely out of the house and in his little car, headed into the country. This, too, was a not uncommon procedure. Cliff was well satisfied with himself. The most suspicious watcher could have found no food for speculation this night. His actions had been the normal actions of an innocent man. He was acting just as he would have acted had he been innocent of the theft of one hundred thousand dollars.

They mounted a gentle acclivity. The broad smooth highway dipped from the crest through a small woods. Overhead the full moon shone benignly over the valley, behind them the city, ringed about by furnaces and steel mills, gems of fire in the setting of silvered night. A red glow in the sky. The man at the steering wheel, calm and self-possessed, eyes focused on the ribbon of road ahead, thoughts busy with the epochal events of the day. Nor did he mention the subject uppermost in his mind until the girl spoke, spoke with a quaver in her voice as her hand closed tremulously about his.

"You—you're free, Cliff?"

"Obviously." The man was a poser; this was too perfect an opportunity to miss. He wished the girl at his side to be impressed with his own granite imperviousness to emotion. Phyllis shook her head; she loved him despite the fact that she knew his weakness.

"They don't suspect you?"

"Certainly not. They couldn't. I went in to the old man and told him the money was gone. I didn't protect myself a bit. Suggested that he had better lock me up. And of course he didn't." He smiled grimly, pridefully. "The only danger point in the whole scheme has been passed, Phyllis. We're safe."

"And I'm frightened."

"Of course. That's natural."

"Aren't you?"

"Not at all." He stopped the car as if to light a cigarette. "You put the money in the vault at the City Trust?"

"Yes."

"When?"

"Immediately after I left the office for lunch."

"You went straight from the Third National to your office?"

"Yes. And the cashier commented on how quickly I got back."

"Fine! Great! Sooner or later they're bound to connect us in this matter, and when they do they'll investigate your actions. It'll disarm them to learn that you got back to the office in record time; that you couldn't possibly have gone anywhere between the bank and your place of business. And now about the vault—you didn't attract any particular attention there, did you?"

"No-o. I'm sure I didn't. There was a crowd there, and I am sure the old man didn't notice me at all. I put the money in Harriet's box, not mine."

He patted her hand reassuringly. "You were a trump, dear. And you're not sorry?"

"No-o—and yes. I know that it is wrong, yet—oh, well, we need the money. It means so much more to us than it ever could to that bank. If we're only not caught."

"We won't be." His narrow, rather hard face was set. He argued as though to reassure himself. "The weakness in anything of this sort is preliminary planning. The average man who sets out to steal one hundred thousand dollars"—the girl winced—"makes plans so enormously elaborate that he cuts his own throat, minimizes his chances of getting away with it. For every detail that such a man plants he sows a possibility of detection. He isn't content with the easy, the safe, the normal. In striving for perfection for absolute safety, he lays traps for himself. Remember this, Phyllis: a detective can make a thousand mistakes and, by doing one single thing correctly, land his man. The criminal cannot afford a single mistake. Understand?"

"Yes." And then the feminine side of the girl flooded to the surface. "Cliff dear, you're so—so hard!"

That pleased him. He wanted to be hard, cultivated a gelid* philosophy.

"Sentiment serves no man well, Phyllis. My hardness has made possible financial ease for us—and consequent contentment. I have no conscience. Neither has the average man. Conscience is the fear of being caught. We are all inherently immoral. It was not wrong for the primitive man to steal. He took what he could get away with. Right and wrong are products of legislation of artificial ethical culture. They are not part of us; we are inoculated with them. They are utterly foreign to us. In taking this money I have committed no natural crime. By statute only am I a criminal. I am not ashamed of what I have done. I would be ashamed of detection."

Silence fell between them. The girl shivered as though with a chill.

"You are very convincing, dear. But I'm afraid that I'm terribly a victim to the morality of education. Of course you've convinced my intellect. But—since this afternoon—I'm afraid you can never convince my conscience."

He flashed her a sudden apprehensive glance. "You're not getting cold feet?"

"No." She shook her head sadly. "It's too late for that."

"But you're afraid?"

"Yes. I'm afraid."

"Then you're silly. We're safe now. The minute you walked through those revolving doors with that hundred thousand in your bag I knew that we were safe. The scheme is successful because of its very simplicity. We are to go ahead in our normal

---

* Cold, emotionless.

ways. There is to be no variation whatsoever in our way of living. In a year we will marry. A year from then I will get a position somewhere else. And then—and not until then—will we begin to make use of the money which we got today. We're safe."

"From the law—yes. But not from ourselves."

"Harping on conscience again?"

"Yes."

"Pff! I have no conscience, no fear of the intangible."

She sighed. "I must agree with you, dear. I've gone too far not to. But I wonder—whether it's worth the price."

He laughed harshly and the car leaped ahead as his finger caressed the gas lever.[*]

"It's fortunate, Phyllis, that I'm practical. The thing that counts in this world is what you have—not how you got it."

They returned to the girl's boarding house at eleven o'clock, stood chatting for a while on the front porch. Cliff wondered whether the man who must be shadowing him was witness to the tableau. He knew that the man must have been bewildered and apprehensive when they went off for a ride together—and pleased by their return. He fancied he could discern the person lolling in the shadows of the big oak across the street. He swung down the steps, whistling jauntily.

Phyllis slept not at all that night. Cliff, serene and untroubled, slumbered heavily. For two years he had planned this thing, had surveyed it from every angle. He had made an intensive personal study of the men with whom he would have to deal: Of Robert Warren, the president; of Garet Jenkins, the cashier; of each member of the board of directors. He had studied their mental processes, had deliberately built up their confidence in him and his integrity. He had known in advance that Warren would do

---

[*] Early automobiles—including the Ford Model T, introduced in 1908 and sold as late as 1927—had hand throttles rather than gas pedals.

just about as he had done and that his opinion would sway the board of directors. He knew that the matter would be hushed up and that the investigation would be conducted with the most rigid secrecy. He knew that detectives would appear the following morning, would remain there for some time—and that they would find nothing. He knew that eventually the conclusion would be reached that there had been, in fact, no robbery at all, but that the hundred thousand dollars had never reached the bank vaults.

He would be watched carefully for one month, two, three. Then the matter would be filed away as an unsolved mystery. Above everything, the bank was not desirous of a scandal. In the absence of sufficient evidence to convict they'd permit him his freedom. And the perfect normalcy of his life would convince them speedily that he was free from guilt.

He reached the bank the following morning at precisely his regular time, not a minute early or a minute late. He held a brief conference with the three assistant paying tellers and apportioned to each his quota of cash from the vault, which was a part of his individual cage. Then quite phlegmatically he answered a summons to the office of the president. And as he entered the door he recognized in the three strangers who faced him the detectives.

Cliff was somewhat amused. He knew that the glances they bestowed upon him were surcharged with deep and dark suspicion. Money had disappeared from the cage of the chief paying teller; ergo, the chief paying teller had stolen it. They'd start out on that theory—and butt their heads against a stone wall. He realized that Robert Warren was talking, that he was being introduced.

"The detectives; this is Mr. Peter Jamieson, representing the bonding company. And Mr. Carl Burton, of the Banker's Protective Association." He hesitated a moment as he turned toward the third stranger. Then: "This other gentleman is also here to represent the Bankers' Protective Association. Mr. Wallace, Mr. Hanvey—Mr. James Hanvey."

Cliff started visibly. Jim Hanvey! He'd heard of the man—a detective with an enviable reputation. But he had envisioned Jim Hanvey as a person tall and sinewy, and with a saturnine face and deep-set flashing eyes. This man——

The hand which the great detective extended to him was limp and clammy, the man himself utterly negative. He was a large man, true; but his shoulders were rounded and from them the coat of his cheap ready-made tweed suit hung like a smoking jacket. Above a thick red neck rose the head—huge, fat, shapeless. Three floppy chins, an apoplectic expression, a wide, loose-lipped mouth. And eyes——

Those eyes fascinated Wallace, not because they were marvelous eyes but because he could not reconcile himself to the fact that they were capable of seeing anything. They were large eyes, and round like a baby's. In color they were a passive gray—fishlike. They rested on Wallace's as their hands met, and then the lids closed slowly over them like a film, rising just as deliberately. It was more an ocular yawn than a blinking of eyes. Cliff felt within him a contempt for the man, instant and instinctive, then pulled himself together with a jerk. He knew that would never do. Jim Hanvey bore an international reputation, such a one as could not be attained through inefficiency.

Jamieson was nearer Cliff's conception of an efficient detective. Medium build, dapper, dynamic, with blazing eyes and a competent manner. He liked Jamieson, knew that he would know how to cope with him. Jamieson was a practical detective, and Jamieson was there in the rôle of a friend. It was most decidedly to the interest of the bonding company to establish his innocence. Burton, too, radiated efficiency. He was tall and broad and had deep-set brown eyes which looked out keenly from under heavy lashes. He was there to convict, but Cliff did not fear him. Burton, like Jamieson, was too normal a man to inspire apprehension. But Hanvey, Hanvey of the slow-blinking, fishy eyes—Hanvey was a disturbing quantity. Cliff didn't like Hanvey.

Hanvey was speaking. Cliff noted that the others deferred to the ponderous, uninspired-looking individual.

"H'm! You're the paying teller, Mr. Wallace?"

"Yes, sir."

"Kind of funny—the hundred thousand gettin' lost thataway, wasn't it?"

Cliff was annoyed. The man wasn't even grammatical.

"Rather peculiar—yes."

"Ain't got any idea how it happened, have you?"

"No."

"No chance of anyone sort of slippin' an arm through the cage window and grabbin' it, huh?"

Bah! the man was an idiot.

"Hardly that."

"Kinder makes us believe that it must have been done by somebody inside the cage. Ain't that so?"

"That is the obvious conclusion."

"Well, now—so it is. So it is." Hanvey produced a golden toothpick, which he regarded fondly. "Awful funny thing how money gits to go thisaway. Awful funny. Ain't it, Jamieson?"

"Yes—yes indeed." Cliff glanced curiously at the competent Jamieson. He fancied that Jamieson would appear annoyed by Hanvey's cumbersomeness. But instead he saw the two other detectives hanging worshipfully upon Hanvey's words.

Peculiar—it was impossible that Hanvey possessed keen intelligence. And yet——

Hanvey nodded heavily. "That's all, Mr. Wallace. I reckon that's about all I need from you."

All? It was nothing—less than nothing. One or two absurd, meaningless questions; a ridiculous voicing of the thought that some one might have stolen a hundred thousand dollars in currency from under his very eyes. And Jim Hanvey was reputed to be a great detective.

Cliff Wallace was bothered. The very somnolent heaviness of Jim Hanvey begot apprehension. He had no idea how to cope with it. The man was too utterly guileless, too awkward of manner. His ponderous indifference must cloak a keen, perceptive brain. Jamieson and Burton—well, Cliff knew just what they were thinking. He'd always know what they were thinking. But Hanvey—never. He didn't even know that Hanvey was thinking. He was an element which the paying teller had not foreseen. Frank suspicion was easy to combat. Through his head there flashed the shibboleth of the Bankers' Protective Association: "We get a man if it takes a lifetime—even though he has stolen only a dollar. It's the principle of the thing."

He shook off the thought of Jim Hanvey, but throughout the day watched the ponderous, big-jowled man lumber about the lobby and through the cages, those great fishy eyes blinking with a deliberation which reminded him of a man making physical effort to remain awake. Occasionally Cliff looked up to find the glassy eyes staring at him through the bars of his cage, the detective's unpressed tweed suit against the marble shelf. His eyes would flash into those of the detective, then would come that interminably slow blinking, and Hanvey would move away apologetically. Once Wallace shivered.

That was the beginning. Hanvey during the days that followed did absolutely nothing. Jamieson and Burton, on the other hand, worked busily and thoroughly. They pored over the list of customers for whom checks had been cashed on the day of the money's disappearance. And finally they came to the pay-roll check of Sanford Jones & Co. They called Cliff into conference with them, Burton doing the questioning.

"Who presented the Jones company check, Mr. Wallace?"

Cliff steeled himself to impassivity. "Miss Phyllis Robinson."

"You are acquainted with her?"

"Yes. We happen to be secretly engaged."

"Ah-h!" Cliff saw a meaningful look pass between the two detectives. "Your fiancée?"

"Yes."

"Did you personally cash her check that day?"

"Yes."

"You are positive about that?"

"Yes. I cash all of the pay-roll checks; and besides, I remember talking to her while she was at the window."

The detectives nodded at each other and Cliff was dismissed. Immediately Jamieson and Burton checked up the movements of Phyllis Robinson on that particular day. They learned that she had cashed the company's pay-roll check as usual and that she had been absent from the office only a short time. Yes, the puzzled cashier was positive of that—he remembered noticing particularly that she'd hardly left the office before she was back with the money. In answer to their query as to whether she had time to stop somewhere en route to the office from the bank, the little man indignantly protested that he recalled every detail of the morning and that she couldn't possibly have done so. "I never knew her to get back so quick before; and she never was one to loiter."

So much for that. The girl had undoubtedly gone straight from the bank to her office. The Jones cashier insisted that she delivered the satchel to him personally. Jamieson and Burton then visited the banks of the city and its suburbs. The Third National was the largest in the district and they went meticulously down the line in the order of importance. At the City Trust they were informed that Phyllis Robinson rented a safety-deposit box. An inspection of her card disclosed the fact that she had not visited the box in two months. Nor had she a box at any other bank. Neither had Cliff Wallace.

News of the investigation, received from the puzzled cashier, via the frightened Phyllis, elated Cliff. He was delighted to know that the two detectives were at work, and supremely confident that they could discover nothing.

But Hanvey did nothing. All day long he lounged about the lobby or sat in one of the cages with his feet propped upon a shelf, surrounding himself with a haze of rancid cigar smoke. And always those blank, stupid eyes were turned upon the cage of the chief paying teller—blinking, blinking.

Wallace did not vary a hair's breadth from the established routine of his daily life. He breakfasted at his usual place at the usual hour, snatched a lunch as he had always been in the habit of doing, dined at his favorite cafeteria, called upon Phyllis Robinson in the evenings and either walked with her or took her riding in his little car.

On Thursday he drew his monthly pay check—two hundred and fifty dollars. One hundred dollars of it he immediately deposited to his own credit in a savings account. He had done this for years.

On Friday he received a shock. It was a light pay-roll day—not more than a quarter million dollars had been set aside for the pay rolls. In the line was Phyllis, satchel in hand. He greeted her as usual, counted the packages of bills and rolls of silver. And then, as he unlocked the little window of his cage to return to her the satchel, he visioned the ponderous figure of Jim Hanvey lolling indifferently over the shelf; round idiotic eyes fixed unseeingly upon him. Fear flashed into Cliff's heart and the color receded from his cheeks. What was the significance of that? Was it possible——With an almost hysterical gesture he slammed shut the window. Hanvey's eyes blinked once, slowly; a second time, more slowly. Then he moved heavily away, playing with his gold toothpick.

That night as Cliff was driving with Phyllis in the country— "That was Hanvey standing by the window today when I cashed your pay-roll check."

The girl shuddered. "Ugh! He's horrid. Like a jellyfish."

"I wonder why he did that? He's never done it before."

"Did what?"

"Hung over the counter while I was cashing your pay-roll check. I wonder if he suspects——"

"That man! He looks like an imbecile."

"Looks like, yes. But he is supposed to be a great detective."

"It's impossible."

"He's getting on my nerves, Phyllis. I can't help but believe that he suspects something. At times I feel a contempt for his obtuseness. Then I know that I'm wrong. He couldn't be what he is and be the fool he looks. And he doesn't do anything. He's never questioned me. He's never questioned anyone. He just sits there and watches and watches—like—like a Buddha."

Nor did the weeks which followed alter the situation. Jamieson reported to the bank officials that in his opinion there had been no robbery. Burton concurred. They had arrived at the definite conclusion that the money had never reached the bank. In answer to Cliff's statement that it had, they admitted that Cliff believed so—but was in error. Cliff refused to be convinced, and thus established more firmly than ever in their minds the fact that he was innocent of complicity in the crime. It was the theory of Jamieson and Burton that in securing the unusually large amount of cash from the District Federal Reserve Bank to meet the heavy pay rolls of that particular day, a miscount had been made at the sending source and the checking up at the Third National had been faulty. True, the accounts of the Federal Reserve Bank showed no surplus of one hundred thousand dollars, but both Jamieson and Burton were optimistic that it would eventually come to light.

Cliff Wallace knew that he had been successful. No hint of suspicion had fallen upon him. The worst that had been said against him was that he had been careless in counting the money as it came into his vaults. He was sorrowful about that—ostentatiously so, just as he would normally have exhibited grief at any suggestion of inefficiency. The bank officials did not blame him. Most of them had climbed the ladder slowly and they were familiar with the nagging routine of the paying teller's cage, the inevitable liability to error. Undoubtedly, they thought, the money would appear eventually. It was absurd to doubt Clifford Wallace. Two detectives had shadowed him meticulously. The orderly existence of the chief paying teller was unaltered. He went his way serenely.

To Wallace it seemed more than worth the trouble. Lying in the vaults of the City Trust was one hundred thousand dollars in cash, an amount sufficient to yield seven thousand income invested with moderate acumen. That meant leisure and ease for himself and Phyllis through life. He did not want anything more. He knew that he would never again be tempted to crime; not that he was morally opposed to it, but because it wasn't worth the danger.

One hundred thousand dollars was adequate to their needs. He had planned this thing for two years. Now it had been worked successfully.

If it only wasn't for Jim Hanvey, those wide-staring eyes. He couldn't get away from those eyes, from the insolent indolence of the man, his apparent indifference to the mystery he was supposed to be solving. All day he lounged around the bank; ignorant, bunglesome, awkward, inactive. He inspected no books, asked no questions, exhibited no suspicion of Cliff Wallace. Yet Cliff felt those inhuman eyes focused upon him at all times. And that incident of Hanvey's presence at the cage when he cashed Phyllis' pay-roll check—that was fraught with deep significance.

"He suspects me," proclaimed the chief paying teller to his accomplice. "He knows that I did it and is just trying to find out how."

She held his hand between both of hers. "I'm afraid, Cliff. Horribly afraid."

"If he'd only say something! I wish he'd arrest me."

"Cliff!"

"I mean it. If he'd arrest me they'd prosecute, and they couldn't possibly convict. They haven't a thing on me. I'd be acquitted in jig time. Then he could go to the devil—Hanvey and those fish eyes of his. I'd be safe then—even if they found out later that I had done it."

"You mean that you couldn't be tried twice for the same offense?"

"That's it."

"Then why not induce them to—to prosecute?"

He shook his head. "I can't. I've tried it, but old Warren and Garet Jenkins are convinced that I'm innocent. Jamieson and Burton both believe the money never got to the bank. And Hanvey just sits around like a hoot owl at noon and does nothing. It's Hanvey I'm afraid of. He knows! The only thing he doesn't know is how!"

Two more weeks passed. Wallace's hope that Hanvey would depart proved ill-founded. The big, awkward man was there at eight o'clock every morning, and there he remained until the books were closed at night. He spoke to nobody save in the most casual way. Every other employe of the bank came to take him for granted. They were interested in him at first, but later accepted him as they accepted the marble pillars which stubbed the lobby. He was big and lumbering and uncouth, and gradually they forgot his reputation as a bank detective.

But Clifford Wallace did not forget. In his eyes there had been born a hunted, haunted look. Hanvey's flabby, rather coarse face had a hypnotic effect upon him. He found himself wondering what obliquitous* course this man was pursuing, what method there might be in his madness of inactivity. He felt like an ill man who finds himself daily in the room with a coffin. Hanvey's stolid demeanor generated an association of ideas that was irresistibly horrible.

It was obvious that Hanvey suspected something, some one; equally plain that he did not suspect anyone else in that bank. It must be, then, that he did suspect Cliff. And then he commenced visiting Cliff's cage.

He did it only a few times. His manner was friendly, almost apologetic. But he had a mean insinuating way of appearing at the cage door and rattling the knob. Cliff would whirl and find those dull inhuman eyes blinking slowly at him.

"Can I come in, Mr. Wallace?" And then once inside the cage: "Jest wanted to pass the time of day with you."

Invariably, then, the same formula. A browsing around the tiny cage. A peeping into the money-stocked vault of the paying teller. "Gosh! That's a heap of money."

"Yes." Cliff found himself on edge when Hanvey was in his cage.

"Never knew there was that much money in the world."

Damn the man! Always obvious in his speech.

---

* Mentally or morally perverse or aberrant; off-kilter.

"Didn't you?"

"Nope. Sure didn't."

Hanvey never mentioned the robbery. His indifference must be studied; all part of a net-spreading process. Cliff was frightened. He recalled the adage that a detective can err a thousand times and yet win; the criminal cannot afford to slip once. He regulated his daily life scrupulously. At the end of another month he again deposited his regular amount of savings. He saw to it that Phyllis did the same. But the strain was telling on him. His appetite had gone, dark circles appeared under his eyes. He wished daily that he'd be summoned into Warren's office to face the thing out with Jim Hanvey. He knew they couldn't convict, that they didn't have a thing against him. Even the box in which reposed their hundred thousand dollars stood in the name of Mrs. Harriet Dare, Phyllis' dead sister. Before her death Phyllis had been authorized in writing to be permitted to the box. Cliff had taken care that the box remained in the name of the estimable and defunct lady.

He became moody and depressed, obsessed with speculation as to what was happening behind the bovinely expressionless face of the detective. The man's countenance was blank, but Cliff was no fool—he knew that it masked an alert mind. True, he'd seen no indication of that alertness, but he knew that it must be so. And Hanvey's inactivity was telltale. Hanvey knew that he had done it, and was waiting with oxlike patience to discover how.

Sooner or later he'd learn. How, Cliff didn't know. But no scheme is so perfect that it can stand the test of unflagging and unceasing surveillance. And when he did learn—Cliff shuddered. He knew full well what they did to crooked bank employes. Robert Warren would be hard in such a situation—very hard, merciless.

Then came another big pay-roll day, and Phyllis' weekly visit with the modest check from her firm. This time Hanvey fell into line behind her. Cliff saw him coming, and his face blanched. Phyllis noticing his pallor turned and stared into the expressionless countenance of the big unkempt detective. The color receded from her cheeks, too, and her hand trembled visibly as she shoved her satchel through the little window of Cliff's cage.

His fingers were trembling as he counted the money. He chatted with Phyllis, the effort being visible and unnatural.

The girl moved away and Hanvey looked after her trim blue-suited figure. Then he turned his froglike eyes back to Cliff Wallace and blinked in that maddening way of his.

"Durned pretty girl."

"Yes." He was short, nerves ajangle.

"Friend of yours?"

"Yes."

"Awful pretty girl."

Hanvey moved away. Cliff staring after his waddling figure restrained with difficulty an impulse to scream. And when he left the bank that day he did something he had seldom done before in his life—he took a drink of whisky. Then he went to see Phyllis.

He was but a nervous shell of himself when he took her riding that night. He was a victim to nerves. Insomnia had gripped him—insomnia interrupted by a succession of nightmares in which he was hounded by a pair of glassy eyes which blinked slowly, interminably.

"It's all off, Phyllis."

"What do you mean?"

"Hanvey knows I did it. Sooner or later he'll figure out how."

"I thought—today—when he hung over the counter——"

"I'm afraid he's about worked it out. We're near the ragged edge."

She commenced to cry. "Cliff——"

"Don't weep. It isn't going to do us a bit of good. The man is driving me crazy. I tell you there's only one thing to do."

"And that is——"

"Confess."

"Oh-h-h!"

He laughed bitterly. "Don't worry. They'll never know you had anything to do with it. You get the money out in the morning. Bring it to me just as it stands—wrapped in brown paper. I'll carry it to old man Warren. I'll offer to solve the mystery and see that the money is returned in exchange for a promise of immunity."

"Will he keep his promise?"

"Absolutely. He's that sort. He'd not prosecute anyway. It would injure the bank's reputation. A bank always prefers to hush up this sort of thing. They prosecute only when it's been very flagrant or when they have to secure a conviction so that the bonding company will be responsible for their loss. So, tomorrow——"

She rested her head briefly against his shoulder. "You're right, Cliff. And I'll be glad when it's all over. So very, very glad. I've been afraid, dear."

She delivered the money to him at eleven o'clock the following morning. It was Saturday; the bank closed at twelve. He saw the eyes of Jim Hanvey blinking accusingly at him through the morning, and found himself trembling. Suppose Hanvey should accuse him at this moment, when he was on the verge of confession?

Noon. The great doors of the bank were closed. Cliff locked his cage, tucked the brown paper package under his arm and closeted himself with the president. During the walk across the lobby he had felt the horrible knowing eyes of the detective fastened upon him, leechlike.

The scene with Robert Warren developed just as he had anticipated. The president readily promised immunity, the cash was produced and counted. Warren was shocked and genuinely grieved. He was considerate enough to refrain from questioning as to the identity of the accomplice, although Cliff felt that the man knew.

Of course, he said, Cliff could consider himself discharged. The matter would never become known; the bank sought no such notoriety. Mr. Warren trusted that this would be a lesson to Cliff; he was sure that conscience had wrung this confession from the young man. Cliff acted his part adequately.

But all the time his heart was singing. A load had been removed. His fear of Jim Hanvey had turned into a deep, passionate, personal hatred. He felt that he'd like to fasten his fingers in that fat, flabby throat.

He swung out of the president's office. The loss of the hundred thousand dollars meant little as against the relief he experienced in the freedom from fear of those mesmeric, expressionless eyes. As he stepped into the lobby he felt them fastened upon him.

Cliff couldn't resist the impulse. Pent-up emotion demanded expression in words. Cliff knew that he must tell this heavy-set, slow-moving man that he had been outwitted. He strode across the lobby and pulled up short before the detective.

"Well, Hanvey, you're too late."

The eyelids dropped slowly, then opened even more slowly. "Huh?"

"I beat you to it." Cliff was gripped by a moderate hysteria. "I've fixed everything—for myself. You don't get a bit of glory. And I wanted the satisfaction of telling you that I've known from the first you suspected me."

Jim Hanvey's fishy eyes opened wide, then narrowed. His fat fingers fumbled awkwardly with the glittering gold toothpick. His demeanor was one of bewilderment and utter lack of comprehension.

"What you talkin' about, son? Suspected you of what?"

Cliff felt suddenly cold. There was a disquieting ring of truth in the drawling voice. Was it possible that this hulk of a man had not suspected him, that the confession had been unnecessary? His trembling hands sought the pudgy shoulders of the detective,

"You've been watching me and my cage, haven't you?"

"Sure."

"Well—why?"

The big man's manner was genial, friendly. His dull round eyes blinked and his voice dropped discreetly. "Jest between us, son, I reckon there ain't no harm in me explainin'. 'Bout three years ago Spade Gormon, cleverest forger in the country, pulled an awful neat job in Des Moines. Then he dropped outa sight. We ain't heard nothin' of him till headquarters got the tip he was operatin' in this district. We knew good and well if he was he'd sooner or later try to slip a bum check over on this bank, it bein' the biggest one hereabouts. So as I know Spade pretty well an' personal, they sent me down here to loaf around until he showed up."

Cliff Wallace's hands dropped limply to his sides. It was hard to understand. "Then you weren't even working on my case?"

"No, I wasn't workin' on your case. An' if you went an' confessed anything, you probably done yourself an awful dirty trick. Far as I'm concerned, son, I ain't even been interested in your case since I got an inside tip it had been dropped."

Homespun Silk

Jim Hanvey was not at all the type of man one envisions when the word "detective" is mentioned. He was immoderately large and shapeless and his cheap ready-made clothes flapped grotesquely about the ungainly figure. Above a collar of inconsequential height but amazing circumference arose a huge head which contained a face of incarnadined[*] complexion, scant and unkempt hair, pendulous jowls and twin chins. His lips were large and loose, ears flappy, and his eyes——

The eyes were the outstanding feature of Jim Hanvey's topography. They were strikingly inexpressive; great sleepy orbs of fishy hue, impressing one with the idea of sightlessness. It seemed impossible that those eyes were capable of vision. They sat glassily in the red pudgy face beneath a hedge of overdeveloped brows. And Jim's blinking—as a matter of fact, he didn't blink; he yawned with his eyelids. An interminably slow process of drooping the lids over the dull-gray eyes, of holding them shut for a moment, and then of uncurtaining them with even more maddening deliberation.

---

[*] Reddened.

Jim emerged heavily from the dilapidated taxicab which screeched to a halt before the ornate portals of the Hanover Apartments. He turned hesitantly toward the taxidriver, who made no effort to conceal the vastness of his contempt. "How much I owe you, son?"

The meter was consulted—a mere matter of form. "Dollar forty."

Jim Hanvey whistled in protest as he counted out one wrinkled dollar bill, a quarter, a dime and a nickel. Then as he waddled into the Hanover he shook his head slowly. "Dollar forty! Holy smokes! An' I thought I knew every professional crook in America."

He walked uncertainly through the cheaply magnificent lobby. The ebony lad at the switchboard eyed him insolently. Jim paused, toying with a gold toothpick which hung suspended from a watchchain of hawserlike* proportions.

"Mr. Arthur Sherwood in?"

"Yeh. Who wants to see him?"

Hanvey's bushy eyebrows arched in surprise. "Why, me, of course."

"Who you is?"

"Hanvey is my name. Mr. James Hanvey."

"Huh!" The boy plugged in viciously, and then, into the transmitter: "That you, Mistuh Sherwood?...There's a guy down here wants to see you....Says his name is James Hanvey....Yeh! Hanvey....All right, suh." He turned back and vouchsafed his information grudgingly.

"Mistuh Sherwood says come right up. Apahtment Fo'-twelve."

Hanvey moved a couple of steps toward the elevator, then turned for a moment. "Son!"

---

* A "hawser" is a heavy rope or cable of the kind used to moor a ship.

"What?"

"Next time I come remember I ain't no guy. I'm a feller."

Sherwood answered Hanvey's ring in person; a slender man of medium height, distinguished in appearance, exquisitely groomed, very much at ease. He ushered his visitor into a richly comfortable library, where he motioned toward a chair, into which Hanvey thumped gratefully. He stared about the room in frank approval.

"Awful soft, eh, Arthur?"

The host smiled, exhibiting twin rows of even white teeth. "Rather comfortable."

"Business must be good."

"It is. Very."

"H'mph!"

Hanvey yawned with his eyes, inspecting the rich furnishings, which gave testimony to the unerringly fastidious taste of the owner. Still gazing Jim produced from a tarnished almost-silver cigar case two projectiles of profound blackness. He handed one to Sherwood, who accepted it gingerly, smelled of it suspiciously, and then emitted a single exclamation of protest.

"It ain't the worst in the world," remarked Hanvey. Sherwood produced a bottle and glasses. Hanvey joined him with gusto. "Here's to you, Arthur. May the judge give you a light sentence."

Sherwood smiled with his lips, but in his eyes lay a faint light of apprehension. He made no comment upon the detective's toast. For a few minutes silence maintained between them, Hanvey draining his liquor at a gulp, Sherwood sipping his with the relish of a connoisseur. It was the visitor who broke the silence.

"It's gonna be pretty tough, Arthur—givin' up all of this."

"Is it?"

"Uh-huh. But you shouldn't have done it."

It was patent that Sherwood was very much on guard. "Done what?"

"Steal them jools off Mrs. Haley."

"I?"

"Yeh—you. It was a pretty slick piece of work, Arthur. But it wasn't quite slick enough."

Sherwood seated himself opposite the detective and crossed one leg over the other. He lighted a cigar of his own, a rich, fragrant, expensive thing.

His tone was quietly argumentative as he replied:

"I think it was slick enough, Jim."

"Aw, Arthur! I'm s'prised at you."

"I was a bit surprised at myself, Jim. As a matter of fact, I don't believe you're going to arrest me for that little affair."

"Why not?"

"You can't prove a thing. And if you arrest me without sufficient evidence to convict, you'll have the double disappointment of seeing yourself made ridiculous while I go free. And safe."

Hanvey nodded agreement. "You're an awful plausible talker, Arthur." He leaned forward in his chair. "Just between friends—you did steal them jools, didn't you?"

"Between friends?"

"Uh-huh."

"Yes, I stole them. But you can't prove it, Jim."

"M'm! I could arrest you now an' say that you confessed you stole 'em."

"It wouldn't help you. Any flatfoot can do that any time he wishes—but it doesn't secure a conviction. What you need, Jim, is evidence—and evidence is the one thing you can't get. If you arrest me and say that I confessed I'll simply deny it, and where will you be? You need proof, my boy; proof."

Hanvey reflected heavily.

"Reckon you're right, Arthur. I was hoping you wouldn't put

me to all the trouble of gettin' it. I was hopin' to get away on a little fishin' trip."

Sherwood was more at ease. "What makes you think I got that stuff?"

"I don't think it, Arthur; I know it. I suspected it, and then I checked up. I'll hand you one thing, son—you sure are—what-you-call-it?—an opportunist."

"Am I?"

"You are. I'm handlin' this affair for the company that Mrs. Haley's jools was insured in, and I've been down to N'Yawlins checkin' up. I reckon I know more about this affair than you do."

"That's interesting."

"Ain't it? An' seein' that you've been so frank as to admit that you done it, p'r'aps you'd like to know what I know about it myself, eh?"

"Yes."

Jim's voice, flat and expressionless, seemed to fill the expensively furnished room.

"Startin' at the beginnin', Arthur, there was Mrs. Grover Haley, wife of the president of the L. R. & C. Railroad.* Hubby traveled the usual route to sudden wealth—engine wiper, fireman, engineer, superintendent. Then he made a killing in oil. They elected him president of the road. Worth close onto twenty millions now. Lives in Chicago. His wife—she ain't exactly one of these here sylphs. He married her when he was a fireman. He's president of the road now, but she's still a fireman's wife. Fightin' all the time to rise up, but not succeedin' specially well.

"This here Mrs. Haley ain't strong on polish, but she's got the

---

* A fictitious railroad; one can only speculate what states or cities the letters stood for. In 1923, Chicago was—and remains—the rail capital of the United States, with more railroad lines serving more cities than any other location. At one point, Chicago had six city-to-city stations.

old ambish* by the tail on a downhill pull. Far as her appearance is concerned—she ain't got any. She's sort of the same upholstery style that I am. An' the only thing she craves in this world is society; none of your pikin'† society, either, but the genuine stuff; the kind that even twenty millions can't buy. For seven years she's been trying to jimmy into the real crowd, an' meetin' with about as much success as an oyster in a hurdle race." He paused briefly. "I've got it pretty straight so far, haven't I, Arthur?"

The other man smiled. "That much is fairly common knowledge."

"Reckon it is. Well, to go on, this here Mrs. Haley starts out from Chicago about a month ago in her private car, headed for Palm Beach by way of Memphis an' N'Yawlins. She carries with her a maid an' a chef an' a butler. Also she carries with her about one hundred and fifty thousand dollars' worth of joolry which she plans to wear all at one time, just to prove that she's a lady. An' about the time she makes her plans a certain Mr. Arthur Sherwood, who is playin' the races down in N'Yawlins, gets wind of it and decides to make a play for them stones.

"Far as I can see, Arthur, you started out without any definite plan. Opportunist—ain't that the word I used before? You figured that all you needed was to get close enough to them jools for a long enough time an' they were yours. An' so, as society is your fad, you went an' had some cards engraved which announced that you was Mr. Albert Grinnell Stoneham, said Mr. Stoneham bein' the son of one of the most exclusive families socially in New York, where they have society as is society.

"You meet the train at Memphis and just after leaving there your card goes back to Mrs. Haley, an' that dame nearly drops

---

* Ambition.

---

† "Piking" in this context means cautious, mean, or cheap.

dead with joy. To make it brief, she lassoes the son of the great Stoneham family and makes him her guest. It looks like the first real break-in she's made in seven years, as it gives her an elegant excuse to drop in on Pa and Ma Stoneham when she gets to New York next time. And so Mr. Sherwood, alias Mr. Stoneham, gets an awful warm welcome on the private car, an' Mrs. Haley wears a hundred and fifty thousand dollars' worth of joolry every time she comes within range of his eyes." Jim lighted another cigar. "Wasn't your fingers itching to grab them stones an' run, Arthur?"

"I'm very fond of jewelry, Jim."

"Sure! Or you wouldn't have taken all them chances. I've checked up, you see. To get ahead: You reached N'Yawlins at eight o'clock. You had been down there at the races, an' you had gone to Memphis to meet that train. The car was going out on a Jacksonville train at six the next morning. An' you asked Mrs. Haley wouldn't she like to go for a sightseeing drive. You went out an' hired a big touring car an' you went for the drive. You gave her an awful good feed at Emil's—they say you know how to order a swell dinner, Arthur—an' about ten o'clock that night you showed up at the Spanish Fort Inn.

"Out there you had a swell time. Bein' known to the head waiter, not to mention the proprietor, the sky was the limit. You had cocktails an' champagne an' maybe even a liqueur or six. Poor Mrs. Haley, thinkin' she was in Rome, done as the Romans did, an', to put it mild an' polite, got sweetly spifflicated. Not drunk, but terribly happy. She found herself sittin' on top of the world an' didn't care who saw her. You left the inn about two in the a.m. an' Mrs. Haley insisted on sittin' in front with you so's she could drive the car. You wasn't particularly keen about it, but you didn't kick hard enough, because same is what she done, the shoffer reclinin' in the back.

"The old dame had started out to prove she could drive—an'

she proved it. I reckon she must have busted sixty sev'ral times comin' into the city. Ol' gal was just naturally havin' a helluva time. That is, she was until you got 'most home. It was there that somethin' happened—because it was there, Arthur, that a cop seen the speed you was goin' at an' tried to stop you. An' poor Mrs. Haley, not carin' nothin' for no cops, with a bunch of drinks inside her, ran into him!

"What happened then, Arthur"—and Jim Hanvey shook his enormous head reprovingly—"was downright unfortunate. The cop was stunned. You stopped your car, an' just when you did the cop moved, indicating that he wasn't so terribly hurt. With which the missus slipped into gear, stepped on the gas an' let 'er rip. Cop fired one time in the air an' you were free. Mrs. Haley drove that car to somewhere in the French quarter, you got out an' slipped the scared shoffer a nice piece of change to keep mum, and back you beat it to the private car.

"That's where good luck played into your hands, Arthur; right plumb into 'em. Bein' an opportunist—Say! That's a swell word, ain't it? I got it out of the dictionary before I come here. Bein' an opportunist like I was sayin', you'd just stuck around with the fat dame, knowin' that sooner or later you'd get a chance at them jools. An' kerflooie, her cop-knockin' experience puts everything in your paws. How? Because you knew darned good an' well that shoffer was goin' to lay pretty low on account of what they'd give him if they ever found out it was his car. The farther away he keeps from the spotlight in connection with that case the more comfortable he's gonna be.

"An' of course Mrs. Haley is now a fugitive from justice down in N'Yawlins.

"You took her back to the private car. She had sobered up more than a little, but the strong stuff was still there inside of her. Her nerves was doin' a shimmy, an' you gave her plenty more to drink.

Finally she went to sleep. When that happened you grabbed the jools an' hopped the car. Mrs. Haley didn't wake up until she was on her way to Jacksonville. It was a couple hours later that she found out the jools was gone—an' you too. The old gal nearly went nuts until she remembered her insurance, then she figured she was sittin' on Easy Street. An' it may interest you to know that the insurance money has already been paid to her; one hundred thousand dollars."

Sherwood sat motionless, staring admiringly at the portly detective. By no slightest physical sign did he give indication of his genuine enthusiasm for Hanvey's deductive powers, although he marveled at them with the frank appreciation of one brainy man for the accomplishments of another.

Hanvey's story was correct to a detail. Sherwood knew the exhaustive search that the detective must have made, the painstaking probing.

And now—"You're working for the insurance company aren't you, Jim?"

"Yeh." Hanvey was very open about it. "We've already paid the money, but we're interested now in gettin' the jools back an' puttin' you in stir. That's why I come to see you."

Sherwood smiled. "You're not going to arrest me, Jim."

"Why not?"

"Because you can't prove a thing."

Jim grinned. "Maybe not just yet. I've talked to Mrs. Haley. Bein' a social climber she ain't any too keen to let it be known publicly that she was imposed on by a faker. That'd make folks laugh at her. An' if, in addition to that, it was ever known that she was the woman who flattened the N'Yawlins cop at the end of a wild party it'd sort of queer her about as queer as could be. An' since she ain't sufferin' only a fifty-thousand-dollar loss anyway—she most certainly wouldn't identify you.

"Y'see, Arthur, it's thisaway: I spotted you easy enough. You are known out at the inn. But nobody knew the dame who was with you. An' it was her that hit the cop. Also, I'm confessin' frankly that the maid an' the chef an' the butler ain't gonna identify you neither. Mrs. Haley has fixed them a-plenty. So she's in the clear, you've got the jools, an' we're stung. That makes us plumb angry, Arthur; bein' rode for a hundred thousand thataway. It just naturally puts it up to me to get you an' the jools both."

"I hope you enjoy yourself trying, Jim."

"I been havin' a good enough time a'ready. But I ain't particularly keen about the job. You're too good a crook to be in jail. But, by gosh, Arthur, you never should of fooled with no woman!"

Sherwood was unimpressed. "You can't find the jewels, Jim."

"Reckon I can. Reckon I can land you too."

"How?"

"Because a crook can't get away with it if the tecs are really after him. You've slipped somewhere. It's just up to me to find out where."

"I'm surprised at you—thinking I've slipped."

"You ain't no different from other crooks, Arthur, except you've got more sense."

"Well"—Arthur rose ostentatiously—"I reckon you want to trot me down to headquarters."

"No. Certainly not. Ain't no use of my arresting you unless you're going to plead guilty."

"Sometimes you're a real humorist, Jim."

"Ain't I? I'm awful cute occasionally. What I really come up for, Arthur, was to tell you how much I know. I want you to see just where you stand. I figured you'd be willin' to help me all you could."

"Certainly, Jim, certainly. Just drop around any old time and talk things over. I'll do all in my power to hinder you."

"Thanks, Arthur. I counted on you for that."

They shook hands; slender, immaculate, polished man-about-town and the mammoth expressionless detective. The contrast was striking. Sherwood ushered Hanvey to the door and bade him a cordial farewell. Then alone, the criminal dropped into a chair and mopped his forehead with a silken handkerchief.

Hanvey had startled him—just as Hanvey had intended. With uncanny intuition Hanvey had pieced together a story so nearly approximating the facts that Sherwood was amazed. And he was now very much on guard. The one hundred and fifty thousand dollars' worth of jewelry nestled in a safety-deposit box at one of the Manhattan banks. It was a box Sherwood had possessed for several years, holding it against just such an opportunity as this. It was rented under an assumed name.

Immediately after the jewel robbery he had boarded a train for New York, but not before he carefully had unset the gems and pitched the elaborate platinum settings into the depths of Lake Pontchartrain. The jewels in their little chamois sack were safe.

From the outset Sherwood had realized that he would have difficulty in disposing of the gems. He was content. A stake of that size was worth waiting for—two years, three, five. But he had not anticipated that suspicion would so readily attach to himself. Now that Jim knew the story, he felt that he must redouble his precautions.

The Mrs. Haley end of the situation was safe. He smiled at recollection of the pitifully gullible wife of the railroad president; the blatant, rather vulgar woman who thought to get into the most exclusive social circles by a display of jewelry. She had been so eagerly responsive to his glib chattering about prominent New Yorkers, had so warmly welcomed his casual invitation to telephone when next she came to New York in order that his supposed parents should have the opportunity of entertaining her.

He had understood fully the value of social position to Mrs. Haley. For years she had struggled gamely, mounting with horrid slowness. She was jealous of her trifling successes. This story, made public in the newspapers and expanded in the dirt-slinging weeklies, would ruin her forever. Safety was possible to her in only one way—she must not identify the man who had been her guest on the private car. And Hanvey had reassured him on that point. That had been the single doubtful link in his safety chain; and he knew now that it was one of the strongest.

He'd have to watch Jim Hanvey for a while. It would be an interesting game, laughing in his sleeve as Hanvey banged his fat head against an endless succession of brick walls. Eventually Jim would tire of the search, and then he would dispose of the jewels one by one. Not in a group, of course—they were of such great value that the attention of the police would immediately be attracted through the kind efforts of stool pigeons—but singly, at distant points, and with utmost discretion. The more Sherwood contemplated the plan the more assured he became. He felt sorry for Jim Hanvey. "Nice fellow too. I hate to see him fall down on the case."

As for the detective, he apparently did not share Sherwood's fear for his non-success. If he had a worry he concealed it exceedingly well behind the pudgy face. Too, he fell into the habit of calling casually on Sherwood at odd hours, and discussing the case.

"Hello, Jim. How's old Sherlock Holmes getting on?"

"So-so, Arthur; just so-so."

"Haven't gathered any definite information, have you?"

"You know durn well I haven't, Arthur."

"You'd better get them to shift you to something else. You'll never get the dope on me."

"Maybe not. An' maybe so. There ain't no tellin.'"

Sherwood leaned forward and rested a friendly hand on Jim Hanvey's knee. "On the level, Jim, you're wasting your time. You know me; you know I'm not a fool."

"Sure, I know that."

"And you know that I've taken every possible precaution. I was careful enough before; I'm doubly careful now. With you on the case, Jim, I wouldn't take a chance for anything in the world."

"You're terrible complimentary."

"I know you, Jim. You ain't half the fool you look. You couldn't be. Now, frankly, I don't expect to cash in on this little deal for four or five years, and——"

"You ain't ever going to cash in on it, Arthur."

The narrow, rather ascetic face of the criminal broke into a broad grin. "Trying to make me apprehensive?"

"No; just talkin' sense. You know the gang I'm working for. It ain't so much the hundred thou' insurance money they've shelled out as it is the principle of the thing. They're just butt-headed enough to be willin' to spend money an' time to get you."

"It's impossible."

"Nothin's impossible. No matter how clever you are, you've slipped somewhere."

"I haven't slipped."

"You think you haven't. An' as for you cashing in, you never will. You're playing a lone hand, Arthur, but I ain't. Real detectives never do. I've got the police of the country helpin' me on this thing, an' every stool pigeon we've got is watching for them jools. They're going to keep on watching. An'"—Jim Hanvey leaned forward earnestly—"you ain't gonna cash in on this deal, Arthur, because there ain't a livin' human bein' who'd buy them jools offen you. Not a single living soul."

Sherwood laughed shortly. He was impressed, and tried not to show it.

"We know every fence who'd handle a deal of that size, Arthur. Every one of them. An' they're all bein' watched. The little jools don't matter, but the minute one of them big ones shows up— we're on a hot trail. An' then Mr. Sherwood does a stretch—worse luck."

"I'll wait."

"So will we. Waitin' is the best thing we do. We're just naturally bound to get you. I'd be doubtful if there was any person in the world you could sell them jools to, but there ain't. Not a one. We've taken care of that. An' the comp'ny has told me the sky's the limit. Besides, Arthur, there ain't so bloomin' many places you could of hid them jools. All the time you're waitin' we're workin'. You can't get away with it. The minute I was sure it was you I knew it was just a question of time before I landed you with the dope. Now if you was willin' to make a clean breast of it——"

Sherwood threw back his head and laughed. "Jim Hanvey! I thought better of you than that."

"A'right." The detective hoisted himself from the depths of a leather rocker. "Have it your own way, Arthur. But I sure do wish it was some other feller than you. I'm awful strong for you."

"I know it, Jim." There was genuine feeling in the other's voice. "It's just a little game; you're on one side and I'm on the other. One of us has got to lose—and I'm plumb sorry it's you."

Alone again Sherwood walked to the window, where he stood looking down into Central Park. Dusk was merging gently into night. The shadowy walks under the trees were dislimning* in the softly gathering gloom. There floated up to his ears the commanding screech of automobile sirens, the clang of passing Eighth Avenue cars, the voices of a group of children. Then into the picture bulked the slouching figure of Jim Hanvey.

---

* Effacing, vanishing.

Sherwood watched the ungainly hulk interestedly. He saw Hanvey enter the park and pause to light a cigar. There was something almost pathetic about the big hulking man, a humbleness that was deceptive to those who did not know him intimately. Too, there was a fairness and squareness which made him popular with the higher class of criminals. They knew he was on the level. He took no unfair advantage of them. He played the game clean. "If I've got to be caught I'd rather Jim Hanvey made the pinch." That was the idea; they were proud of their friendship with Jim Hanvey. They played clean with him and he with them. He looked out for them after he arrested them; saw they were given a square deal; didn't forget them when they were doing time. A lonely man, Jim Hanvey; big and ugly and ungainly—and eagerly friendly. His best friends stood high in the criminal social register. Outside the underworld he had no intimates.

Sherwood saw him walk on slowly, in the lumbering gait of a man too bulky for his feet. And gradually the big figure was lost in the gloom. He was there—then gone. Sherwood turned away from the window, "It's a dirty shame. He would have made a wonderful crook."

He pondered over his recent conversation with the detective. Jim's utterances were worthy of serious reflection; Jim was not given to trickery of speech. Besides he knew Sherwood too well to bluff. He understood that Sherwood would play a waiting game.

Sherwood was willing, but a trifle disturbed. He hadn't anticipated having the robbery traced to his door so promptly. There had been no opportunity to dispose of even a few of the gems. And he wasn't too well supplied with cash. Of course with Jim watching every move it would be impossible to pull another job; he'd have to lay low and take things easy. Worse luck.

Jim was right of course. At present there was no one to whom he could sell the jewels. No professional fence would handle them, and if an amateur took over the jewels he, Sherwood, would be lucky to get ten thousand dollars. "And I'll never let them go for that; not if I have to wait ten years."

He visited Jim Hanvey a couple of days later. "I've been thinking over our little talk, Jim."

"That's good."

"Suppose I handed the jewels to you, would you forget that you knew who took them?"

"Wish I could, Arthur, but it isn't possible. We want you."

Sherwood shrugged. "I'll just have to wait then."

"That's foolish. I'll get you sooner or later. You might as well come clean and start serving your time now. Every day you put it off is just that much time wasted."

"I've got plenty of time, Jim."

"Yeh, reckon so. I hardly thought you'd 'fess up."

"Not a chance."

"I'm real sorry for you, Arthur. All that trouble, all that risk—and you ain't gonna get nothin' out of it."

"I'll make out very well."

"Nope. You can't sell 'em, an' there ain't no other way of realizin' on your investment of time and effort."

Sherwood knew that he must hold on for a long, long while. It was awkward, but necessary. He was too clever a performer to worry about financial stringency. Jim was after him now as keenly as he was after the jewels, even more so. Of course he had never intended turning the jewels over to Hanvey; had quizzed him solely for the purpose of finding out whether it was the man or the jewels they were seeking. The fact that it was the former made greater caution imperative.

Jim was using the police too. That was further embarrassment. The police system bothers criminals, it is so extensive and comprehensive, a system of surveillance that eventually wears a man down. Playing lone hands, Sherwood knew that the advantage would always be with the criminal. But fighting against the individual brilliance of a detective and the inexorable patience and scope of the nation's police departments, a man had to watch his step pretty carefully.

Sherwood was willing—but it was deucedly uncomfortable.

Jim had impressed him. There was no one to whom he could sell the jewels; not for several years, at any rate, not a soul. Unless, perhaps——Sherwood nodded slowly. "It's worth thinking over," he told himself.

Two days later Sherwood's telephone buzzed, and Jim Hanvey's monotonous droning voice came to him over the wire:

"That you, Arthur?"

"Yes."

"This is Jim Hanvey."

"Yes."

"Busy?"

"Not particularly."

"How 'bout droppin' over to my rooms a minute. I got somethin' to show you; somethin' real interestin.'"

"Coming."

"Right away?"

"Pronto."

A taxi, a swift journey uptown to West 110th Street; Jim Hanvey's three-room apartment—a stuffy affair grotesquely furnished and vilely kept; three rooms which sagged under the heavy odor of Jim's cigars.

Sherwood swore fervently and threw up the windows in the tiny parlor.

"Jim, you shouldn't."

"What?"

"Smoke those cigars indoors."

"Oh! Them? Gosh! I like 'em."

"The other tenants don't kick?"

"Dunno. The janitor done time once in Joliet,* an' him an' me is buddies. He was a awful rotten yegg,† but he's a swell janitor. That just shows——Anyway, you ain't interested in him; n'r me neither for that matter. I got somethin' to show you."

"So you said."

"C'mere."

Sherwood trailed his host into the dining room. Jim motioned him to a chair. "Just got one thing to ask, Arthur; that is that you use your eyes—not your hands."

"Whatever you say, Jim."

"Good." From the capacious hip pocket of his voluminous trousers Hanvey extracted a little chamois sack. Sherwood's eyes narrowed slightly. Chamois sack! Jewelry! Hanvey, apparently unmindful of his visitor, droned on:

"Just you watch, Arthur—but remember, hands off."

With a quick deft motion he opened the sack and spilled its contents on the imitation-mahogany table. The fishlike eyes of the detective were focused vacantly upon Arthur Sherwood, who had started involuntarily from his seat. Then Sherwood caught himself, controlled his nerves with an effort and tried to smile.

"What's the idea, Jim?"

Hanvey's glassy eyes were turned to the table top, upon which glowed and flamed a handful of magnificent gems—matched

---

* The Joliet prison (officially, the Joliet Correctional Center) operated from 1858 to 2002 and housed murderers such as Leopold and Loeb and John Wayne Gacy (as well as "Joliet" Jake Blues of *The Blues Brothers*).

† Short for "yegg-man," this slang term originally referred to tramp-thieves, but its usage broadened out to include criminals generically. Etymologists are in disagreement about whether the name stemmed from a criminal named Yegg or another named Yeager, but it was adopted by William Pinkerton, son of the founder of the Pinkerton Detective Agency, who used it regularly in a popular series of speeches between 1900 and 1907 discussing the rise of American crime.

pearls, diamonds of rare cut and brilliance, a huge blood ruby, twin emeralds of enormous size and clarity, deep oriental sapphires. The eyes of the detective closed slowly, sleepily, then opened with maddening leisureliness.

"How you like 'em, Arthur?"

Sherwood appeared at ease, but his nerves were under a terrific tension. "Very much."

"Look familiar?"

Sherwood nodded frankly. "Yes."

They were familiar; stone for stone they were the jewels he had stolen from Mrs. Haley—stolen from her, stripped from their mountings, and which at that moment he could have sworn were safe in a box at one of the city's largest banks. There was no mistaking them—the ruby, the big diamond with the odd workmanship.

"What are they, Jim?"

Hanvey grinned genially.

"Paste."

"Paste?"

"Sure. Can't you tell?"

"Where did you get them?"

"Had 'em made from the descriptions the insurance company has. I think they look grand—for paste."

Sherwood stared at the glittering gems as though hypnotized. And while he gazed Hanvey's huge hand went out and swept them back into the chamois sack. "Awful good imitations, I think, Arthur."

Sherwood laughed weakly. "They are. Mighty clever."

The sack was returned to Hanvey's pocket. "I got to be trottin' along downtown, Arthur. That's all I wanted of you—just to show you them imitation jools."

Sherwood was nervous. He more than half expected to be

arrested, and he drew a deep breath of relief as he stepped into the street. He walked swiftly toward the corner, turned sharply, and saw Hanvey emerge from the apartment house and follow him. A slight frown corrugated the criminal's forehead.

He was frankly worried. Hanvey was too insistent about the brummagem* quality of the gems. Doubt assailed him. Perhaps they were the genuine stones. It was impossible—but if they were imitations they were wonderful. Suppose Hanvey had discovered the location of his safety-deposit box and the name in which it was held? Suppose he had actually secured the gems?

Sherwood hailed a passing taxi and entered. As he did so he saw another cab ease around the corner. Jim Hanvey overflowed the back seat, cigar between his pursy lips. Sherwood spoke swiftly to his driver. "See that cab yonder?"

"Yeh."

"Lose it and you get twenty dollars."

"Cinch."

At the same moment Hanvey was speaking with his own driver. "See that cab up ahead—the one the good-lookin' feller is just gettin' into?"

"Uh-huh."

"Foller it an' you get five dollars."

"Cinch."

The chase started. Both cabs swung into Riverside Drive at moderate speed, Sherwood's driver playing a careful game until such time as he might find an opportunity to elude pursuit in a traffic jam. Along Riverside they went, turning eastward to Broadway on Seventy-second Street, thence down that thoroughfare to Park Circle. It was there that luck played into Sherwood's hands. His cab crossed Park Circle just as the traffic policeman

---

* Cheap, counterfeit.

raised his hand. It took Hanvey fully a half minute to exhibit his credentials to the policeman, and by that time Sherwood had sped eastward on Fifty-eighth Street, turning downtown on Sixth Avenue and doubling back uptown via Fiftieth Street and Ninth Avenue.

Sherwood was confident that he had eluded Hanvey, but he was taking no chance. As a matter of fact, additional precaution was unnecessary. Hanvey's taxi reached Fifty-eighth, Jim glanced down the avenue through an endless line of cabs, touring cars and busses, and motioned his driver to a halt. "Needn't go no farther, son. They've got away. How much?"

"Dollar eighty."

Hanvey handed him a two-dollar bill. "Keep the change." Then, as he started across toward the Subway kiosk, he glanced at his watch. "Three-thirty—hmph!"

He entered the Subway and rode uptown. When he alighted it was to walk to Central Park West and seat himself on the steps of Sherwood's apartment house. He was smiling slightly and there appeared to be a faint sign of life in his dead fishy eyes. Sherwood had proceeded with meticulous care. He left his taxi on West Sixty-fourth Street, took a surface car to the Pennsylvania Hotel, entered the Subway via the lobby of that hostelry, rode downtown and thence to his bank, where he secured access to the safety-deposit box held by himself under the alias of Roger Clarkson.

His examination took but a moment. The jewels were there, every last one of them. He sighed relievedly. Then as he left the bank he found himself worrying. He realized that Jim Hanvey had some deeply ulterior motive, that he had not gone to the trouble and expense of securing the paste duplicates without making them a part of an elaborate trap. Hanvey's very frankness had been disquieting. Paste, said Hanvey, made from the insurance company descriptions. Well, Hanvey had told the truth. But why?

Sherwood was apprehensive. Here had entered the first element the criminal was unable to understand. Until this moment he had felt a bit sorry for Jim Hanvey's heavy blundering, his bovine indifference and his lethargy. But now—

Still seeking a solution Sherwood rode uptown on the Elevated and then walked to his apartment. As he turned in at the door the monster figure of Jim Hanvey hoisted itself from the marble steps.

"Hello, Arthur."

"Jim! You here?"

"Naw! I'm over in Brooklyn huntin' for the other end of the bridge."

Sherwood took his friend by the arm. "Come upstairs a minute, Jim. I want to chat with you."

"Sure."

Hanvey selected the most comfortable chair and crashed into it. Sherwood walked to the window, put up the shade and turned toward the Gargantuan figure of his friend. Sherwood's face was in shadow, that of the detective in the full glare of daylight—as expressionful as putty.

"I've been trying to figure out your little play, Jim."

"Have you?"

"Yes. And I don't get the answer. About the only idea I can see behind it was that you showed me those imitations to make me go down to the vault where I have the real stones to reassure myself."

"You're hittin' on all six so far, Arthur."

"And that you'd trail me there and find out what box——"

"Arthur Sherwood! I'm plumb disappointed in you—knockin' me thataway. You don't honestly think I thought I could trail you through the streets of New York, do you?"

"It didn't seem so, Jim—unless you were attaining your second childhood. But I couldn't figure out any other reason—and you did try to follow me."

Hanvey shook his head slowly. "Nope."

"In that taxi?"

"That wasn't my idea, Arthur." The detective's big spatulate fingers drummed lightly on the table. "All I was doin', Arthur, was to make sure that you was tryin' to shake me!"

"A-ah!" Sherwood's thin lips compressed. Hanvey waved genially. "Think it over."

Sherwood thought it over. Then: "Well, I was trying to shake you. Where does that get you?"

"A heap of places, Arthur. 'Cause how? 'Cause the minute you tried to shake me I knew good an' well you was doin' it because you was headed for the vault where you had the jools hid. Of course it is a vault—no crook of your intelligence would hide 'em anywheres else. So the minute you gave me the slip I come on back here an' waited for you."

"Ye-e-es." Sherwood was puzzled. "But why?"

"Because, Arthur, I laid an awful clever trap for you, an' you fell into it. You don't mind my callin' myself clever, do you, Arthur? I really do think it was an awful good stunt I pulled."

"Just what was it, Jim."

Hanvey glanced at his enormous watch. "Just this: At some time between 3:45 and 4:30 this afternoon you went to your bank box. You signed your card—under an alias, of course. An' tomorrow mornin' I start out inspectin' the vault cards of every bank in New York. I'll get help from headquarters, an' eventually we'll check up on every man, woman an' child who entered a bank box in that three-quarters of an hour."

The detective grinned in boyish approval of his own acumen. "'Tain't gonna be such an easy job, Arthur, but it ain't gonna be so hard neither—me not carin' particularly about time in this case. Of course I know the box is in a Manhattan bank, because you got back too quick to have gone to Brooklyn or even Jersey

City. Jerry Naschbaum, chief of the headquarters identification force, will let me have a few good men to help. In one week, two weeks mebbe three, we'll check up on everybody who entered a bank box between 3:45 and 4:30 today. An' when we've done that, Arthur, we'll have you. See?"

Arthur saw. "I wish some one else was on this case, Jim. You're too blamed painstaking."

"Better 'fess up now."

"No; I'll take my chances."

"Ain't gonna get you nowhere. You can't sell them jools; there ain't a soul in the world would buy 'em offen you."

"Maybe not." Sherwood opened the door invitingly. "Sorry you have to be going, Jim."

"I'm sorry myself, Arthur." He turned at the doorway. "I'm kinder cute yet, ain't I?"

"I hope not, Jim," was the answer.

It did not take Sherwood long to realize that he was nearing the end of his rope. He might have known that Jim Hanvey was going to trap him. That had been a clever trick of Jim's, and it promised definite and fairly immediate results. Hanvey was right; the task of checking up would be a slow and difficult undertaking, but Sherwood knew the police system sufficiently well to understand—and fear—its tirelessness. Eventually they'd complete their check-up, and when they did——

Sherwood admitted to himself that he must dispose of the jewels. Thought of transferring them to another box was out of the question. They'd discover that eventually. The thing to do was to rid himself of the gems. But Jim Hanvey had insisted that he could not sell them because there was no market. Jim had spoken truly. No market. "Oh, confound Mrs. Haley and her jewelry!"

Sherwood caught his breath suddenly. Mrs. Haley! Puffy, ponderous Mrs. Haley! The poor, bewildered, self-sufficient

Mrs. Haley, who had lost one hundred and fifty thousand dollars' worth of jewelry and been partially reimbursed with one hundred thousand dollars of the insurance company's money. Sherwood smashed his right fist into the palm of his left hand.

"There's my market! I'll sell the jewels back to Mrs. Haley!"

He paced the room, his brain running riot with the sardonic daring of his scheme. He knew Jim Hanvey was not infallible. Jim had been so confident that no one would buy the jewels—so confident that he had completely overlooked Mrs. Haley.

And Mrs. Haley would buy. He'd make her buy. No one would think of looking to her for the gems. She could have them set in new mountings and no one would ever be the wiser. He'd sell them to her for fifty thousand dollars, and she'd be fifty thousand dollars winner on the transaction. Then Jim Hanvey could search all he pleased.

He telephoned Mrs. Haley. She was decidedly disinclined to meet him. He assumed a threatening tone. She consented fearfully. They met at Port Chester, he going there by train and she by automobile. She refused frankly to have anything further to do with him.

"Very well, Mrs. Haley. When they arrest me I'll tell the whole story. What happened in New Orleans for one thing; then about your refusal to identify me—I know they've shown you my picture. It will be a choice morsel for the newspapers, and a wonderful story for the society weeklies. You'll be laughed out of the country."

"But if they find out that I've bought them back from you——" The woman was on the verge of hysteria. She was horribly frightened.

"They won't. You're the last person on earth they'd think of in connection with those jewels. You buy them. They can search all they please and they can't get the goods on me. They won't even arrest me because there'll be no evidence to convict. And you will be fifty thousand dollars to the good."

"I can't."

"You can."

"Well, I won't."

A steely light crept into his eyes. "You will! You must!" Eventually she consented. There was nothing else she could do. Petrified with terror, fearful of losing the tiny bit of social recognition for which she had so valiantly struggled, inordinately afraid of arrest in connection with the New Orleans escapade which had assumed Brobdingnagian proportions in her eyes—she agreed to meet him in the private dining room of a quiet hotel, bringing with her fifty thousand dollars in cash, which was to be exchanged for the jewels. And then, apprehensive and nervous, she left him.

Sherwood returned to the city, exultant. His plan had worked. It was safe, supremely safe. For, even should she be eventually discovered in possession of the jewels, she would never dare tell the true story.

But Jim Hanvey had not been idle. He made careful investigation and then spent the entire afternoon chatting with the presidents of the four New York banks where Mrs. Haley maintained personal checking accounts. "She'll cash a big check here in the next few days," explained the detective to each of them. "A thunderin' big check; an' she'll take the money in legal tender. Minute she does, telephone my apartment. Ask for a feller named Henry Jones. He'll take the message an' get in touch with me."

And then Jim Hanvey personally took unto himself the task of watching Mrs. Haley.

It was not difficult. Suspecting no surveillance Mrs. Haley conducted herself so that a blind man could have shadowed her. Mrs. Haley's single major sorrow in life was the stubborn refusal of her husband to take up his residence in New York. Her apartment was a sop, and during her occasional sojourns in the metropolis she expended a vast amount of effort in the task of letting people know that she was somebody. Purple limousine, uniformed chauffeur and footman, shrieking clothes and diamond-studded lorgnette* combined to make Hanvey's self-appointed task absurdly simple. And on the morning of the third day following, the man called Jones notified his superior that only a few hours previously Mrs. Haley had personally cashed her check for fifty thousand dollars.

Jim received the report with a nod. He was lolling comfortably in a taxicab owned by the police department and driven by one of his own operatives. "Yeh! I knew somethin' was about to break. I follered her down to the bank an' seen her when she went in. She's in yonder now"—he nodded in the general direction of the gingerbready apartment house—"an' she'll be comin' out directly. Beat it, Henry."

Henry beat it. The purple limousine appeared. So, too, did Mrs. Haley. Twenty minutes later she entered a modest downtown hotel. Hanvey waited until she had crossed the lobby in the wake of a bellhop and disappeared into an elevator. Then he followed and exhibited his credentials to the manager, receiving from that startled dignitary a bit of helpful information.

"There's a man in that private dining room already, isn't there?"

"Yes, sir."

"Good. I'll trot along up."

He allowed them ample time for conversation. And when he opened the door with a master key furnished by the hotel management it was to interrupt an interesting tableau.

By the table stood Mrs. Haley, clutching in her two hands the sack of jewels. Sherwood was busily engaged in counting the money she had paid over to him. Neither moved.

---

* A pair of glasses with a handle.

Hanvey closed the door gently. His wide-open, fishlike eyes blinked with amazing slowness. Mrs. Haley choked, spluttered and collapsed into a chair. Sherwood's eyes met Hanvey's levelly. The criminal was apparently emotionless, a game loser. Very quietly he took the sack of jewels from the nerveless hands of Mrs. Haley, returned her money and extended the jewels to Hanvey.

"There has been no transaction here of the kind you think, Jim. I am handing over the jewels of my own accord, and confessing to the robbery. There is no need to drag this lady's name in the mud."

Hanvey bowed with ungainly grace. "Always a gent, eh, Arthur? I'm proud of you." He turned to Mrs. Haley. "I reckon it wasn't ever your fault, ma'am. An' me an' my friend Mr. Sherwood here will see that you don't get no rotten publicity out of it."

She was dazed, but volubly and tearfully grateful. Sherwood, calm and dignified, questioned the detective.

"You've got me, Jim. I had a hunch that I wouldn't get away with it. But I have a professional and academic interest in the matter. There are one or two things I don't quite understand."

"Always at your service, Arthur."

"First and most important"—Sherwood's voice was quietly conversational—"what made you think I planned to sell the jewels back to Mrs. Haley?"

Hanvey shook his head reprovingly; "I'm s'prised at you for not knowin' such a simple thing as that, Arthur. The reason I knew you was gonna sell them jools back to Mrs. Haley was because I suggested it to you."

"You suggested——" Then Sherwood smiled in frank admiration. "You mean you suggested it when you said——"

"Sure," interrupted Hanvey pleasantly, "when I kept repeatin' that there wasn't nobody in the world you could sell 'em to—I meant nobody except Mrs. Haley."

Common Stock

Gerald Corwin emerged from the elevator, glanced apprehensively about the ornate lobby of the hotel and walked swiftly toward the dining room. But as he handed hat and cane to the checker a huge, ungainly figure bulked before him and a mild, pleasant voice brought misery where a moment before there had been contentment.

"Gonna eat now, Corwin?"

Gerald sighed resignedly. Too thoroughly a gentleman to display consciously his frank distaste, he was yet too poor a dissembler wholly to conceal it. He merely nodded and strode disgustedly in the wake of the obsequious head waiter, with Jim Hanvey waddling cumbersomely in the rear.

Corwin was disgusted with the whole affair, and particularly that phase of it which placed him under the chaperonage of the ponderous and uncouth detective. Not that Jim had been obtrusive, but the man was innately crude, and Corwin despised crudeness.

One could readily understand his antipathy. The two men were as dissimilar as an orchid and a turnip. Corwin, about thirty years of age, was tall and slender and immaculate, shrieking the word "aristocrat" in every cultured gesture. He was unmistakably a gentleman, a person to whom aesthetics was all-important, and he could not fail to consider Jim Hanvey thoroughly obnoxious.

Jim was all right in his way, perhaps, but never before had Corwin been forced into intimate association with a professional detective. He was resentful, not of the fact that Jim Hanvey was a detective, but because the man was hopelessly uncouth. Jim was an enormous individual and conspicuously unwieldy. He wore cheap, ready-made clothes that no more than approximately fitted his rotund figure. He smoked vile cigars and wore shoes which rose to little peaks at the toes. But Corwin felt he could have stood all that were it not for Jim's gold toothpick.

That golden toothpick, suspended as a charm from a hawserlike chain extending across Jim's vest, had fascinated Corwin from the commencement of their journey to Los Angeles. It was a fearsome, flagrant instrument, and Jim Hanvey loved it. It had been presented to him years before by a criminal of international fame as a token of sincere regard. Otherwise unemployed, Jim was in the habit of sitting by the hour with his fat fingers toying with the toothpick. Gerald had once hinted that the weapon might better be concealed. His insinuation resulted merely in debate.

"Stick it away? Why?"

"A toothpick——"

"Say, listen, Mr. Corwin; have you ever seen a handsomer toothpick?"

"No, but——"

"Well, I haven't either. That's why I'm proud to have folks see it. It's absolutely the swellest toothpick in captivity."

No arguing against that, but from the first hour of the acquaintanceship Corwin reviled the fates which decreed that for two weeks he should be under Hanvey's eye.

The thing was absurd of course. Corwin, fearless and no mean athlete, was well able to take care of himself and fulfill the delicate mission with which he had been intrusted—a mere matter of securing a proxy from Col. Robert E. Warrington and returning with it to New York in time for the annual meeting of the stockholders. He was not a simpleton and there was no doubting his integrity. Why, then, this grotesque and goggle-eyed sleuth?

Matter of fact, Jim had appeared wholly disinterested since their departure from New York. All the way across country he had slouched in their drawing-room, staring through the window with his great, fishy eyes. Those eyes annoyed Corwin. They seemed incapable of vision. They were inhuman, stupid, glassy eyes which reflected no intelligence. Corwin fancied himself the victim of a stupendous hoax; it was unbelievable that this man could rightfully possess a reputation to justify the present assignment.

The meal was torture to the fastidious younger man. There was no denying that Jim enjoyed his dinner, but the enjoyment was too obvious. Jim caught the disapproving glance of his companion and interpreted it rightly.

"'Sall right, Mr. Corwin. Eatin' ain't no art with me. It's a pleasure."

Corwin flushed. Suddenly he discovered that Jim was not listening. Hanvey had turned slightly and was gazing into a mirror which reflected a section of the huge dining room. Corwin followed the direction of his gaze and saw that the object of his scrutiny was a man of medium size but muscular figure who was searching for a table.

Hanvey was interested, and as an indication of that interest he blinked in his interminably deliberate manner, lids closing heavily over the fishy eyes, remaining shut for a second, then uncurtaining even more slowly. And finally, when the newcomer had seated himself, Jim nodded toward him and addressed Corwin.

"Yonder's the answer," he said.

Corwin shook his head in puzzlement.

"To what?"

"Me."

"I don't quite understand."

"See that feller who just come in?"

"Yes."

"It's him."

Corwin inspected the newcomer with fresh interest. The man was of a type, one of those optimistic individuals who futilely struggle to acquire gentility and who fondly believe they have succeeded. In every studied move of the man one could discern mental effort. Even the hypercorrect raiment was subtly suggestive of a disguise. There was nothing flagrantly wrong with the man, just as there was nothing quite as it should be. Corwin, himself not an overly keen student of human nature, could yet fancy the stranger's manner of speech—careful, precise, stilted, rather malapropian,* with here and there a moment of forgetfulness, with its reversion to downright bad grammar. He turned back to Hanvey.

"Who?"

"Billy Scanlan, alias Gentleman William, alias Flash Billy, alias Roger van Dorn, alias, a half dozen other things. He's done time in Joliet and Sing Sing. He's a good friend of mine." The faintest suggestion of a smile played about the corners of Jim's mouth. "An' he's why your crowd hired me to trail you out here."

It was quite plain to Hanvey, but Corwin was puzzled.

"I don't yet understand."

"You don't? Gosh, son, there couldn't anything be any plainer!

---

* A malapropism is a mistaken pairing of words (e.g., "neon stockings" instead of "nylon stockings"). Mrs. Malaprop was a foolish, mixed-up character in Richard Brinsley Sheridan's 1775 play *The Rivals*.

We ain't never discussed what brought you out here, but I know all about it just the same; an' since you prob'ly won't answer no questions, I'll tell you what I know. The Quincy-Scott gang started a drive recently to grab off the control of the K. R. & P. Railroad from McIntosh and his crowd. Before McIntosh woke up the Quincy bunch had coralled every loose vote, enough to give them a control in the forthcomin' stockholders' meetin'. When McIntosh got wise he knew that his only hope was Colonel Warrington out here in Los Angeles, the colonel ownin' about ninety thousand shares of common stock. So he telephoned the old bird and found out that he wasn't interested in the fight one way or the other; that he'd already been approached by the Quincy-Scott combination an' had turned 'em down cold an' final, which seemed to indicate that with a little proper persuasion he'd be willin' to deliver a proxy to McIntosh. It bein' 'most time for the meeting an' things bein' pretty desperate, they sent you out to get the proxy from the ol' gent, his proxy gettin' there meanin' victory for McIntosh, an its failure leavin' the vote control with Quincy an' Scott. Ain't it so?"

Corwin was staring at Hanvey in amazement. The pudgy detective had been speaking disinterestedly, casually, but he had the most intimate facts at his finger-tips. Corwin nodded before he thought, then bit his tongue.

"I'm not at liberty to say whether or not you're correct, Mr. Hanvey."

"Sure you ain't. You're dead right, son. Don't you never spill no beans to nobody no time. I wasn't tryin' to pump you. I got the dope straight from headquarters. I was just tellin' you so you'd understand that I know why I was sent out with you, an' so you'd understand too."

Hanvey paused, and as though that ended the matter he extracted from an elaborately engraved and sadly tarnished silver-plated cigar case two huge black invincibles,* one of which he reluctantly extended to his companion. Corwin declined, and Jim sighed relievedly as he tenderly returned the cigar to its place. He lighted the other, inhaled with gusto and blew a cloud of the smoke into the air.

"I still don't understand, Mr. Hanvey."

Jim jerked his head toward Scanlan. "Billy's been sent out by the Quincy gang. His job is to keep that proxy from getting to New York in time for the stockholders' meeting."

"O-o-oh!"

Corwin's jaw hardened, his sinewy frame tensed and a fighting light blazed in his fine, level eyes.

Jim grinned.

"They ain't gonna try no rough stuff. That ain't Bill Scanlan's way of workin'. He's one of the smoothest con men in the known world, but he ain't rough—not Billy. He's smooth as butter."

"Then how——"

"Easy enough, son. He'll be on the same train that carries us back east, an' before we get to Chicago he'll swipe that proxy. At least that's what he's figurin' he's goin' to do."

Matters were clarifying slightly in the brain of young Corwin. But his curiosity was still unsatisfied.

"If I may ask, Mr. Hanvey, how do you know that he is the Quincy-Scott agent?"

Jim shrugged his fat shoulders.

"Easy enough. Y'see, it's this way: When the good Lord manufactured me he forgot to hand me out any good looks an' he slipped me entirely too much figger. But he didn't find that out until too late, so what he did to make up for it was to give me a mem'ry. I've got a mem'ry like a cam'ra, son. I just naturally

---

* At least two popular inexpensive cigar makers, King Edward and White Owl, marketed cigars with the brand name of "Invincibles."

don't forget things, an' I've sort of built up the rep of knowin' more professional crooks than any other ten men put together. McIntosh knew that the other crowd would engage a professional crook to get the proxy away from you, it not bein' no job for an amachoor. He was sure to foller you out here, an' the way he was plannin' to work was to scrape an acquaintance with you, you never suspectin' nothin', which would have made things pretty easy for Billy. I just trailed along to sort of point out to you the feller you wasn't safe with, an' Billy Scanlan is him."

Gerald Corwin felt a fresh respect for the fat man with the bovine expression, and a bit of his resentment vanished at the same time, for he now understood one or two things which before had left him wholly puzzled and more than a trifle resentful.

They finished their meal in silence. The check paid, they rose and started from the dining room, but Hanvey took Corwin's arm.

"C'mon over an' lemme introduce you to Billy. It'll sort of make things easier for him, bein' introduced formal-like, an' the poor feller's got a tough enough job on his hands as it is."

Startled but obedient; Corwin followed, and he saw the expression of incredulous amazement, not untinged with apprehension, which flashed into Scanlan's face as they paused by his table.

"Hello, Billy!"

Scanlan rose slowly. His jaw was set and it was plain that he was struggling to orient himself to this bizarre situation. He strove to make his tone casual.

"Hello, Jim!"

Hanvey was exceedingly gracious.

"Lemme introduce my friend Mr. Corwin. Mr. Corwin is the feller you was sent out here to watch, Billy. Mr. Corwin, shake hands with Mr. Scanlan."

Awkwardly the two men—one an innate gentleman and the other a student at the school of gentility—shook hands. Corwin was a trifle sorry for Scanlan. The man seemed afraid of Jim Hanvey.

"I'm pleased to meet Mr. Corwin."

"Sure you are." The voice of Hanvey chimed in genially. "Didn't you come all the way from New York just for that? An' wasn't you wonderin' how you was gonna work it? That's me—always ready to help out a friend, Billy—so I up an' introduces you fellers."

"It's real kind of you, Jim"—Scanlan was choosing his words with scrupulous care—"but I don't quite—er—comprehend what you're driving at."

"No?" Hanvey's bushy eyebrows arched in surprise. "I'd sure hate to think that you wasn't tellin' me the truth, Billy."

"I really don't understand your—a—innuendoes. I'm in Los Angeles on a vacation and without no definite objective."

"Sure, Billy, sure! I know that. You're a gent of leisure, you are. But if you could grab off that fat wad the Quincy-Scott people hung under your nose, you wouldn't have no objections, would you?"

Scanlan's hand dropped on Hanvey's shoulder and he gazed earnestly into the eyes of the detective, Corwin for the moment forgotten.

"Honest, Jim, I'm runnin' straight. I ain't plannin' a thing. So leave me be, won't you?"

"I ain't aimin' to bother you none, Billy. Goodness knows, you're too much of a gent to be in jail. Only it just struck me that I was doin' you a favor by introducin' you to Mr. Corwin, him an' you both bein' genuine swells an' li'ble to have a heap in common."

Suddenly reawakened to consciousness of Corwin's presence, Scanlan pulled himself together.

"Mr. Hanvey is bound to have his little joke, Mr. Corwin. A very interesting chap, isn't he?"

Corwin inclined his head gravely.

"Very."

Hanvey regarded them amusedly.

"You fellers like each other?"

They nodded.

"That's fine! I'm sure glad!" He turned away, then swung back suddenly. "By the way, Billy, we're leaving on the California Limited Friday morning, ten o'clock. We've got Drawin'-room A in Car S-17. I'm tellin' you so you can get your reservations early on that train. Eastern travel is awful thick these days."

They parted from the bewildered Scanlan. In the sanctuary of Hanvey's room Gerald Corwin voiced his displeasure.

"You are probably a very great detective, Mr. Hanvey——"

"Naw! Not me! I'm just a fat, lucky bum."

"But it strikes me that you volunteered some valuable information unnecessarily."

"To Billy?"

"Yes."

"How so?"

"About our reservations east. Why did you tell him the correct day?"

"I never lie to a crook," said Jim gravely. "It ain't fair. Besides, if they're good enough crooks to be worth lyin' to a feller ain't gonna get away with it. Billy will check up, an' once he found I'd lied to him he'd lose all confidence in me."

"But I don't see what difference it makes."

"That's 'cause you're a business man, son. Detectives an' crooks know the value of tellin' the truth."

"You didn't have to tell him who I was."

"No-o, that's true. But it saved him a heap of trouble."

"I don't understand your desire to save him trouble."

"It's this way, Mr. Corwin: The less trouble Billy has to take the more time he'll have for thinkin', an' the more he thinks the worse off he is. Thinkin', son, has ruined a heap of happy homes, an' don't you forget it."

Hanvey was right. At that moment Billy Scanlan was slumped in a chair in the hotel lobby, smoking cigarette after cigarette and wondering what it all meant. He knew Jim Hanvey of old, was familiar with the working methods of the ponderous, slow-moving, quick-thinking detective; and he knew that Jim had told the truth. Of course he'd check up, but that was a mere formality. All the more prominent criminals knew that Jim Hanvey did not lie. That was one explanation of the high esteem in which they held him—because he played fair.

Scanlan was worried. He had been intrusted with a definite mission, one well suited to his peculiar talents. His job was to secure from Gerald Corwin the proxy which Corwin was to receive from Col. Robert E. Warrington and to deliver that proxy to the men who were fighting to wrest control of the K. R. & P. from the McIntosh interests. That was all. The sky was the limit so far as he was concerned. His professional reputation was at stake. Besides, the reward offered by the Quincy-Scott crowd was stupendous, and Billy was sadly in need of ready cash—and plenty of it.

The presence of Jim Hanvey complicated matters somewhat in the way of accomplishing a task already difficult and delicate. But Billy was game and not entirely averse to matching wits with the Gargantuan detective. So he waited patiently in the lobby, watching the elevator bank, and eventually he was rewarded when Gerald Corwin descended, walked swiftly to the street and hailed a taxi.

As he drove off, Scanlan stepped into another cab.

"Follow that cab ahead. Keep about a block in the rear. When he stops you stop."

As Scanlan drove off, he glanced over his shoulder in time to

see the ungainly figure of Jim Hanvey climb laboriously into yet
a third taxi. He did not quite fathom Jim's motive in following,
but he didn't care particularly. He knew that Jim knew he'd trail
Corwin. So much for that.

Corwin's taxi driver, evidently aware that his fare was unfamiliar with the vastness of Los Angeles, selected a circuitous route
to the Wilshire Boulevard address of Colonel Warrington. He
drove through the traffic to Pico and via that important thoroughfare to Western Avenue, swinging across then to the fashionable
Wilshire section, a tremendous area of spotlessly white homes,
immaculate lawns, stiff and artificial gardening and aggressive
affluence. Before the gates of a huge home, the grounds of which
occupied an entire block, Corwin's taxi stopped. Gerald retained
his man and entered the Warrington mansion. A block farther
down Wilshire Boulevard Scanlan's taxi halted, and a half block
behind that Jim Hanvey left his taxi.

Jim, alone of the three, dismissed his driver. And then, slowly
and purposefully, puffing on a cigar, Jim waddled up the street
toward Scanlan's automobile.

"'Lo, Billy!"

"Hello, Jim!"

"Have a good ride?"

"Pretty good."

"Just wanted to let you know I follered you, Billy. All I done
it for was to make sure you was watchin' young Corwin yonder.
I'll be trottin' back to town now." He addressed Scanlan's driver:
"Which street car do I take to get back to town?"

The driver vouchsafed the desired information. Scanlan could
not forbear a question:

"Where's your taxi, Jim?"

"I let it go. Taxis are terribly expensive." And Hanvey moved
heavily away.

Scanlan's vigil continued for more than an hour. Then through the gates of the Warrington home swung a limousine. It stopped briefly while Corwin alighted, paid his taxi and then returned to the big car. The route into the city was more direct this time, and Scanlan followed Corwin and Colonel Warrington into one of the larger Broadway office buildings. He saw them enter the offices of a law firm and knew that Corwin had won the first move of the game by persuading Warrington to issue his proxy in favor of the McIntosh interests.

From his vantage point in the marbled hallway Scanlan kept watch. Eventually he saw a young man emerge from the offices of the firm of lawyers and enter a smaller office down the hall which was marked "Real Estate & Insurance. Notary Public." A second young man returned with the first and in his hand was a small notarial seal. It was obvious to Scanlan that if there was a notary in the law firm he was out at the moment. Alone again, Scanlan ascertained the name of the notary—Leopold Jones.

When Warrington and Corwin descended in an elevator a few minutes later Scanlan did not follow. Instead he produced from his pocket an income-tax blank and went with it to the office of Leopold Jones. Of that young gentleman he requested an attestation of his income-tax return.* Mr. Jones found Mr. Scanlan an engaging talker and they chatted for several minutes. When Mr. Scanlan eventually departed Mr. Jones was happily unaware of the fact that in Mr. Scanlan's coat pocket reposed his, Mr. Jones', notarial seal.

From the office building Scanlan visited the city ticket office of the Santa Fe Railroad. He learned readily enough that Drawing-room A in Car S-17, California Limited, for Friday morning had been sold the day previous to a very fat gentleman. He bought Compartment C in the same car. He returned to the hotel.

---

* Income tax returns never required notarization or "attestation."

Thus far things appeared propitious for Mr. Scanlan.

Jim was a hindrance, of course, and a grave one; but Scanlan operated on the theory that no vigilance is so keen that it cannot be eluded. There remained nothing now save the trip east. At some time between the departure from Los Angeles and the arrival in Chicago it was incumbent upon Mr. Scanlan to secure from Corwin the Warrington proxy.

That night—Wednesday—the three men dined together, Corwin's distaste swallowed up by his keening interest in the peculiar friendship existing between Hanvey and Scanlan. Corwin had always held the idea that criminals and detectives clashed on sight; that the former were habitually in flight and the latter constantly in pursuit. To see them chatting amiably about topics in general, reminiscing over past escapades of Scanlan and exploits of other criminals and swapping theories on unsolved crimes was astounding. Corwin found it hard to reconcile himself to the fact that at the moment the portly detective and the would-be-gentleman crook were engaged in a battle of wits. He later discussed the matter with Hanvey.

"Why don't you arrest Scanlan?"

"Arrest him? He ain't done nothin.'"

"He's planning to."

"You can't arrest a man for what he's got in his head. If you could the jails'd be overflowin.'"

"You could arrest him for that McCarthy affair I heard him telling you about. He confesses he was involved in the swindle."

"Aw, you know I wouldn't touch him for that! He just passed that dope on as a friend."

"But I didn't know that policemen and criminals were friends."

Hanvey smiled wistfully.

"'Bout the only friends I got in this world, son, are crooks. Most of them are servin' time. Some of 'em I put there. But we're friends. This here solid gold watch charm—that was given me by one of the niftiest con men in the world. I sure hated to send him up."

They checked out of the hotel Friday morning. Billy Scanlan was at the station when they arrived. The heavy train rumbled under the shed and they settled themselves for the three-day journey to Chicago. At Hanvey's invitation Scanlan joined them in the drawing-room and they became absorbed in a game of setback* at half a cent a point.

Hanvey and Scanlan waxed violently enthusiastic over the game——"King for high." "Trey low?" "Well, dog-gone your ornery hide——" "You're a rotten setback player, Mr. Corwin; y'oughta learn somethin' 'bout the fine points of the game."

Nothing to indicate that a crisis was approaching, no outward manifestation of the drama which was imminent. Occasionally Corwin reassured himself by touching his coat, in the lining of which was sewed the envelope containing the proxy which controlled a railroad. Once Hanvey saw the gesture and he laughed.

"It's safe all right, son. It'll stay safe unless you lose your coat."

Corwin flushed angrily. Hanvey rightly interpreted his anger and extended a fat and reassuring hand.

"I wasn't giving no dope away. Billy knew where you had the proxy, didn't you, Billy?"

Scanlan nodded.

"Sure! It's the regular place."

Both men—detective and criminal—were vastly amused by Corwin's obviousness, and Corwin knew it. But he didn't care. Perhaps the lining of a coat was the regular place to keep a valuable document; certainly it was a safe one; and Hanvey might have been more careful than to remove the last vestige of doubt from

---

* Also known as pitch or auction pitch, this bidding, trick-playing card game originated in the mid-nineteenth century.

Scanlan's mind. Corwin knew that Scanlan could not possibly get the proxy. Such a thing was impossible during the day, and at night Corwin planned to use the coat as a pillow.

Following a light breakfast the next morning, Corwin made his way forward to the club car for a shave. He removed coat, collar and tie, for the moment unmindful of Scanlan. When the hot towel was removed from his face and fresh lather applied he noticed Scanlan sitting with two other men, awaiting his turn for a shave. Next to Scanlan was Jim Hanvey. Corwin sighed relievedly.

The barber shaved the right side of Corwin's face, then turned him in the chair to get at the other side. As he did so Scanlan cast a glance of simulated impatience at the waiting men, rose, donned coat and hat and left the club car.

But the coat which Scanlan wore on leaving the car was Corwin's!

In five minutes' time he returned. Corwin was just emerging from the chair. Hanvey was slumped in a corner immersed in the very-female pictures of a weekly periodical. Scanlan removed Corwin's coat and extended it to that young gentleman.

"Took your coat by accident, Mr. Corwin. Just discovered my mistake."

Corwin's face blanched. He grabbed the coat and touched the spot where the proxy had been. For a single wild instant Corwin contemplated bodily assault, and only the hulking figure of Jim Hanvey and his slow, drawling voice prevented.

"What's the matter, son? What's the matter? You look all het up."

"This thief—"

"Whoa, son, whoa! That ain't no kind of a name to call a crook."

Corwin whirled on Hanvey.

"You don't know what you're talking about! This man has that proxy! He just stole it from me!"

Jim was unperturbed. He turned mildly reproving eyes upon the amused countenance of his friend.

"You didn't go an' do that, did you, Billy?"

Scanlan grinned.

"Mr. Corwin seems to think so."

"Well, I'll be dog-goned! Let's git together an' kinder talk things over."

Back through the swaying, grinding cars went the procession, Scanlan leading, Hanvey next and Corwin bringing up the rear. Corwin was in a cold fury. He felt that he was being made ridiculous—they were laughing at him. He didn't like the looks of the whole business anyway. What assurance had he that Hanvey and Scanlan were not confederates? They were suspiciously intimate, and Hanvey must have seen Scanlan——In the privacy of their drawing-room Corwin's sinewy figure towered over Scanlan.

"If you don't give me back that proxy I'll break every bone in your rotten body."

Jim restrained the young man.

"Them's awful harsh words, Jack Dalton."*

Corwin shook him off.

"I think you're as crooked as he is. I've had my suspicions from the first, and I'm not going to allow any pair like you to make a monkey of me."

It was Scanlan who spoke.

"Just what are you going to do about it, Mr. Corwin?"

"I'll do a-plenty!"

"Giving me a licking isn't going to get you anywhere except in

---

* James "Jack" Dalton, a.k.a. "the Tiger," was the melodramatic villain of the popular play *The Ticket-of-Leave Man* by Tom Taylor (1863). "I know you, James Dalton" was the catchphrase of the hero, Hawkshaw the detective, and the name "Jack Dalton" became a moniker for daring thieves around the world. That there was also a notorious Dalton gang—brothers, none of whom was named Jack—who robbed trains in the late nineteenth century only burnished the legend of the mythic criminal.

jail. We're in New Mexico now; and if you lay a finger on me I'll have you dumped in the Albuquerque lockup tonight; and you can't do the same to me, because you haven't got a lick of proof."

"Will you let us search you and your compartment?"

"Surest thing you know!" He turned to the detective. "C'mon, Jim. Get busy."

Hanvey shrugged and reached for one of his black cigars.

"Ain't gonna waste my time, Billy. If you've got that proxy there ain't no use of my searchin' for it now. I've just got to think things over and get a hunch where you put it. Then I'll get it."

"Do you mean," interrogated Corwin furiously, "that you're not even going to search this man?"

"I do. I mean just that exact thing, son."

"Well, I will!"

Scanlan meekly submitted to the search. Once as Corwin's trembling, clumsy fingers probed into a pocket he deliberately winked at Hanvey, and at the conclusion of the personal search Scanlan led the way to his compartment. Twenty minutes later Corwin, dispirited and dully angry, returned to the drawing-room, where he found Hanvey gazing stolidly out of the window. The detective spoke without turning his head.

"When you git peeved, son, you sure git peeved all over."

The younger man did not answer. He slouched opposite and tried to think, to piece together the ends of this tangled skein. He was distrustful of every one, particularly of the slothful Hanvey. Jim's only other remark did not add to his comfort.

"You sure was careless with that coat, Mr. Corwin—awful careless."

Hanvey was right. He had been careless, inexcusably so. True, there had been a feeling of safety in the knowledge that Hanvey was also in the barber shop; but there was small solace in the thought that it wasn't entirely his fault that too great confidence had been placed by his employer in Hanvey's ability. And now, should Hanvey fail to recover the proxy; he—Corwin—was ruined, a brilliant career abruptly and ignominiously terminated.

Meanwhile, in Compartment C, behind a locked door, Scanlan was busy. He obtained a table from the porter and then proceeded to open his suitcase, to unpack it, to remove a false bottom and extract from the space disclosed a sheaf of legal appearing documents. Each of these was strikingly similar to the proxy which lay beside them on the table.

Then slowly and painstakingly Scanlan prepared a duplicate proxy, being very careful that his forging of Colonel Warrington's name should be patently a forgery. The finished job was a masterpiece. No one unfamiliar with Warrington's signature could guess that this was not genuine, yet a comparison left no room for doubt that Scanlan's work was a forgery. Carefully he inscribed the attestation, affixing thereto the impress of the notarial seal he had stolen from the office of Mr. Leopold Jones. That done, he viewed his handiwork with pardonable pride. He next destroyed the other blank proxies which had been prepared by the Quincy-Scott crowd in New York, placed the forged proxy in the false bottom of his suitcase and put the genuine proxy in an outside pocket of his coat.

At lunch time Scanlan found Hanvey sitting alone at one end of the diner while Corwin sulked at the other. The crook paused by the detective's table and cheerfully accepted Hanvey's invitation to join. Jim nodded toward the tragic figure at the other end of the car.

"You sure have played tarnation thunder with that, kid, Billy."

Scanlan shook his head. Naturally tender-hearted, he was genuinely regretful. "Business is business, Jim."

"Yep, so it is. Kinda tough on the kid, though. He feels bad, knowin' he played right into your hands. An' I ain't feelin' any too spry myself." The detective's dull eyes turned toward his companion and blinked slowly. "Where have you got that proxy, Billy?"

Scanlan laughed.

"I haven't admitted that I have it."

"No-o. An' I didn't ask you to admit nothin'. The point bein' that you can't get away with it, kid. I'll have you held when we get to Chicago and search you—a search that is a search."

Scanlan registered apprehension.

"That ain't fair, Jim. You ain't got a lick of proof that I have the proxy."

"Nope. But I intend to get it."

From the diner Scanlan went back to the observation platform to think things over. He did not relish the prospect of an additional thirty-six hours on the same car with Hanvey. He contemplated dropping off at Albuquerque, then thought better of it. Jim would merely remain with him. And then an idea came.

At eight o'clock the train pulled into the handsome station at the capital of New Mexico for a one-hour layover. Scanlan walked swiftly up the street toward the post office. There he prevailed upon a registry clerk to accept a letter. In a long envelope he inclosed a note to Phares Scott and with it the proxy he had that day stolen from Gerald Corwin. He sent the document both special delivery and registered. It would get to New York a day or two late, perhaps, but still in ample time for the meeting. Besides, it was not essential that it get there at all. It was only necessary that the McIntosh forces be deprived of its possession.

Scanlan would have destroyed the thing in preference, but he knew that he would have difficulty in collecting his fee unless the document itself was produced.

But even though Billy Scanlan had left the train at Albuquerque, Hanvey and Corwin had not. Hanvey, making quite sure that Scanlan had gone, entered Scanlan's compartment in Corwin's company. The manner of the big detective had momentarily lost its sluggishness. He questioned Corwin.

"Where'd you search?"

Corwin told him. Jim shook his massive head.

"How 'bout his suitcase?"

"I looked in there, of course."

"Sure—of course you did, son. Naturally. But let's us try it again."

Jim dumped the contents unceremoniously on the seat. With deft fingers he went through every garment and even inspected the contents of the rolled traveling case.

"You see," commented Corwin resentfully. "I told you nothing was there."

Hanvey paid him no heed. He had closed the suitcase and was inspecting it carefully. Then suddenly he turned it over and thumped it with a heavy, spatulate finger. His pursy lips creased into a smile.

"Think we got somethin', son."

"What?"

"We'll see."

The suitcase was reopened and Hanvey fumbled inside for a moment. Then a button unfastened here and one there and he removed the false bottom. He extended the envelope to Corwin.

"Better see that he don't get another chance at it, son."

With fingers that trembled the younger man spread open the forged proxy, never questioning its genuineness. There it was—Warrington's signature, Jones' attestation, the notarial seal. Corwin seized Jim's hand and wrung it gratefully. His voice was choky.

"I've been a rotter, Mr. Hanvey. I suspected you of being a confederate——"

"'Sall right, Mr. Corwin. 'Sall right. Don't slop over."

"I can't help it. I feel like a cur."

"Gwan!" Hanvey was touched by the boyish gratitude of his young friend. "Let's get this stuff back in here. Scanlan'll spot that we have the thing, but it wouldn't be decent to leave his stuff all spread out like this."

Ten minutes before leaving time Scanlan returned to his compartment. He opened his suitcase, discerned the disorder—and grinned. Then, pretending disappointment and fury, he rapped on the door of Drawing-room A. Inside he faced Corwin.

"You wanted to start something a little while ago, Mr. Corwin," he snapped, "when you thought I copped a paper from your coat. Well, I'm here to say that whenever you're ready you just wade right in, because, no matter what I've done, I never robbed a gent's suitcase."

A hard, chill smile appeared on Corwin's lips. He rose slowly. From the window seat Hanvey viewed the tableau amusedly.

"Get out!" ordered Corwin.

"Put me out!"

"Get out or I shall!"

Scanlan's eyes met those of the other man, and Scanlan discreetly withdrew.

But that night Scanlan lay in his berth, smoking and smiling. Success had blessed his strategy. The Warrington proxy was en route to New York by registered mail, the envelope specifically marked "For Delivery to Addressee Only." Better still, Jim Hanvey thought he had recovered the document. There was the strongest point in Scanlan's favor—the fact that Jim was smugly contented. Now all he had to do was to assume the attitude of a man thwarted. He was a trifle sorry for poor old Jim, yet it was no lack of acumen on Jim's part, but rather a superlative cunning on his own.

During the final twenty-four hours of the journey to Chicago, Gerald Corwin clung to the supposed proxy with a pitiful grimness. Alone with Hanvey in their drawing-room, he sat with his hand against the pocket of his coat. He shaved himself. He slept with the coat for a pillow.

"He got it once," he explained to Hanvey. "He won't again."

Jim smiled.

"Once ought to be enough for any man."

"What made you think of a false bottom to that suitcase, Mr. Hanvey?"

"Same thing that made Billy think of the lining of your coat. Plumb obvious. Gosh! I'll bet Billy's ravin'."

Corwin was frankly admiring.

"And I thought you were no good! I even thought you might be double-crossing McIntosh!"

"That's right, son; that's right. Never trust nobody an' you'll never get a shock. That's my motto. The honester a person is supposed to be the easier he can crook you."

They reached Chicago at noon of the following day, Hanvey and Corwin boarded the Pennsylvania for New York. Scanlan secured a berth on the New York Central. Freed from the Scanlan menace, Corwin thawed slightly and attempted to make late amends to his benefactor. He even summoned sufficient courage to request a closer inspection of Jim's gold toothpick and to say complimentary things about the fearful weapon which had been anathema to him. Jim bloomed under the praise of his decoration.

"Feller that gave me that had sense," he said earnestly. "It ain't only beautiful—it's useful."

Corwin repressed a shudder.

"I suppose it is."

The gratitude of the younger man was pathetic. He grimly determined to invite Jim to dinner some night—the ultimate test of his fortitude.

They reached New York on time and repaired immediately to

the offices of the K. R. & P. There Gerald Corwin delivered over to Garet McIntosh the Warrington proxy. McIntosh congratulated the young man and assured him of the directors' appreciation. But before leaving the room Corwin made a straight-eyed confession.

"You must thank Mr. Hanvey," he said. "The proxy was stolen from me on the train and Mr. Hanvey recovered it."

"Good!" McIntosh dismissed Corwin with a nod and reached for his notebook. "How about it, Hanvey?"

Jim grinned. "Don't listen to nothin' the kid says, Mr. McIntosh. He's game all through, that lad. But it was funny."

At that moment Billy Scanlan faced Phares Scott and gave a detailed report of the success of his mission. A gleam of admiration appeared in the steely eyes of the financier.

"Good work!" he commented briefly. "You'll get your pay when the proxy arrives."

The following day at noon, Scanlan presented himself at Scott's office. His reward was paid in legal tender——"To avoid the embarrassment of a check." Scanlan nodded and pocketed the money.

"The proxy?" he questioned.

"We've destroyed it. Simply wanted to look it over to make sure we were safe."

That night Billy Scanlan celebrated. The following morning he awakened with a violent headache, and was aroused by a ringing of his telephone.

"Jim Hanvey," announced the slow, drawling voice on the other end. "Can I come up?"

Jim came. He regarded Scanlan interestedly.

"I judge they paid you off all right," he commented.

"They did," admitted Scanlan. "What about it?"

"Nothin'; nothin' in particular." Hanvey glanced at his watch, a tremendous affair, gaudily engraved. "Only that the stockholders' meetin' takes place in just about one hour, an' as a friend I advise you to beat it an' beat it quick."

Scanlan sat upright, hands pressed against his throbbing forehead.

"Me beat it?"

"Uh-huh."

"What for?"

"Takin' pay from the Quincy-Scott crowd for somethin' you didn't do. They're li'ble to get awful sore."

"What are you talking about, Jim? You know good and well I got away with it."

Hanvey shook his head. "Nothin' of the kind, Billy; an' I'm advisin' you as a friend to beat it—an' stay put."

The eyes of the other man narrowed.

"You must be gettin' into your second childhood, Jim. Do you mean to tell me that you haven't yet found out that the proxy you stole from my suitcase was a fake?"

Hanvey's voice was quite matter of fact.

"Oh, that? Sure, I knew all the time that was a fake."

"Well, then——"

"What you ain't never stopped to realize," explained the detective, "is this: The proxy you swiped from young Corwin wasn't no good either."

Scanlan rose abruptly.

"What do you mean—no good? Old man Warrington executed it——"

"Sure he did! An' the next day he executed another to McIntosh. That second one was the only one worth the paper it was written on. It nullified the first, an' I had it in my pocket all the time. An' when that real proxy appears at the meetin' today the gang you were workin' for is li'ble to get all het up. You see, Billy, you and Corwin both had the wrong dope. I wasn't on that train to keep you from gettin' that proxy off Corwin; I was there to see you did get it so you wouldn't bother me none, me bein' the real messenger."

Headache forgotten, Billy Scanlan leaped for his suitcase and commenced a frenzy of packing.

"I might've known you were too easy, Jim! I might've known it! Anyway, they paid me off yesterday———"

"That's what tickles me," replied Jim; "you gittin' paid for that proxy. It's a swell joke on them fellers. An' say, I got somethin' to show you. You know young Corwin was awful grateful for what I done."

"He should have been."

"He was. He sent me a present this morning. Ain't it swell?"

And beaming with pride Hanvey exhibited the gift of the fastidious Gerald Corwin.

It was a gold-handled toothbrush.

Helen of Troy, N.Y.

THE first summer blast of a Southern springtime failed to inspire Jim Hanvey to hallelujahs. The mammoth detective lounged uncomfortably in his tiny apartment, cursing the unkind fates which had first been too liberal in their apportionment of avoirdupois and then caused him to be temporarily located in that section of the country where the intense heat makes for healthy cotton and lethargic humanity.

Southern spring is a season of constant doubt and surprise. One goes to bed innocent of sheets and arises shiveringly at three in the morning to resurrect blankets from a moth-ball depository. Overcoats are one day in order, and on the next palm-beach suits are inspected longingly. On Wednesday the fresh young leaves will struggle against the near-frost of the previous night, and on Thursday wilt before the ravages of unseasonable heat. Winter does not merge gently into summer. The thermometer fluctuates uncertainly like a woman torn between the competitive allure of two bargain counters.

Today it was hot, genuinely and unreservedly hot, and Jim's physique had never been intended to withstand heat. He slumped miserably in a wicker chair, puffing disconsolately upon a cigar and staring with fixed distaste at the weather forecast: "Clear. Continued warm."

A profound sigh escaped from the recesses of Jim Hanvey. "O death, where is thy heat?"*

Jim was capable of intense feeling, and this day that capability was working overtime. He was utterly and supremely unhappy both as to the present and in contemplation of the future. If this was April, what, then, would July be?

He scarcely heard the clangor of his telephone, and only when that instrument had sent its raucous summons dinning into his ears for the third time did he conscript sufficient energy to hoist himself from the wicker chair. His voice was not at all friendly.

"'Lo!"

"Hello!" A queer, interested expression flitted over Jim's features. Woman's voice. Hmph! "Is that Mr. Hanvey?"

"Almost."

"This is a friend of yours, Jim."

"Ain't got any friends today. Too hot."

"I'm coming up."

"That's fine. Apartment 4-B. Door's unlocked. Walk right in."

"Good!"

"And, say?"

"Yes?"

"Don't expect me to get up. When the mercury climbs this high I stay put."

He recrossed the room and slumped down into his chair again; but no longer did his face reflect the misery of the flesh.

His florid countenance was wrinkled speculatively. The voice of the woman had been vaguely familiar; memory probed

---

* Hanvey misquotes the King James Bible ("Oh death, where is thy sting?" from 1 Corinthians 15:55).

inquisitively into the past. Jim shook his tremendous head from side to side.

"She called me Jim an' said she was a friend of mine."

Pudgy fingers toyed idly with the hawserlike watch chain connecting his timepiece and himself.

The front door opened. Footsteps sounded from the hallway. All outward indication of interest fled from Jim's face leaving it as expressionful as the visage of a cow at milking time. Then the woman appeared in the doorway, and instantly Jim recognized her. The heartiness of his greeting was thoroughly sincere.

"Helen of Troy." He smiled and added, "New York."

The woman swept across the room and pressed a light kiss on the forehead of the detective.

"Dear old Jim! It's good to see you again."

"Yeh, ain't it? Lord! I'm hot." Jim's eyelids drooped with exasperating slowness over his fishy orbs, held shut for a moment, then opened again. "Step over yonder, Helen. Lemme give you the once-over."

The woman obeyed, and Jim nodded approvingly.

"Million dollars—plus, Helen. That's you."

She was far from unattractive as she stood by the window. True, she was not of the general type which inspires the plaudits of a connoisseur; but for all practical purposes she was there seven ways from the ace.* In the first place she was blond— magnificently and unyieldingly blond from the shrieking crown of gold upon her head to the tips of her long, slender dead-white fingers. She was amply supplied with a figure which had been apportioned liberally and with an eye to ensemble rather than lissomeness.† The effect was not to be denied: Floppy white

---

* A popular phrase with no discernible meaning.

---

† "Lissome" means supple, limber.

panama with orchid trimmings; an elaborate street dress of white and orchid crêpe de chine; orchid stockings of chiffon, and white shoes. She pridefully submitted to his inspection and thrilled to his comment.

Said he, "Once seen, never forgotten."

"You think I'm looking well, Jim?"

"Terrible good. Terrible." He mopped his forehead. "How do you stand this heat?"

She laughed.

"We've lived South ever since we were married. That's six years."

"And three months," he amplified. "Ever since Johnny finished that last stretch. Me, I'd just as lief be in stir.* Sit down. How's Johnny?"

The woman's face clouded slightly.

"It's about him I came to see you, Jim."

"Much obliged to Johnny." He relighted his cigar. "What's he doin' now? Con?"

She shook her head.

"We've been straight ever since we hitched up. You ought to know that, Jim."

"Ought to. Just thought maybe he was keepin' away from my line. I'm with the Bankers' Protective now, you know."

"I know it; that's why I came to you."

He stretched out.

"Spill it, Helen. I'm all ears—all ears and perspiration, I mean."

"You've always been a friend of ours, Jim. You play square. You sent Johnny up once, but he didn't hold that against you; it was all his fault for gettin' caught. And he made a regular killin' that time, Jim—you remember they never did get the stuff. Well,

---

* "I'd just as soon be in jail."

when he got out we decided to get married and go straight. Of course we didn't know how we'd like it, but we did think it was worth trying—understand?"

"Sure! Novelty. Any time you didn't like it you could turn crooked again."

"That's it. Well, I've liked it, an' so has Johnny. No dicks worryin' us, everything running smooth. It's been a real nice experience, Jim. I never would have believed there was so much fun in bein' honest. And after a while—well, it sort of gets to be a habit. Now I've come to the point where I wouldn't change for anything."

She paused. He blinked with disconcerting slowness.

"Well?"

She leaned forward tensely.

"Johnny's planning to pull a job!"

"Huh?"

"Johnny's planning to pull another job. He's got a chance for a neat killing, and he's going to try it."

Jim's head rolled sorrowfully upon his fat shoulders.

"That's too dog-goned bad! After runnin' straight this long!"

"It is too bad, Jim. That's why I've come to you."

"What's why?"

"I want you to keep him straight. I know I can trust you, so I'm going to slip you the whole works, and I want you to steer him off. There ain't a bit of sense to his going crooked again. We've got all the money we need; but the thing looks so easy—you know how it is."

"Uh-huh. I know. What you expect me to do?"

"The job he's planning, Jim, is a bank job. That would bring you into it."

Jim's lips drew into a protuberant circle and a low whistle escaped.

"Bank job, eh? His old line. That's plumb silly."

"I've told him so; told him a dozen times. But he says it's a cinch. Sure thing. Bah!"—bitterly. "It's a sure thing he wouldn't get away with it."

"But he thinks he can."

"That's it. I know just how he feels, Jim. I've felt that way myself a dozen times when I've seen some dame out at the race track wearing a million dollars' worth of sparklers. I'd remember how good I used to be at that sort of thing and my fingers would just naturally itch. It seemed a shame to pass it up. But"—righteously—"I've given temptation the go-by, Jim. I haven't pulled a job since I got hitched up to Johnny, though I've had chances enough. You always have when you're running straight. Sometimes I've felt like I'd give everything I had just for the sport of reducing the weight of some fat dame to the extent of a coupla carats. Well, the bug's got Johnny now. Things have played into his hands and he's rarin' to go. I told him you was down in this part of the country, but he only laughed. 'Reckon I can get away with this in spite of Jim Hanvey,' he said. The poor fish! You know good and well, Jim, there ain't any crook can buck you and get away with it, is there?"

Jim grinned.

"What you tryin' to do—vamp me?"

"Lord forbid! It would be too much trouble for the result."

"That sounds more like my frank friend. Now please continue to go on."

"I'm going to give you a straight steer on this job of Johnny's. I want to leave it all in your hands. You ought to be able to head him off. I know I'm foolish to be so dead set on honesty and all that sort of romantic stuff, but I can't help it. Reckon I've been seeing too many movies or something." She leaned forward tensely, giving off an aroma of heavy and expensive perfumes, her fingers glittering with an imposing array of rings. "I want to stay straight, Jim—I sure do! And I want Johnny to do likewise."

Jim reached for a fresh cigar and settled back comfortably in his chair.

"You don't mind these, do you, Helen?"

"We-e-ll, I haven't any right to kick when I'm asking you a favor."

"Thanks."

He snipped off the end of the cigar and lighted up with gusto.

"Since Johnny turned straight he's been gambling," she explained. "No rough stuff, nor nothing like that. Of course I'm not claiming that he hasn't rung in the works once in a while when he's hooked a particularly easy mark or that maybe he hasn't managed to read the backs of a few cards; but that's all part of the profession. The point is he hasn't been crooked—understand?"

"Sure! I get you."

"Last two seasons he's been oralizing* down in New Orleans—both tracks there: Fair Grounds and Jefferson Parish. Business has been pretty good, but nothing extra. New Orleans is a wise town on horses. They're the very devil on backing the favorites and that's awful tough on the bookies. Anyway racing has kinder got into Johnny's blood. He started off last year by buying a few cheap platers—called himself owning a stable. And finally he come into a two-year-old that is a colt. Lightning Bolt is the name. Y'oughter see that angel run!

"Major Torrance clocked that baby one time in a workout and wanted him; wanted him bad. Johnny didn't hanker to let him go. They talked price, but nothing come of it. Everybody knew the old gent was nuts on Lightning Bolt and was gonna get him sooner or later—everybody except him. And just recently Johnny

---

* "Oralizing" simply means reading something out loud. The slang usage here appears to refer to touts who work the horseraces and orally offer their betting odds.

found out that the major had booked passage for Europe on the Homeric, sailing out of New York day after tomorrow—Thursday. Also that Torrance's stable was bein' shipped North for the New York season. And that's where Johnny fell."

She paused, one white-shod foot tapping the floor. Jim sat in supine silence, apparently oblivious of her presence.

"Yes," she continued tensely, "that's where Johnny took his tumble. He told the major he'd sell Lightning Bolt, provided the old geezer would buy all the rest of his stable—four other horses. The price for the bunch was eight thousand dollars. The deal went through. Those horses went North with the Torrance stable the other day when the season ended in New Orleans. Old man Torrance sails from New York in a couple of days. Of course you can prove up on all of this; the real point being that Johnny holds the major's check for eight thousand dollars."

Her voice died away. Out of the silence which followed came Jim's drawling voice:

"An' one little teeny letter added onto an eight makes an eighty."

The luxurious blonde glanced sharply at the big man in the wicker chair, her eyes narrowing slightly.

"What made you think——"

"Two an' two always did make four, sister."

Her fingers interlaced nervously.

"That's the layout, Jim. He's planning to raise that check and make a get-away——" Her voice trailed off. "And that isn't all."

"No?"

Jim's query was a mere indication of interest rather than an effort to extract further information.

"Not all, Jim. It's this way——" She hitched her chair closer and laid one ringed hand on Jim's knee. The ponderous man seemed unmindful of it—for a moment. Then he moved away. "Just before Johnny turned straight and married me he pulled one last big job. It was regular and all that. The poor sucker they caught was hog-tied; he didn't dare let out a yap. Johnny made a clean-up on it and with that amount added to what he had he retired with about a quarter of a million bucks." There was conscious pride in her final declaration: "Johnny never was a piker."

"He sure wasn't, Helen. Great chap, Johnny."

"That quarter of a million has been salted away in Liberty Bonds. Johnny bought 'em at about 84 and they're pretty near par now. He's dead stuck on 'em; says when they jumped in value it was the first honest money he ever made. He never would touch 'em. Kind of superstitious. But, Jim, he's planning to dig into 'em now."

"Yeh?"

"He's got a chance of opening a big gambling place down near Juarez. Things like that take cash—a wad of it. So Johnny is fixing to borrow on his Liberties."

"Borrow?"

"Yes. He's superstitious about them, like I told you, and he don't want to sell. He figures he can borrow two hundred thousand on the things. Then he's going to raise that Torrance check from eight thousand to eighty. That'll give him $280,000 in cash—more than enough for what he wants. He'll sink a heap of that into the business, and at the first opportunity he plans to come back, redeem his Liberties and salt 'em away again. Understand?"

Hanvey was apparently not listening. He stared moodily through the window, lower jaw drooping, the ash on his cigar perilously lengthy. Finally he turned his glassy eyes upon her.

"How c'n you look so cool when it's so durned hot?"

She bit her lip.

"Do you understand, Jim?"

"Eh?" He blinked with interminable slowness. "Oh, about

Johnny an' his gamblin' house an' the Liberty Bonds an' all that? Sure, that's easy. Johnny's just naturally plannin' to get wicked again, ain't he?"

"And I don't want him to. There ain't anything in the world like being honest, Jim; I've found that out. It's the grandest feeling I've ever had. I wouldn't turn crooked again for anything in the world—unless we really needed the money. I don't want Johnny to. He's been out of the game so long he's liable to pull a boner and lose what he's got."

"You sure spoke a mouthful then, sister. That's a downright crude stunt Johnny is figgerin' on pullin'. Of course, him plannin' to beat it into Mexico, anyway——"

"I'd hate to live there. Never did like Mexican cooking—chili an' hot tamales and all that sort of thing. And the climate——"

"Hotter'n this, ain't it?"

She didn't answer. For a few moments silence held between them, tense silence punctured only by the ticking of the cheap alarm clock on the mantel and the bellowing of a group of boys playing in the street below.

"You've got to help me, Jim—got to help me keep Johnny straight. He'll listen to you where he laughs at me."

"Awful glad to do a little job like that, Helen. I'm real anxious Johnny shouldn't turn crooked again. He's got brains enough to make an honest livin'. Lemme see—when's he plannin' to pass this bum check?"

"Two or three days. You see, Jim, he'll borrow the two hundred thousand on his bonds—borrow it from a local banking house—Starnes & Company. When he deposits their check for that amount he'll deposit along with it Major Torrance's check for eighty thousand; and the eighty-thousand one being so much smaller than the other, they won't pay a whole lot of attention to it. Then he'll check against the total sum.* Ain't that clever?"

"Awful!" He inhaled deeply. "Awful clever! A good check for two hundred thousand and a bum one for eighty, passed right through the bank. Then he checks against 'em. Johnny sure uses his head for somethin' more than a hatrack."

She rose and threw a light scarf across her plump shoulders.

"You promise to keep him straight, Jim? You promise?"

"Sure! Sure I promise, Helen! Dog-gone this weather!"

She made her adieus and swung down the street toward the city's largest hotel. One or two traveling men ogled her and she expanded to the pleased consciousness of the effect she was creating. It had always been thus, ever since her girlhood in Troy, New York. Blessed with voluptuous blondness, men had always flocked about her. Adulation had been all in all to her until the advent of Johnny Norton, and to him she capitulated utterly.

Johnny had been an honest and efficient wooer. They teamed up and knocked about the country until he made his final big killing. Then they married and turned straight; but the strain of the past five years had been terrific.

Helen rapped on the door of her room and Johnny opened it in person. He was a small man, slender and wiry and very much of a dandy in his lavender silk shirt, his white sport shoes and his aggressively checkered suit. He kissed her dutifully, then stepped back, twisting his near-mustache.

Three other men lounged about the room. There was Slim Bolton, a card sharper, whose practice had been largely confined to transatlantic liners; Happy Gorman, who had attained fame— and a jail sentence—by means of an astoundingly clever oil-stock

* A standard auditing technique, to add up all of the debits and credits and check against the totals.

swindle; and Connie Hawes, one-time counterfeiter and generally expert flimflam artist. Their eyes were focused interestedly upon the Junoesque figure of the woman who stood with her back against the door, enjoying to the ultimate her calcium moment.*

"Well," she announced pridefully, "Jim Hanvey fell for it!"

There was a moment of tense silence.

At last, Johnny Norton pulling nervously at his mustache, voiced the question which was uppermost in the minds of all of them:

"You sure?"

"Positive! You know how it is, boys. Jim has got only one weakness and that's his heart. It's softer than mush. He fell for that going-straight stuff like a tabby for a fresh box of catnip. Honest, it was a shame to take the money."

Johnny grinned.

"He promised to keep me straight?"

"Yeh. Reckon it was the first time poor old Jim was ever asked to do anything like that." Her face clouded. "I sort of hate to put it over on him this way. I'm awful strong for Jim."

"So are all of us." It was Connie Hawes speaking. "But what could we do about it? It was a cinch we'd have trouble with Jim, so the best thing was to throw him off the track."

Slim Bolton rose and walked to the window. He spoke without turning.

"Reckon this stuff ain't exactly in my line," he commented; "but I never did understand the reason for wising Jim up. I'm not saying you fellows are wrong, but it looks to me like we are running an unnecessary chance."

Johnny Norton made no attempt to conceal his contempt for the slender one.

---

* Another slang phrase of obscure meaning.

"If you had more than one brain in your head, Slim, they wouldn't have barred you from the steamships. The reason Jim had to know it was this: He's chief of the detective force of the Bankers' Protective Association. Bein' down in this part of the country, it was a dead cinch he'd be called in the minute anything irregular happened."

"But nothing irregular——"

"Nothing irregular me eye! I borrow two hundred thousand dollars on a quarter million dollars' worth of Liberty Bonds. The banking house sends 'em over to the bank by messenger for rediscount. You fellows bump the messenger and make a get-away with the bonds. Bond robbery from a banking house which is a member of the Bankers' Protective. Jim Hanvey is called in of course, and first thing he asks is where did they get the Liberty Bonds. And when they tell him that a gent named John Roden Norton borrowed the money he would be most likely to smell a mice; even two or three mices."

"But when this happens——"

"Pff! You fellows are gonna lay low. And Jim already knows all about my borrowing the two hundred thou. He even knows about the Juarez proposition, and at the very moment you fellows are grabbing off the bonds I'll be with Jim Hanvey. Get that? He not only is gonna be set easy on borrowing the coin, but he's also gonna be right with me when the fireworks are being shot. What's the result? I've got a clean slate with Jim. I even let him induce me not to raise Torrance's check—swell chance I'd have raisin' that bird's paper—and so Jim will be lovin' me real sweet and you guys will be beatin' it to the border with them quarter million dollars in bonds. You fellers will cash 'em in somewheres—"

"How about the numbers? They ain't registered bonds, I know, but the minute that many are stolen the banking house will notify the B. P. A. to watch out—"

Helen of Troy had been too long in the background. She didn't like it. All her life she had been accustomed to having men stare at her and hang upon her words, and so now she took the floor again and gave explanation to Slim Bolton, who had but recently been impressed into service as the necessary fifth member of the party.

"I and Happy worked out that game," she explained. "Happy is awful keen on stocks and bonds and things like that, so he knew that we'd have to watch out for those numbers. So what we'll do is this: Johnny, here, has already made arrangements for the loan—told the banking house just what he wants the money for—and on Thursday he's to swap the bonds and his note for the cash. He's due to be on hand at eleven o'clock in the morning, but he ain't gonna be. He's gonna get there about half-past one, the banks in this burg closin' up at two o'clock. He'll hand over the bonds to the president of the banking house and that bird will check over the bond numbers with Johnny, Johnny having them written down formal-like on a piece of paper.

"And here's the point, Slim: The numbers that Johnny reads out will be the numbers of the bonds all right, but the numbers he reads won't be the numbers that are written down on this slip of paper.

"Minute he does that he's gonna ask the banker to give him the check quick so he can deposit before the bank closes, with the result that the banker will accept that list and will give Johnny's slip to the bookkeeper for entering in the journal. In other words, the numbers that they'll enter up won't be the numbers of the bonds at all, and there won't be any check when you get away with 'em. Chances are the banking house has already made arrangements to rediscount at one of the big banks, and they'll be anxious to shoot the collateral right around there; so the whole thing will slip through real pretty."

"And if it don't?" questioned the pessimistic Slim.

She stamped her foot irritably.

"Then it'll simply be a harder matter to dispose of the bonds. They're in thousand-dollar denominations, and it would take time, but not be dangerous. Anyway you boys are to cash in as soon as you can, shoot the two hundred thousand back to Johnny and then Johnny redeems his bonds and hikes down there to join you. We can't lose."

"Us fellers do the rough work," commented Connie Hawes. "That ain't ever been exactly in my line."

"I'm putting up the kale, ain't I?" queried Johnny. "That ought to count some."

"It does. But——"

"But nothing!" snapped Helen of Troy. "The way you boys talk about flunking this thing you almost make me ashamed of being a crook."

Meanwhile, in the very limited confines of his room, Jim Hanvey had been doing considerable thinking. He sat as Helen had left him, overflowing the old wicker chair, puffing solemnly upon the long-extinguished stump of his cigar, fat fingers fiddling with his watch chain.

Jim was interested; so interested that for a few moments he almost forgot the intense heat. He had been asked to keep a crook on the straight and narrow.

"Gee! Johnny was a good workman in his day. Funny what wimmin will do to a guy."

He was surprised that Johnny had remained straight for this length of time. He didn't blame the lad, of course—was sincerely glad that he had done so. Helen was a woman in a million, just such a one as Jim secretly craved for a wife. She was comfortably large and full-blooded and richly blond. "And wise. I'd hate to be married to a boneheaded dame." He lighted his cigar stump absently. "Swell-lookin' frail* like her could almost make me turn crooked. No wonder she's kept Johnny straight."

More peculiar than that, however, Jim reflected, was the fact that Helen herself had forsaken the rose path. She had been a clever dip⁺ in her day—none superior—and a smooth worker in other lines. He recalled the Starkman blackmail scheme; they'd never been able to hang a thing on Helen for that—or Johnny either. Old Starkman's lips had been tightly sealed, and not through indifference to money.

"That bimbo didn't love a dollar no more than he did his last pair of pants. Helen sure had him dead to rights, some way."

Here was Helen going straight and coming to him for assistance that her husband might not step from the road of rectitude. Jim's massive head rolled heavily from side to side in wonderment.

He spent the evening at a movie, finding himself aroused to spontaneous applause at that portion of the picture which disclosed the husband returning home just in time to prevent the elopement of his wife and the chauffeur, the latter having turned out to be an old lover in disguise. There was a saccharine scene which resulted in a dramatic choice between the men, the woman designating her preference by nearly strangling her husband while that gentleman beamed happily upon the discomfited lover as he slunk miserably away, presumably to another household where, perchance, the husband might not return home thus inopportunely.

Scenes of that sort were vastly impressive to Jim. He hated bad sportsmanship, and the villain-chauffeur in this picture had been a bad sport. Crookedness Jim loved. He admired a clever crook and worshiped a good woman. There was something massively pitiful about the man as he gazed raptly upon the silver screen in

---

* Slang for a woman, used as early as 1899, according to the *New Partridge Dictionary of Slang and Unconventional English*.

---

† A pickpocket.

the picture show; something inexpressibly sad in his demeanor, his abject loneliness. Jim himself would have been the last person in the world to realize the void in his life. Keen as he was in analysis of others, he was no master of introspection. When he emerged from the picture theater it was in the grip of a warm, sentimental glow. His simple, direct nature had been stirred to the roots. At that moment he desired nothing in life so much as to insure Helen the retention of that happiness which a few brief years of honest living had brought to her.

The following morning—Wednesday—he visited the banking house of Starnes & Company, where Johnny's loan was in the process of negotiation. He discovered that Joseph P. Starnes, the president, was handling the matter personally and that Johnny had explained frankly to Mr. Starnes the use to which the money was to be put.

"It is no concern of mine," explained Mr. Starnes crisply, "what Mr. Norton does with that money. As a matter of fact, it has been my experience that a professional gambler is highly trustworthy. In the second place there is always the chance that his venture will prove unprofitable, in which case I shall have recourse to my collateral. It is excellent collateral, Mr. Hanvey; as good as money. This house is safe—entirely and thoroughly safe."

"H'm! Guess you're about right, Mr. Starnes. Just wanted to know if you was wise to what this bird wanted the money for."

"Of course I am." Mr. Starnes' manner was curt. He had an instinctive antipathy to this hulking representative of the Bankers' Protective Association; had more than once seriously considered suggesting to that organization that the man was mentally unfitted for the responsibility of his position.

"And if I were not it would make no difference. Liberty Bonds form security which we cannot question."

Jim rose.

"I ain't gonna argue about it."

"There's nothing to argue."

"Certainly not. Of course there ain't. That's why I ain't gonna argue about it."

That evening Jim dropped in at the hotel where Johnny and Helen were registered. He telephoned to their room and was bidden to come up. His call abruptly terminated a hectic pinochle game then in progress, leaving Happy Gorman a heavy and disgruntled loser. When Jim entered the room he discovered Johnny playing solitaire and Helen seated by the window, reading a fashion magazine. A significant glance passed between the portly detective and the lavishly blond woman. Johnny rose at sight and posed for a moment with one hand gripping the card table, a slight frown showing.

"'Lo, Jim."

Johnny was a most excellent actor. Apparently he was enormously surprised at the presence of the Gargantuan gentleman who bulked in the doorway. It was Jim who punctured the silence:

"Ain't you glad to see me, Johnny?"

"Why shouldn't I be?"

"I'll bite. Why?"

"If you think you've got anything on me—"

"Aw, g'wan, Johnny! You know durn well that I know you've been goin' straight since you and Helen got hitched up. Just heard you were in town an' dropped in for a social chat."

Norton appeared relieved. He heaved an impressive sigh and motioned his visitor to a chair.

As though for the first time, Jim took notice of Helen. He held her two hands in his and stared approvingly.

"Helen of Troy! By gosh, Helen, you're prettier than ever! You've put on flesh, but you've been careful where you put it."

"That's all that counts, isn't it?"

"Yep. Some wimmin are downright careless. How're you an' Johnny gettin' along?"

"Mighty well."

"Who you doin' for a livin'?"

"The public. Johnny's been makin' a book down in New Orleans. It's a lot of work and a heap of expense, but we've managed to make ends meet."

Jim eyed the cards longingly.

"How 'bout a little three-handed game of setback?"

Chairs were drawn up. They played for a cent a point. It was midnight when Jim paid his losses—eighty-one cents—and rose to go.

"This is the life," he commented heartily. Then his face grew serious. "Keep it up, Johnny. There's nothin' to this crooked stuff."

"I know that, Jim," returned Norton fervently. "I'm off it."

The door closed behind the detective. Assured that he had departed, Johnny crossed the room, took his wife in his arms and implanted a smacking kiss upon her willing lips.

"Hook, line and sinker!"

"It is a dirty shame to take him in that way."

"Sure! But it's him or us, and there ain't any use of it being us. We'll be on Easy Street when this deal is finished."

They slept but lightly that night. The following morning early there was an executive session in Johnny's room. Slim Bolton was there, pessimistic as ever; Happy Gorman, melancholy but game; Connie Hawes, steely-eyed and emotionless.

"There's nothing to worry about," reassured Johnny. "Everything's chicken."*

"For you—yes."

Helen of Troy whirled on the speaker.

---

* An old saying, "everything is chicken but the gravy" means that everything is acceptable except for one grievance; shortened here, Johnny means that everything is all right.

"You can welch* any time you want. It's Johnny's idea and Johnny's jack.† If you ain't game to go through with it———"

"Aw, dry up, girlie! Who said anything about welching? I just wanted you to know that we aren't going it blind. If we didn't need the money so bad———"

"If people didn't need money there wouldn't be any crooks," she said tartly. "Now let's check over the plan."

They put their heads together and for the next fifteen minutes their earnest voices hummed steadily; five clever—if warped—brains planning the betterment of themselves and the discomfiture of a single, lonely, unwieldy detective.

"It's rough," summarized Happy Gorman, "but it looks like a cinch."

They separated. Slim Bolton went to a downtown garage, where he took out a car bought by him three days before. Slim knew more than a thing or two about automobiles, and for two days had been devoting his energies to the task of tuning this car up to the notch of perfect performance. He drove downtown and parked opposite the office building which housed the firm of Starnes & Company, bankers and brokers.

Slim took his post in the automobile at about eleven o'clock. At 11:30 he was joined by Happy Gorman, strong of arm and melancholy of face.

At 11:45 Connie Hawes appeared. He was dressed in a loose-fitting tweed suit, his coat tailored with a vent back so as to afford a maximum of action liberty. He nodded briefly to the two men in the car, then strolled around the corner and stationed himself outside a barber shop where he controlled a view of the building which held the Starnes offices. At 1:20 o'clock the figure of

---

* To renege, usually on payment.

---

† Money, stake.

Johnny Norton came into view. He was walking up from the main business thoroughfare of the city and carrying a package which the men knew contained the Liberty Bonds. From the corner of his eye he took note of the fact that his three confederates were on duty. He turned into the office building and five minutes later was ushered into the private office of Joseph P. Starnes. That gentleman greeted him effusively, but it was patent, too, that Mr. Starnes was very much on guard.

"You're late, Mr. Norton."

"Sorry," explained Johnny suavely. "I overslept, and I've been busy checking over these bonds." He produced a knife and deftly cut the twine which bound the bulky package. "I suppose you have the note prepared."

"Yes."

Starnes reached for the bonds. His sharp eyes, glittering from beneath bushy brows, inspected them closely. There wasn't a doubt of their genuineness. He counted them three times. Mr. Starnes was thoroughly reassured. His firm was on the verge of negotiating a very profitable loan. They were to receive 7 per cent interest from Johnny, rediscount the bonds at 5 per cent and thus make a clear 2 per cent profit, plus brokerage commission, without the embarrassment of tying up any of their cash reserve.

"Amount correct?" questioned Johnny crisply.

"Yes."

Johnny glanced at his watch.

"It is almost time for the bank to close, Mr. Starnes. If you'll make out my check for two hundred thousand and let me sign the note—I want to make my deposit today."

Starnes reached for a memorandum pad.

"I'll have to take these numbers down."

Johnny was frigid under the strain.

"I have a list here, Mr. Starnes. If you will just check the bonds themselves."

"Good!"

Unsuspiciously Joseph P. Starnes checked the numbers on the bonds as Johnny Norton read from the list. It was considerable of a memory feat on Johnny's part, and he would not have been equal to it save for the fact that he worked with a key system. He read the numbers swiftly, each number that he read being the actual number on a bond which the banker checked off. But the numbers which Johnny called out were not the numbers which he had on his list.

The hour of two was approaching. Johnny again suggested that he desired to make his deposit that day in the First National. Starnes sounded the buzzer for his bookkeeper.

"The Norton note, please, and the check."

They were duly produced. Starnes innocently reached for the list of bond numbers which Johnny had unostentatiously laid atop the bonds and extended the list to his bookkeeper.

"See that these are entered up, Mr. Mathews. These are the thousand-dollar Liberties which we have accepted as security for the loan to Mr. Norton here."

The bookkeeper departed with the incorrect list of bonds. Johnny Norton was grinning inwardly. He scribbled his name on the note and accepted the Starnes check for two hundred thousand dollars. He shook hands and departed. Slim Bolton and Happy Gorman saw him swing down the street en route to the First National. At two minutes before two o'clock Johnny deposited to his credit the Starnes check. Then he returned to the hotel—and Helen.

She was exultant at his report of success, and immediately they set the stage for a new drama. From the depths of his trunk he produced several dozen blank checks of the Crescent National of New Orleans. These he placed on the writing desk beside Major Torrance's check for eight thousand dollars, which was also on the Crescent National. A half dozen pens were next laid out carefully and several bottles of ink, all approximately of the color used originally by the unsuspecting horse owner, who was at that moment a victim to *mal de mer*.* Then, with brow furrowed, Johnny went to work. The spell of it gained upon him; he forgot for the moment that this was not seriously undertaken. His fingers, clumsy through lack of practice, labored over 8's and 0's similar to those made by the major.

"It's a dog-goned shame," commented Johnny, "that I ain't really trying something like this."

Helen gazed pridefully upon his handiwork.

"Come off that, dearie! Jim'd have you in less than no time."

"I know, I know; but I'm awfully tempted." He shoved his chair back from the writing desk, lighted a Turkish cigarette and walked to the window, where he posed for a moment, carelessly twirling his close-clipped mustache. "Better telephone Jim, Helen. We want this thing to be an alibi."

She called the number of Jim's hotel apartment house. The switchboard operator there answered.

"Mr. Hanvey's apartment, please."

There was a brief pause and then the operator's voice: "If you'll hold the telephone for a moment I'll connect you. Mr. Hanvey has just went up in the elevator."

Helen nodded violently at her husband, signifying that Jim was at home. In the transmitter she fired a question: "How long has he been out?"

"I don't know. I've just been on duty a half hour. If you wish——"

---

* Seasickness.

Then came a violent buzzing, a pause and a drawling, lazy voice from the other end:

"Hello! Who's this now?"

"Jim?"

"Yeh?"

"This is Helen."

"Is it?"

"Oh, Jim"—she pulled out the tremolo stop—"you promised to help me keep Johnny straight—you promised!"

"Well, I'm doin' my best."

"You haven't done enough. He's working now, Jim—right now. Do you understand?"

"On that paper?"

"Yes. Understand?"

"Sure; sure I do, Helen! I ain't so thick I can't see the joke when one clown slaps another in the pants. What you want me to do about it?"

"Come down and stop him. He'll listen to you."

"There ain't many folks will." Brief silence and then—"I'll come. It's awful hot for walkin'———"

"Take a taxi."

Came Jim's answer, heavy with sarcasm: "Too durned expensive for an honest detective."

His receiver clicked on the hook. Helen flung herself across the room and into her husband's arms.

"It worked, dearie. He just came in, which means he ain't hanging around Starnes & Company. He probably followed you when you left there, to get an idea if you were up to anything special. Saw you return to the hotel, and he went home. You've got an alibi. And now—now we'll let him save you from going crooked! Oh, honey, we're getting away with it!"

He patted her shoulder fondly.

"You sure are a dandy wife, Helen! Great ol' girl!"

She bustled into the dressing room.

"I'll be on the watchout for Jim in the lobby. Remember, Johnny, if you act your part right he'll never suspect you of being in on this deal, even if something should go wrong."

As she arranged her hat Johnny Norton glanced across the housetops in the general direction of the downtown business district.

"Gee, I'd give something to know what happened down yonder!"

It was worth knowing, for there had been action a-plenty. All three of the waiting men had witnessed Johnny's departure from the offices of Starnes & Company, and they saw Johnny walk to the bank via the route which they knew the messenger would take. The quintet had planned this affair to a detail. They knew, for instance, that securities of unusual value held by Starnes & Company were daily taken to the First National Bank by a trust-worthy messenger.

This messenger was little more than a glorified office boy despite his maturity. Too, he was a creature of habit. He daily departed the Starnes & Company suite about 2:30 o'clock, and being methodical took the shortest possible route to the First National. It was upon this habit of the messenger's that much of their scheme was based.

There were two routes between the Starnes corner and the First National, located two blocks away. The obvious one was down Elm Street one block to Main, and thence along that cheap thoroughfare to Pelham Street. The other was one block north on Ashmore and thence across on Pelham to Main. The latter route was several steps shorter, less traveled, and therefore easier. It was this second route which the Starnes messenger was in the habit of taking.

Almost identical in distance, the two routes were entirely dissimilar. Elm Street was a principal thoroughfare, something which could not be said of either Ashmore or Pelham. Those two blocks were lined with shoddy secondhand stores, groceries, markets and third-rate cafeterias.

At thirty-three minutes after two o'clock the Starnes messenger emerged from the big office building and started northward on Ashmore. He walked with a peculiar shuffling gait, and in his right hand he clutched a brown leather satchel. The moment he appeared Slim Bolton slipped into reverse, backed his sedan into the traffic, turned into Ashmore and followed. He saw Connie Hawes detach himself from the doorway of a barber shop and fall into step behind the decrepit and unsuspecting messenger.

Slim was driving parallel to the slow-moving messenger. His car veered toward the curb. A trifle ahead of the man, Slim stopped his car and immediately slipped into second in preparation for a quick get-away. Happy Gorman, every inch the gentleman in appearance, opened the rear door of the sedan and hailed the little old man.

"Pardon me, stranger," he said politely, "but would you mind telling me which way I go to reach the best hotel?"

The messenger paused and quite innocently moved toward the curb and the car. He recognized that this man must be a tourist. Connie Hawes closed in on him from the rear.

"The best hotel?" repeated the messenger, pleased at having been questioned. "It's two blocks down that way, and then———"

The world went black before his eyes. Connie Hawes struck as he leaped. The messenger pitched forward into the opened door and Connie flung him out of the way as he darted by and grabbed the satchel. A spectator, rigid with terror, emitted a shriek of horror. The messenger crumpled grotesquely in the gutter—stunned.

Slim clamped down on the accelerator and sped forward.

There was no traffic policeman on that little-used corner. Another pedestrian shouted, but no one knew what caused his excitement. The car whirled eastward on Pelham Street, turned north at the next corner and then rounded the block and sped southward over the viaduct. A crowd had collected about the figure of the stricken messenger, who was now struggling back to consciousness. Excitement was intense, but explanations given the belated policeman were incoherent. The officer notified headquarters that a messenger for the Starnes banking house had been hit on the head and robbed, but he had no clue as to the identity of the assailants and knew nothing of the affair save that the escape had been made in an automobile. And the three criminals, speeding across country, little appreciated the measure of their safety. They drove at reasonable speed for thirty miles. At the first little town Connie Hawes alighted, carrying the satchel. The car proceeded. Twelve miles farther south Happy Gorman left the car. Slim drove into the next town, parked his car at the curb, strolled nonchalantly into a drug store, where he consumed an ice-cream soda, and twenty minutes later boarded a New Orleans-bound train. In the second Pullman* he saw Connie Hawes and Happy Gorman, but by no slightest gesture did these men indicate an acquaintanceship with one another.

They knew that they were safe, but took no chances. Time enough for that after their trip westward from New Orleans, when they should have attained safety on the far side of the Mexican border.

Events of some importance had been occurring contemporaneously in the city from which they had so abruptly departed. Immediately on receiving the telephone call from Helen of Troy, Jim Hanvey left his diminutive apartment. The heat had become more intense; the sun baked down from a sky unmarked by clouds.

---

* A luxurious rail car, usually a sleeping car.

Walking, for Jim, was far from a pleasure. He rolled uncomfortably down the street, his tiny*, fishlike eyes blinking with interminable slowness, fat hands flapping awkwardly against his pants legs with each lumbering step. He turned in at the hotel lobby and there found Helen. She crossed eagerly toward him, futilely searching his puttylike face for any indication of suspicion.

"You understand what I wanted with you, Jim?"

"Yeh, sure I understand, Helen. But it does seem to me Johnny might've been considerate enough to pick a cooler day to go crooked on."

"He's working now. He's all excited, looking like he's sorry he wasted all this time going straight. He's a wizard with other folks' checks, Johnny is."

"M'm-h'm! Clever boy. What you want me to do?"

"Go up and talk to him."

"Alone?"

"I'll go with you."

"He won't get peeved at you for tipping me off?"

"I don't care if he does," she returned virtuously. "I always have believed that honesty was the best policy—when you don't really need money."

"Yeh—and when you get away with it."

They entered Johnny's room without the formality of knocking.

Johnny backed against the table, jaws working in true movie-villain fashion. His hands, groping behind his back, scraped the checks into a heap in a crude attempt at concealment. Helen, too, gave evidence of the fact that the art of the actor is not yet dead—or even ill. She raised pitiful eyes to her husband's face.

"I know you'll hate me, Johnny; but I tipped Jim off."

He simulated great rage.

---

* Hanvey's eyes are earlier described as "large, and round like a baby's"; this different description may signify that Hanvey was squinting in the sun's glare.

"Snitched on me, eh? Damn you———"

"Whoa, Johnny! Easy there, son! I hate to hear ladies damn-you'd when I'm around."

Johnny turned his offended attention to the detective.

"It's none of your business———"

"I hope not, Johnny; but it most likely would have been if Helen hadn't telephoned me."

"I did it for your sake, Johnny," she chimed in. "I have been very happy during the last six years, unhaunted by the fear of prison cells."

Jim turned to her, a quizzical light in his glassy eyes.

"Who wrote them words?"

She flushed.

"I don't know; but they're just what I feel." She threw her arms around Johnny's neck. "Please, dearie, for my sake, for the sake of our happiness, listen to Jim! We've been straight for so long. You couldn't get away with no forgery job now, dearie; you're all out of practice."

Jim waddled heavily across the room and took the batch of half-written checks from Johnny's unresisting hand.

"Lemme see how good you are now, kid. You used to be real clever." He inspected them closely. "T'chk! T'chk! They just can't come back, Johnny. That's awful rough work. I'd have got you in no time at all. Yeh, tough luck, son; but I reckon you'd be wise to run straight from now on. You've lost your touch, Johnny."

An expression of genuine sorrow crossed Johnny's face.

"On the level?"

"Surest thing you know!"

"Well"—and Johnny sighed—"I s'pose I might as well keep on like I've been going. Much obliged, Jim."

Helen's hysterical squeal of delight filled the room.

"You promise, dearie—promise to keep straight forever and ever?"

"Amen!"

She turned her attention to Jim, clasped one of his hands between both of hers.

"I don't know how to thank you, Jim. You've been wonderful, marvelous!"

Jim blushed boyishly.

"Gee, Helen, lay offen that stuff! When a good-lookin' dame begins sayin' sweet things to me I ain't got no more backbone than a nickel's worth of ice cream."

"But, Jim——"

The telephone jangled.

"That's for me," Jim announced.

"You?"

"Uh-huh! I was expectin' a call an' I told the apartment house operator she'd find me here."

Helen and her husband were ill-at-ease. In a trice they had ceased to be sorry for the ungainly detective. There was something so cumbersomely positive in his manner; such a degree of assurance.

"Hello!"

It was Hanvey at the telephone. The two others strained their ears, but without result. And Jim's face told them no more than they could have learned by watching the lee side of a cantaloupe.

"Yeh, Jim Hanvey speaking....Uh-huh....You don't say so!... When?...Clear?...You done what I suggested?...Well, that proves you ain't the absolute ass I thought you was, Mr. Starnes."

He clicked the receiver on the hook and turned away. He lighted a fresh cigar and jerked his head toward the telephone. "Funny thing," he commented disinterestedly.

"Yes?" They spoke eagerly in chorus.

"Messenger left the Starnes offices a few minutes ago. Coupla roughnecks bumped him on the bean, grabbed his satchel and made a get-away." If he discerned their mutual signs of relief he gave no indication of the fact. His voice droned on monotonously. "Old man Starnes is a stiff-necked idiot, but this time he was wise. He took my advice for once."

"Your advice?"

"Sure! Y'see, with you dumping a quarter million dollars in unregistered Liberties with him, there was always danger that some crooks might get wise to it and try to make a haul. So I suggested to Fat-head Starnes that he stick them securities in his own vault for a while instead of sendin' 'em down to the First National as he usually does. In view of what just happened, I think I was kinder clever—real awful clever." He paused apologetically. "You ain't got no objections to me callin' myself clever, have you?"

They did not answer, a premonition of disaster had robbed them of speech.

"Y'see, Helen, them naughty crooks might of got away with Johnny's Liberty Bonds. Might of, I said. But they didn't. All that was in that satchel was a few registered bonds which ain't worth duck soup s'far's negotiatin' 'em is concerned."

Helen's face was dead white beneath her plentiful make-up.

"Johnny's Liberty Bonds are still at Starnes & Company?"

"Yeh, sure!"

"You wouldn't lie to me, Jim, would you?"

"Aw, Helen, you know I wouldn't! Fat men are rotten liars."

"You suspected that the bank messenger was going to be robbed?"

He nodded.

"I had a sort of a hunch thataway."

She turned dejectedly. It was Johnny Norton who launched the next question:

"How did you get wise, Jim?"

"Me? It was easy this time. A lady tipped me off; a terrible pretty blond lady." Helen winced. "'Bout as much of a tip-off as I needed, anyway," continued Jim softly. "Y'know, Johnny, things occur awful funny sometimes. I happened to drift into the Starnes offices just after you left, and would you believe it, the list of bond numbers that old bird had didn't tally with the bonds at all. It was real peculiar. So I just suggested that they hold 'em there a while for the bookkeeper to enter 'em up. Y'know, a banker ought to be more careful than Starnes was. He never knows when he's li'ble to get gypped." He turned toward the door. "Yeh, Johnny, if I was you I'd stay on the safe side of things. You've lost your touch, son—lost it complete."

Helen of Troy stared at her husband and he returned her gaze with one equally miserable. Jim Hanvey posed heavily in the doorway, the fingers of his right hand fiddling with his massive watch chain. He regarded them benignly. Then he blinked with maddening slowness.

"Didn't you come to me, Helen, an' ask me to keep Johnny from goin' crooked?"

She nodded.

"Well," drawled the big man, "I only done what you asked me, didn't I?"

Caveat Emptor

JIM HANVEY lolled upon a park bench, his ample and ungainly figure entirely surrounded by landscape. The fingers of his right hand clutched the stump of a cigar which for downright meanness was in a class alone. His fat and florid face was wreathed in contentment and his fishy eyes were partially curtained by heavy lids from beneath which Jim stared amusedly at a group of very small children who romped in shrill disdain of a sign which warned all and sundry that that particular grass was not to be trod upon.

The sun of early September was dropping slowly to rest behind the interminable line of apartment houses on the farther side of Central Park West. It sprinkled in golden radiance through the red leaves above Jim's uncovered head and mottled the rich green carpet beneath his enormous feet. Jim's eyes closed slowly as he luxuriously stretched his Gargantuan frame. Then the eyes opened to rest upon the trim figure of a little girl of six who stood regarding him with an expression of grave but frank interest.

"Hmm!" Jim pulled himself together. "Good evening."

The child made no answer. A spot near Jim's midsection held her undivided attention. The unwieldy detective matched the child's gravity with his own. She was a pretty little thing whose raiment, even to Jim's untutored eyes, bespoke extreme affluence. At length, with absolute ease of manner, she moved forward and touched with her fore-finger, the gold toothpick which hung suspended from the heavy watch chain spanning Jim's ill-fitting vest.

"That's pretty," she commented abruptly.

Jim's face lighted with pleasure. It was seldom indeed that his pet bit of personal ornamentation received so genuine a compliment.

"Ain't it?"

"Yup. Awful pretty." Then, doubtfully. "What is it?"

Jim touched a button and a wicked and glistening point appeared. "A toothpick," he explained.

"What's that?"

"It's—well, you see———" His face went blank. "Just a toothpick, that's all. Solid gold."

"Oh!" said the child. "I see."

Jim felt relieved. He fancied it might be difficult to explain a solid gold toothpick and he thanked goodness for the youngster's erudition. She continued to finger the bauble approvingly but, so far as she was concerned, the conversation was at an end.

The silence proved somewhat embarrassing to Jim. It was entirely too impersonal for his friendly nature. "What's your name?"

"Pauline."

"Pauline what?"

"Pauline Lathrop."

"That's a pretty name, Pauline. Where do you live?"

A touch of imitative snobbishness displayed itself in the answer of the little girl. "Riverside Drive. My father is a very rich man and we have three automobiles."

"Wonderful. Astounding. And what is your father's name?"

"Mr. Noah Lathrop. He's an emporter."

"An emporter, eh?" Remembrance came to the detective. "Sure. Sure enough he is. A joolry importer, isn't he?"

"Yup. An' we got three automobiles."

"That certainly is wonderful, Pauline. I'm awful glad to know about them automobiles. I guess your daddy's business must be awful good."

"No," confessed the child frankly. "Father says it's gone to hell."

Jim was a trifle nonplussed. "That's too bad. I'm real sorry to hear it, Pauline."

Once again the wordless, contemplative stare of the child. "You're awful fat."

"So I've heard."

"And you look ugly," she finished. "But you ain't."

"That's a relief. I ain't no blue-ribbon entry, at that."

"I like that gold thing," continued Pauline. "But I bet you ain't got three automobiles."

"No. I bet I ain't."

"My Father has, and he says——"

"Pauline!" The voice of a woman came inquiringly through the soft air of a gradually gathering dusk. "Oo-oh! Pauline."

"That's my nurse," she explained to Jim Hanvey. "She gets twenty dollars a week. Her name is Mary."

Jim's eyes turned slowly toward the trim little uniformed figure which was bearing down upon them. Faint stirrings of recollection occurred in the detective's brain. The figure—the face—the voice——And now Mary had taken Pauline's hand.

"I told you not to run away from that summerhouse. I've been looking everywhere for you." She exhibited genuine concern—and relief. Pauline appeared not at all interested.

"This man has got a gold toothpick," she announced triumphantly. "But he ain't got three automobiles."

The nurse turned toward the big man with a smile of quiet apology on her lips. Her eyes met the glassy orbs of the detective; and the smile congealed. The color receded from her cheeks and it was patent that she was struggling to recover a poise suddenly lost.

The detective blinked with maddening slowness. "Hello Mary," he said. "How's Tim?"

The trim little woman in the nurse's uniform stood rigid for a moment. Then she turned to the child. "Run on and play with the other children a few minutes," she ordered. Pauline obeyed willingly enough. The nurse stood regarding Hanvey apprehensively, and eventually the mammoth detective punctured the silence.

"Why the disguise, Mary?"

She spoke in tones so low as to be scarcely audible. "It isn't a disguise, Jim."

"No-o? Last time I seen you——"

"Never mind that," she said nervously. "I'm runnin' straight now. Lay off."

"Goshamighty, Mary—I ain't aiming to do nothin' else. I'm just curious."

"I tell you everything's all right."

"Sure it is. But why the job? What you doin' nursin' a kid?"

He could discern the struggle which she was undergoing. And finally she seated herself beside him. "There ain't a thing wrong, Jim. Honest there ain't. I've just been workin' since they sent Tim up."

"He's in stir?"

"Didn't you know?"

"I heard somethin' about it—but the case wasn't exactly in my line as I remember. Gov'ment, wasn't it?"

She nodded. "Smuggling."

"Shuh!"

"They caught him with the goods. He pleaded guilty. He's

doing a two-year stretch in Atlanta.* He left me flat—that's why I went to work. I got a nursing job because I naturally like kids. I had to do somethin.'"

"Mm!" Jim's face betrayed no particular interest. If there was doubt of her in his mind he did not show it. "Funny—you workin' as a nursegirl while Tim is doing a stretch. Well—I sure hope you stay on the straight an' narrow. It don't pay awful good but it's real safe."

She sighed with relief. "I'm not pulling anything, Jim. I'm on the level—anyway until Timmy gets out."

She summoned her youthful charge and they walked off together toward the Seventy-second Street gate. Jim stared speculatively after them. He groped blindly for a match and relighted his cigar. Then, as he inhaled deeply, he gave vent to an expression of doubt——

"Wonder what she lied to me for?"

His somnolent eyes half closed and as he lay back in his seat there came to him the faint limning of the picture in which she had appeared at the occasion of their last meeting—a bank job in Omaha, a successful bank job in which he knew that she had been the brains of the gang. Jim held a great admiration for that little woman; she was courageous and she was clever; she played her cards well and she played them boldly. That last case had been one of his few unsuccessful ones and he had been more than half glad of it. He had been out to get them, but, failing, he felt nothing of resentment—only a keen admiration for the brains which had outwitted him.

But a few minutes since he had seen Mary Lannigan flustered for the first time in the several years of their acquaintanceship. That discomfiture bespoke guilt. Hanvey's fat fingers groped for the gold toothpick so lately admired by Pauline Lathrop.

---

* A federal prison that opened in 1902 and continues in use in 2020.

That golden horror was of inestimable assistance to Hanvey in moments of mental stress. Mary working as a nursegirl. Hmph! There was something behind that—bound to be. Jim Hanvey was reputed to know intimately every worthwhile crook in the country and he counted Tim and Mary Lannigan as among his very best friends. Jim knew, for instance, that Tim had a young fortune* salted away and that it was not at all necessary for his wife to work as a menial while he enjoyed the hospitality of the United States government. That being the case, Mary's present occupation was the cloak for something. He was sorry—darn shame Mary couldn't keep straight. Good kid. "An' dog-gone her—she's gone an' got me all interested."

At first Jim determined to play hands off. He wasn't a policeman; it was no duty of his to make trouble for crooks who were not engaged in work which held his immediate attention. But there was something bizarre in the very thought of this excessively clever little woman acting as nursemaid to a snippy little girl who boasted of her father's trio of motor cars. Two other facts paraded before him, demanding that he adduce something from their proximity to one another.

One of them was that the father of the girl whom Mary nursed was a jewelry importer.

The second fact had to do with Tim Lannigan's incarceration for smuggling. Smuggling was not in Tim's line.

That night Jim reluctantly omitted his regular picture show and did a little investigation. Information came readily to hand principally because Jim knew just where to turn. When he retired near midnight he knew considerably more about Mary Lannigan's job, but there were one or two blank spaces which had aroused his curiosity beyond measure.

---

* Again, slang of uncertain origin, though from the context, Hanvey evidently means "considerable fortune."

One vital thing he had learned—and that was that the name of Noah Lathrop had been mentioned more than casually in the case which resulted in Tim's journey to Atlanta. Just what Lathrop had to do with it no one could adequately explain, but there was undeniably a sinister significance.

He was at the park again the following day but Mary and the child did not appear. The next afternoon Jim was on Riverside Drive at the hour he knew a nurse would naturally go walking. Pauline recognized him first, nor, in the eagerness with which she greeted him, did he lose sight of the apprehension which blanched the pretty face of Mary Lannigan.

"That," proclaimed the tactful Pauline, designating Jim's gold toothpick, "is vulgar."

"G'wan. Why?"

"Gentlemen," she explained, "do not use *gold* toothpicks."

Jim turned quizzically to Mary. "Ain't she the bright kid?" He grew serious then—"Come out of it, Sister. I ain't gonna eat you."

He walked with them to Central Park. In response to his unspoken command, Mary sent Pauline to play with the other children and she and Jim sat together on the bench. It was Jim who spoke first, after he had lighted one of his offensively fragrant cigars.

"Get me straight, Mary—I don't want to cause you no trouble…but you've got my curiosity aroused something terrible."

For a moment she didn't answer. She sat staring at the path where her toe was etching aimlessly in the dust. And finally she faced him with a flash of her old-time spirit. "I want you to lay off, Jim. I'm not pulling anything crooked."

"If you're runnin' straight I ain't got no choice, have I?"

"Yes—you have."

"How you make that?"

"You can queer things for me—and," earnestly, "I don't want 'em queered, Jim—I don't want 'em queered."

There was a little break in her voice which puzzled him. She was deeply moved—that, in itself, was a novelty. He took her hand gently between both of his enormous ones and patted it as a father might have done.

"I ain't tryin' to butt in on your affairs, Sister, but I'd like to get the lowdown on this. I'll say right off—wait a minute, I'll come clean with you before you spill anything. You got me curious night before last with that straight stuff an' all. I know—an' you know I know—that Tim has a pile salted away which means that I didn't swallow your bunk about needin' the twenty-per-an'-cakes you're gettin' for nursin' that kid which has a father who owns three automobiles.

"As I say, that sort of started me off an' I did a little checking up on my own hook. I learned, among other things, that Noah Lathrop's name sort of figured in the smugglin' case which sent Tim South—that indicatin' pretty clear that you ain't workin' in Lathrop's house for no reason which ought to make Lathrop comfortable. So knowin' what I know, if you want to loosen up— why, go right to it Sister an' I'll be all ears, like any other jackass."

Her head was bowed and it was plain that she was thinking intensively. On the grass nearby the children romped, their shrillings cutting through the balminess of the September evening. From Central Park West came the clanging of Eighth Avenue cars and the occasional sirening of automobile traffic. A man and woman on horseback rode down the bridle path near them and a park policeman strolled by and ostentatiously looked away as he, with considerable surprise, recognized the obese Hanvey.

At length she commenced speaking, her voice coming as though from a great distance. "It's important, Jim, first of all, that you understand I'm telling the truth. If there's anything I say that ain't true—it ain't because I think it ain't. I'm giving you the works as I know 'em. I'm telling you—well, first of all, because I want to get it off my chest. And second, because you'd get wise anyway. And third, because—Oh! just because.

"I'll commence right at the beginning Jim. It started six months ago when Tim went to Europe. You know he's a real gent and every once in so often he works the card graft on the big steamers—not often enough for them to know him. Only when business is dull.

"Well, he was over there loafing around waiting for a certain party to sail for America again, this party being the grandest sucker which ever stood a couple of raises for the privilege of drawin' to an in-between straight. About that time Mr. Noah Lathrop was in Paris doing some jewelry buying. He goes over there once or twice every year. His firm is one of the biggest on Maiden Lane. And in Paris at the same time Lathrop and Tim were, was Walter Yeager."

"Yeager?" Hanvey exhibited keen interest. "In Paris?"

"Yeh. All set for a job. An' get this, Jim—I aint tryin' to get Walt in bad. He's had a tough enough time already. But even if Walt does run foul of trouble I can't help it. I'm out to do what I can for Tim…that's all I'm thinking of."

Again that little catch in her voice. Jim closed his glassy eyes sleepily and motioned for her to continue.

"To hold a long story down, Walt Yeager was onto something soft in Paris. He pulled the job and got away with it—about three hundred and fifty thousand dollars worth of stones that are stones. It turned the Paris police inside out and stood 'em on their ear. It was as nifty a piece of work as you've ever heard of, an' Walt got away with it in a way you'd be proud of if you knew the details.

"Well, there was Walt with the jewels and nothin' to do with 'em. The European markets had nine eyes peeled an' Walt didn't dare bring 'em to this country because when he came through the customs there'd be a stir and a talk—and flooie! So, Walt hearing that Lathrop was doin' his semi-annual buying, an' knowing that he wasn't more than ten miles above a shady transaction, went to him, confessed that he had stolen jewels and asked him what they'd be worth in cash, delivered at Lathrop's New York office.

"Lathrop was interested, of course. It was a graft for him. He'd run no risk buying the stuff in New York and since his house has a first class rep he knew he could slip 'em on the market one by one and the trade would never be no wiser. They dickered around for awhile and agreed on one hundred and forty thousand dollars cash, F. O. B. Maiden Lane. And that's where Tim was pulled into the deal.

"Walt Yeager wasn't willing to declare those jewels at the customs and he wasn't game to try and smuggle 'em. So he told Lathrop that in order to carry the deal through Lathrop must hire some one to do the smuggling. Yeager and Lathrop both inquired around and learned that Tim was over there—he bein' at that time in Bremen waiting for his sucker friend. He had gone there from Paris. Lathrop went to Germany, found Tim and offered him five thousand dollars for the job of smuggling.

"Tim grabbed it. It seemed like a cinch. And that's where Lathrop done Tim dirt—because," she turned her blazing eyes on Jim Hanvey—"the dirty crook never told Tim that the jewels he was supposed to smuggle was stolen goods!"

Jim nodded heavily. "I see....Lathrop was dishonest. Even with Tim."

"Exactly. And he played safe seven different ways. He saw to it that Tim and Walt Yeager engaged passage on a French liner for New York and he had it framed with Walt that he wasn't to say a word to Tim until they were pretty close to the customs when all Walt was to do was to turn the stuff over to Tim, watch Tim smuggle it through and then get it back from him and deliver it to Lathrop. Tim was to make the trip knowing that some one was going to slip him some jewels just before they got to customs.

And as true as I'm telling you, Jim, he didn't know it was nothing more than a smuggling job. It never occurred to him that there might be something behind it.

"Lathrop never even come back on the same ship with them. He sailed a week ahead from Southhampton. Tim and Walt came over together from Havre* and a couple days before they reached New York, Walt slipped Tim the stuff.

"Well, there ain't any use botherin' you with details about how Tim tried to work it. It's enough to say that they nabbed him. Caught him dead to rights. Tim was sorry, but he wasn't really worried. He knew all he had to do was to get in touch with Lathrop on the Q. T. and a heap of influence would be used to get him a fine instead of a jail sentence and that Lathrop would pay the fine. But—" her hand went out and tightened grimly over Jim's flappy paw—"Lathrop welched. Welched like a dirty yeller dog. He said he didn't know Tim, hadn't never seen him before, and had nothing whatever to do with the case. Meanwhile Tim, feeling secure, had pleaded guilty to the smuggling charge.

"And it wasn't until after he pleaded guilty to that, Jim—and Walt Yeager had disappeared—that Tim learned how bad he was in. Because the jewels he had admitted smuggling were the ones which had been stolen in Paris and they were recognized instanter. That's where Tim was crossed up. It wasn't that they nabbed him for smuggling—he was guilty of that and willing to take his medicine. But he wasn't mixed up in the robbery....

"And here's the lay of the land now. Tim got two years in the Federal prison for smuggling. He's been there seven months. The jewels have been returned to Paris. Yeager has disappeared. Noah Lathrop swears he don't know nothing about anything crooked.

---

* Southhampton was (and remains) a major terminus for passenger ships, about seventy miles southwest of London. Le Havre was a major port in the Normandy region of France, heavily damaged in World War II.

And when Tim gets through serving his smuggling time, Jim—they're going to send him back to Paris to stand trial for stealing them jewels."

Her voice trailed off. Jim blinked with maddening slowness and turned his apparently sightless eyes upon a pert little squirrel nearby. But his voice was charged with keenest sympathy—

"They've got him dead to rights, sure enough, ain't they, Mary?"

"Yes," with fierce bitterness, "they have. He hasn't a leg to stand on. It's twenty or twenty-five years in a French prison for him. He was in Paris when the robbery occurred—no chance to prove an alibi. He tried to smuggle the stones. He was caught red-handed. He confessed to the smuggling. Lathrop was in the clear—what's Tim's word against his? And I—well, I don't mind the two years Tim is doing: he went into that with his eyes open…but Jim—I'm out to save Tim from doing a twenty-year stretch for something he never even knew about. That's what I'm doing, Jim. Now do you understand?"

Jim nodded a ponderous affirmative. "I sure do, Mary. I sure do. But I still don't quite savvy this nurse stuff."

Her voice came crisply now in response to the warm friendliness of the detective's tone. "Any man who will do what Noah Lathrop did is the dirtiest kind of a crook. He's poison mean and low-down and rotten. You never knew a first class crook who would welch like that, did you?"

"No-o. Not no decent crook."

"Neither did I. And I figured out if Lathrop was that crooked—it wasn't the first time. He's a prominent man and he's proud. He must have slipped before. It's a certainty that some time in his life he's done something just as rotten as the trick he pulled on Tim. Oh! I wouldn't be kicking if he'd come clean with Tim in the first place and told him it was stolen stuff. It was the double-crossing and then the welching that hurt. And the fact that Tim is innocent. A crook has a hard enough life serving time for what he really does, let alone what he don't do.

"That's why I worked around and got this job as nursegirl in Lathrop's home. I've got a room on the place, and I'm watching, Jim—I'm watching close. I'm learning a heap about that bird. He's rotten all the way through—a cheap, piking, safety-first crook. Smug and self-satisfied and so stuck on himself I want to kill him sometimes. Of course he don't dream I know Tim Lannigan or that I'm anything except what I seem.

"And some day, Jim, I'm gonna get something on Noah Lathrop—something that he'd rather die than see come out. And when I do I'm gonna make him sing. I'm gonna make him come out in the clear and save Tim from doing that stretch in France." She threw her arms wide in an unconsciously dramatic gesture—"That's why I'm working as a nursegirl in his house, Jim—that's why."

Pauline Lathrop appeared and demanded two cents with which to purchase an apple-on-a-stick. She accepted the money from Jim but again expressed her disdain for the vulgar toothpick. "And your cigars smell terrible."

Jim sighed. "I reckon they do. But I like 'em."

"You're a funny man," said the child.

Pauline departed joyously to purchase her confection. Jim turned friendly eyes upon the tiny, indomitable figure of the little woman by his side. He *tchk'd* once or twice and mopped his forehead with a lavender handkerchief.

"You'll lay off me, won't you, Jim?"

"Huh?"

"You'll give me a free hand in this matter, won't you? Let me play it my own way?"

He thought for a moment before replying. And then, slowly and deliberately he shook his head. "Nope."

He saw her figure stiffen, watched the delicate hands ball into tiny fists. "Jim…." There was horror and unbelief in her tone.

"Nope, Mary—I ain't gonna play hands off in this little game of yours. Not for a minute. I can't." He, with difficulty crossed one enormous leg over the other. "But I tell you what I will do," he volunteered conversationally.

"What?"

His voice was toneless.

"I'll help you."

For a second she did not move. "You—you'll help?" she choked.

"Sure."

"H-h-help me to clear Tim?"

"Sure."

She faced him then, her face flushed and radiant, the light of happiness flaming from her fine eyes. "Jim Hanvey!" she said, "I love you for that!"

He fidgeted in embarrassment. "It is kinder funny—a detective workin' for a crook. But it's something I've always wanted to do. Of course, I mightn't be of any help——"

"You will, Jim. You will. Oh! it's wonderful. I've been so alone——"

"Aw! dry up, Sister. It's my job to nab the whole bunch of you when you've done something to be nabbed for. But I like you— every one of you—and I'm damned if I can sit back and see you go up for something you didn't do. Specially when you've been double-crossed by an honest man."

And long after she and little Pauline had disappeared beyond the traffic of Central Park West, long after gray dusk had merged gently into velvet night, long after the shrill playcalls of children had been superseded by the low-toned dialogue of occasional passing couples and the insistent, rhythmic *k-chnk, k-chnk* of oarlocks from the adjacent lake—long after all of that Jim Hanvey sat upon his park bench and mused upon the vagaries of circumstance.

Jim Hanvey had experienced a long, a colorful, a varied career. Now, for the first time, he found himself embarked upon a professional enterprise on behalf of a criminal, the object of his attack being a person in that class of society for which men such as Jim Hanvey served as bulwark.

The situation was bizarre—rather outrageously so, but it held an irresistible appeal to Jim. He was a lonely man who counted his friends among those whom he professionally hunted. The better class of criminals knew Jim and liked him. They outwitted him if they could—but they played straight with him, just as he did with them. To most of them it was a source of wonderment that he had not long since joined their ranks. In answer to their frank questionings he invariably returned an answer astounding in its simple logic——

"A feller is either born crooked or straight. I was born straight—that's all. You can't blame me for that any more than I can blame you for bein' crooked."*

But now he was to attain the unspoken ambition of many years: he was to expend his talents in an effort to free one of his criminal friends from an unjust charge. Let Tim Lannigan serve his time for smuggling—he was guilty. But Jim had checked up on Mary's story and knew that she had spoken the truth. That being the case it behooved him to see that Tim served a sentence for what he had done and was extricated from the predicament into which he had blundered.

---

* The line between investigator and miscreant is often a thin one. Sherlock Holmes himself remarked on this in "The Adventure of the Bruce-Partington Plans" (which first appeared in the *Strand Magazine* for Dec. 1908, reprinted in *His Last Bow*, Arthur Conan Doyle, ed. [New York: George H. Doran, 1917], 131): "It is fortunate for this community that I am not a criminal…"

That he had undertaken a task of no mean proportions was plain to him. In this particular matter the position of Noah Lathrop was impregnable. There was no possible proof that Lathrop had connived with Walter Yeager to purchase the stolen gems. There was even less proof that Noah had hired Tim to do the smuggling. Certainly there was no chance to enlist the services of Walt Yeager. It wasn't Walt's fault, anyway. He had played fair with both Tim and Lathrop by the tenets of the criminal code. It was unfortunate that Lathrop had betrayed Tim—but it was too much to expect that Walt would do anything so absurdly Quixotic as to confess to the robbery in order to save Lannigan. And there wasn't even an outside chance to convict Yeager of the original theft.

Mary Lannigan had the correct idea. A man as crooked as Lathrop had shown himself to be in this instance had been crooked before. He would be crooked again. He had indicated that he was moulded of conscienceless stuff. Somewhere in his past there must be a skeleton which he would not care to have displayed. And in order to prevent that display he might even be willing to confess his guilt as a smuggling accessory. In that way—and in that way alone—Tim Lannigan could be saved from facing trial—and certain conviction—for the crime which he had not committed.

Jim first of all boarded the Southern for Atlanta where he had two long and earnest conversations with Tim Lannigan. Tim's story verified that of Mary in every way. The big, handsome, red-headed crook was pitifully embarrassed at the knowledge that Jim was working for him. Too, he made no attempt to conceal his emotion at tidings of Mary's activity in his behalf. Jim found him bitter against Lathrop and not at all so against Walt Yeager. "Poor Walt! He was crossed up pretty near as bad as I was. And he's flat now. Gosh! To think of getting away with a job like that and then have a falldown. It's tough!"

"Sure is," agreed Jim.

Acquainting himself with Noah Lathrop's personality without meeting that gentleman was a more difficult undertaking. He made occasion to be near him two or three times when Lathrop was unconscious of the sleepy-eyed surveillance. Jim found Lathrop a rather undersized, slender man of obtrusive pomposity and disagreeable manner. He spoke in a loud, nasal voice which carried unpleasantly a considerable distance and his utterances were all dogmatic. Jim found his Great-I-Am* attitude annoying and at the same time amusing. There was a laughable similarity between father and daughter. Jim could well fancy the boast of the man—

"I pay four thousand a year for my apartment on the Drive and I maintain three cars." Jim's big fingers fumbled with the gold toothpick. Somehow, it seemed a little less vulgar than Pauline had led him to believe.

Jim held frequent conferences with Mary Lannigan. She had nothing to report but there was no lessening of confidence or determination. He was amused by her grim defiance—the indomitable will to power behind the masklike manners and pretty, girlish face. No wonder the smugly complacent Noah Lathrop was unsuspicious of the dynamite within his house; to all appearances Mary was merely an innocuously pretty young woman temporarily engaged in the nursing profession—against the day when she would be carried off to wife by some six-foot truck driver.

"I know I'm right, Jim. The man's rotten all the way through—and he handled this affair in a way which proves that it ain't the first time he's pulled something. Sometimes when I watch him I get mad enough to scream—I can imagine him chuckling to himself about his cleverness. Not a thought for the man who he

---

* The name of the divinity, taken from the first of the Ten Commandments: "I am the Lord thy God."

thinks is going to do the long stretch in France. Her teeth clicked suddenly. "Oh! what's the use of letting myself get all worked up? I guess my game is to lay low and keep grinning."

"You said it, Sister. And when you get something on him—talk it over with me. We'll make him dance a hornpipe."

She looked up gratefully into his expressionless eyes. "You can do that, Jim. Until you promised to help I was only a crook without a chance. I didn't know what I was going to do when I found what I was hunting."

Jim shrugged. "It's you who's got to do the discovering Mary. Just keep those bright eyes wide open——"

"I sure ain't gonna do nothin' else."

"—And let me know every least little thing that goes on. Listen in on his dining room conversation all you can. A feller as stuck on himself as that bimbo—an' as crazy about hearin' himself talk—is certain to blab something around the house." Jim lighted a cigar. "He may even have some interesting papers lyin' around."

"No," she said with perfect candor, "I've searched everything. Even the safe."

"Good." He rose heavily to his feet. "Keep it up, Sis. We've got all the time in the world, plus—an' the best thing we can do is to use it. By the way, how's my little friend Pauline?"

The girl made a wry face. "Ugh! Nasty little minx."

"Huh!" grinned Jim, "think what she'll be like at forty."

A fortnight dragged by. Jim busied himself with routine matters without, however, allowing the main focus of his attention to waver from the Lannigan matter. Occasionally he made it a point to meet Mary in the park. She had nothing to tell him and he talked things over with her only for her own sake—to keep her courage and optimism keyed to the proper pitch. There was something heroic in her doggedness. He shook his head in wonderment at the thought that until recently she had been playing a lone hand—just as grim, just as determined—"I sort of reckon," he mused, "that she sort of might be what you'd call kinder crazy about that Tim Lannigan."

It was not until another week had passed that anything happened. It was early October and the air was chill with the portent of coming winter. Jim Hanvey was sprawled on the lounge in the untidy living room of his apartment reading the pugilistic news in a current sporting weekly. The air was fetid with the odor of his vile cigar, his stockinged feet were cocked upon the table and he had allowed his flowered suspenders to drop comfortably about his tremendous waist. It was a considerable effort to answer the summons of the telephone and his voice was none too gentle—

"Hey! Hello! What you ringin' so much about?"

"Jim? This is Mary."

His expression altered like magic. He caught the nuance of excitement in her carefully modulated tones.

"Yeh?"

"Are you alone?"

"Entirely."

"Can I come up—now?"

"You tell 'em. I'll fix it with the telephone boy so's he won't start no scandal."*

A half hour later she was with him. She threw open the window despite his protest. His eyes were fixed steadily upon the attractive vividity of her face. Then he yawned and appeared to sink into an indifferent lethargic doze. It was only when she had drawn up a chair and placed her hands on his arm that the sleepy eyes uncurtained with an indication of interest.

"A'right, Sister—shoot."

---

* The "telephone boy" would be the hotel operator who put the call through to his rooms and hence knew that Mary had called him (and undoubtedly listened in). This is a joke that the boy might gossip about her visiting his apartment.

She found difficulty in selecting a starting point, and when she did eventually speak it was with an incoherence which was rather unusual—"He's slipping, Jim—and I'm watching."

"You don't say."

"Yes—I do. I knew it would come...if I just watched close enough. Of course I've had to keep pretty much out of the way and I haven't learned all that I might, but—"

"At that," interjected Jim dryly, "you learned a heap more an' a heap faster than I am now."

She laughed—a semi-hysterical little quaver—and pulled herself together. "Jim, Noah Lathrop is up to something."

Jim nodded in satisfaction. "Good."

"He's had a visitor at the house for the last two evenings. Who do you think it is?"

"How many guesses do I get?"

Her eyes burned into his, her voice trembled. "Teddy Nelson!"

Jim nodded ponderously and, although his expression lost none of its impassivity, his tone indicated a lively interest.

"Teddy Nelson, eh?"

"Yes—Teddy. And they're talking turkey."

"Teddy usually does."

The girl sat back and inspected the bovine face of the detective. "You got any recent suspicions of Teddy?"

Jim's head inclined. "Have you?"

"Yes."

"What?"

Unconsciously, she lowered her tone. "He's got the Rawlings' pearls."

Jim yawned with his eyes. "Right the first time, Sis. You take the head of the class."

"You knew?"

"Sure. An' I ain't the only dick which does. They've been

watchin' Teddy ever since them pearls were stolen. The only reason they didn't nab him long ago was because they didn't know where he had 'em cache'd—it wasn't gonna do 'em a bit of good to grab Teddy unless they got the pearls, too."

She shook her head slowly—"I didn't know they suspected Teddy of that job...."

"There ain't but a half dozen men in the country could of done it," explained Jim, "an' Teddy was the only one with a perfect alibi, so they knew it was him. But it ain't Teddy they're after—it's the stuff."

"So-o...and you think he's trying to sell 'em to Lathrop?"

"It's a cinch. He can't sell 'em nowhere's else. There ain't a fence would dare handle 'em and the easiest way they could be put on the market would be through a first class wholesale jewelry house. Yeh—I reckon Mr. Noah Lathrop is just about aimin' to slip his head into a noose."

The girl rose to her feet and paced the room. "It's the first thing I've discovered...I wish I thought he'd dare buy those things—I wish we could catch him with the goods."

Jim's toneless voice came as though from another room. "You keep those eyes of your'n peeled, Mary. If he's gone this far with the deal the chances are he'll go through. An' if you can get wise to the hour when they pull it I'll be on hand...."

"You think they'll do it at home?"

"Surest thing you know. A guy as keen as Lathrop ain't riskin' a deal like that in his office; he wouldn't even let Teddy come there if he knew what he was comin' for. Yeh, Sis, I reckon they'll put it through at home. So all you got to do is watch an' keep me posted."

"And what will you do?"

"My durndest—that's all I can promise."

"That's more than enough, Jim—a heap more than enough."

Jim flushed slightly—"Don't you go countin' on me too strong.

You can remember at least one case where I fell down something awful an' there ain't no certainty I won't flop this one."

Mary had the grace to blush. "I'm sorry about that, Jim."

"Ah gwan! I ain't. It was a pleasure to have you put it over me. Say, listen—some day I want the lowdown on that, Mary."

The girl departed and then for three days he heard nothing from her. On the fourth day she telephoned him to meet her in Central Park.

"Teddy was there again last night."

"Sure enough?"

"Yes—for three hours. And this morning I heard Mr. Lathrop breaking a dinner engagement he had for tonight."

"So you sort of reckon maybe tonight's the night?"

"Yes....I'm pretty sure it's an attempt to sell Lathrop the Rawlings' pearls. I did a bit of listening last night and I heard something of what they were saying—about having the cash there....I guess poor Teddy is glad to get them off his hands at any price."

"Yeh—I reckon he is. They ain't nothin' now but a liability. Hmm! Reckon I better stick around this evenin'."

They put their heads together then in an earnest discussion of details. And when Jim rose heavily to his feet a half hour later and waddled away through the trees the girl looked after him with an expression which would have brought a warm glow to the sentimental heart of the big detective had he glimpsed it. Somehow the sun seemed to shine with unusual friendliness that afternoon upon the slim figure of the girl in the nurse's uniform, and she felt suddenly very close to her big, handsome husband in the Atlanta prison.

She had never quite recovered from her amazement at Jim's position in this case. She had always liked Jim but the idea that he might some day assist her—a professional criminal—in a matter involving the possible freeing of her criminal husband—had been beyond the realm of possibility.

True, thus far Jim had done very little and that little with his customary modest unobtrusiveness. His chief aid had been in moral support, in a willingness to talk things over. What had really been accomplished had been the result of her own unremitting vigilance…but the hour was approaching when Jim was to play a leading rôle. At the moment of denouement she would have been sadly handicapped without him—and she knew it, for there was no possible chance of publicity without an airing of her own unsavory reputation.

With Jim as an ally all was different. The very knowledge that he was helping her imparted a strength and a courage far beyond anything she had theretofore experienced. And he had promised to be watching from across the street that night—to be awaiting her signal.

Darkness settled early over the Drive, a deep, cloudy darkness punctured by the faint twinkling of lights from the Jersey shore, the sparkle of apartment house windows, glaring arrows of brilliance from the headlamps of speeding automobiles and lumbering busses. From a window in the Lathrop apartment Mary Lannigan fancied that she could discern the overlarge figure of Jim Hanvey bulking in the gloom across the way. She returned to her own little cubbyhole of a room and waited—waited, it seemed, for an eternity.

And eventually there came the ringing of a telephone and Lathrop himself answered. She heard his voice bidding the operator to send the gentleman up. A few minutes later Lathrop opened the door of his apartment and then Mary heard footsteps in the hallway and she opened her door in time to see Lathrop and Teddy Nelson disappear into the library.

Jaw firm and eyes steady, Mary Lannigan proceeded with

meticulous care. Fortunately, Mrs. Lathrop was out that evening— "Gadding about like she always does...." and the butler was attending to affairs of his own. Mary had been left in charge of the complacently sleeping Pauline. She crept to the door of the library and applied an ear to the keyhole.

From inside came the wellnigh unintelligible murmur of voices. Occasionally one or the other of the men would become argumentative. It was plain that they were bargaining. Mary fancied that she could see the long-sought-for string of Rawlings pearls through the keyhole...and once she fancied that she heard the rustle of new paper money.

It was then that she went to a front window and, using an electric torch, flashed to Jim Hanvey the agreed signal. She tiptoed into Pauline's room and assured herself that the child was sleeping soundly. Then into the hallway again to resume her vigil.

After an interminable wait there came a light tapping on the door. She opened it softly and admitted the mammoth detective.

"Goshamighty," he whispered, "that boy downstairs didn't want to let me come up." He patted her shoulder reassuringly. "How's tricks?"

She detailed developments in a voice barely above a whisper. He nodded ponderous approval. "Fine stuff. Here's where ol' sleuth gits in his dirty work, ain't it?"

She designated the library door. "What'll I do? Jim?"

"Just stick around to look after the remains—if any."

"You're not expecting anything rough?"

"Naw....Teddy ain't that kind unless he's changed a lot. But I'm gonna stage an awful play just to see whether a feller which owns three automobiles can turn green."

She led him to the door and then withdrew into the shadows of an adjacent room. Jim patted down the ill-fitting coat which hung so grotesquely around his girthful figure and rapped once upon the door.

For a dramatic instant he stood motionless, then flung open the door and entered—blinking like a monster owl in the brilliant light.

Before him was an interesting tableau. Lathrop, motionless, was bending across the table inspecting a string of magnificent matched oriental pearls. Beside him was a pile of crisp, new one-hundred dollar bills. His lean, rather saturnine, face, still reflected the avarice of a moment since although an expression of stark terror was now slowly robbing him of his naturally aggressive unpleasantness.

Opposite sat Teddy Nelson—suave, dapper, perfectly at ease. Nelson's experienced eyes rested briefly upon the intruder and a close observer could have noticed the visible effort with which he pulled himself together. Too, it was Nelson who broke the portentous silence. That insouciant criminal rose to his feet, bowed with exaggerated politeness and spoke in a quiet conversational tone—

"Mr. Hanvey—this is indeed a pleasure."

Jim was enjoying himself thoroughly. He produced a pink silk handkerchief and mopped his forehead. "'Lo Teddy."

Nelson waved a comprehensive hand toward Lathrop, the pearls and the money. As yet the astounded jewelry importer had not moved; he sat staring in bewilderment from one to the other.

"You will notice, Jim," said Nelson, "that you have nothing on me. My host is in possession of the money and also of the pearls which I presume you are seeking."

Hanvey grinned. "You're a hard egg, Teddy."

"You are hunting for some pearls, are you not, Jim?"

"I are."

"Well—in all probability you have them. I am willing to

explain, Jim, that I never saw those pearls before—I'm as positive of that as I am that I shall never see them again." He made a rueful little grimace. "Business is pretty rotten these days."

Lathrop was getting a grip on himself. He rose unsteadily and addressed the detective. "Who are you?"

The suggestion of a sneer wreathed Nelson's lips. "You're a pretty good little staller yourself, Lathrop."

"What are you talking about?"

All sign of amusement departed from Teddy Nelson's face. He whirled furiously upon Lathrop. "You know damn good and well what I'm talking about. You trapped me into your apartment and brought a dick here—all right, so much for that. You thought you'd have me with the goods and you'd get the glory of having nabbed me. Why you poor fish, they've been after me for six months for this little job. They've laid off because they didn't know where the pearls were. They've got 'em now—but by God! they didn't catch 'em on me. They're in your hands. You've got the money. I'm broke. There ain't a piece of evidence against me. And Jim Hanvey is square. I'm asking him to make you prove that *you* didn't steal those jewels."

Lathrop stammered. He stared first at Nelson, then at the lethargic Hanvey. "A—a detective?" he muttered.

"Uh-huh." It was Jim who answered. "A regular, honest-to-Gawd detective." He flashed his badge and strode over to the table. He inspected the pearls briefly. "It's that Rawlings' stuff, ain't it, Teddy?"

Nelson shook his head. "You can't prove anything by me, Jim. Say listen—" he became very earnest. "Did this half-size imitation of a cigar clerk double-cross me?"

Jim shook his head slowly. "No-o. Not hardly. Because when you stop to consider things—that would have been a bum play for him. Y'see, Teddy, we've been watchin' this bird a long time—he was sort of mixed up in that Tim Lannigan affair and we figured he was worth lookin' after. An' we knew you had the Rawlings' stuff. So when you and him got together we figured that two and two was pullin' their usual act. Y'see, we've got you, Teddy, for the Rawlings job—while all we send Lathrop to jail for is receivin' stolen goods."

Lathrop tried to speak—and could not. His mouth opened and closed—then opened and closed again. His adams-apple bobbed alarmingly. His voice, when it did come, was shrill with hysteria—

"It's a lie—a lie! I don't know anything about this man. I don't know anything about Lannigan. What he said I did was true—I was trying to prove that he stole these jewels."

"The dirty liar...."

"Lay off, Teddy," advised Jim. Then, to Lathrop—"You might as well come clear, buddy. I know how much money there is in that little pile and I know what bank you drew it from and at what time this morning. I know, too, that this ain't the first time you've pulled a stunt like this—but I know it's gonna be the last. Now Teddy, if you come clean I'll see that things are made light for you—light as I can have 'em made. Give me the lowdown on the job."

Nelson eyed the detective levelly. "Straight, Jim?"

"Here's my hand on it. No promises—only the best I can do for you."

"Well," Nelson cleared his throat, "in that case I'd better come clean. There ain't no use confessing that I stole them pearls off old man Rawlings about a year ago. You know that an' the insurance company detectives know it. They knew it so well that there wasn't a chance for me to dispose of them through the regular channels, so when I heard that Lathrop was inclined to use his position as an honorable man to get away with an occasional dirty little job, I went to him and offered to sell and sell cheap—"

"No! It isn't true...." Lathrop's face was pitiful. "Nelson, please! This will all be used against you."

"Sure—sure. And it'll be used against you, too," explained Jim casually.

Lathrop cowered as Nelson continued the story of their negotiations. When he finished Hanvey returned his attention to the figure of the terrified jeweler.

"My family—my child—my business—"

"You're a fine slice of limburger," complimented Jim. "I suppose you've been weeping your eyes out thinking about Tim Lannigan, haven't you?"

"Lannigan?"

"Yes—Lannigan, the lad you double-crossed—got him to try an' smuggle in stuff that he didn't know was stolen. Well, you're clear of the Lannigan case but we'll make you sweat for this. Ten years, maybe."

"Please...for God's sake—anything but that—"

Jim regarded him steadily. "Tim Lannigan is a good friend of mine, Lathrop. One of the best friends I have. It just occurs to me that we might make a little deal....Interested?"

"Yes. Yes. Go on."

"Well—all we've been after in this Rawlings affair is the stuff. We don't care particularly about sending Teddy Nelson up. And since we've got the pearls...how about this: You sit down there and sign a confession that you hired Tim Lannigan to smuggle in those jewels. You can say that you didn't know they were stolen—that it was simply a job on your part to beat the customs. That'll be proof enough that Tim didn't know they were stolen—and, of course, proof that he wasn't mixed up in the original robbery which'll keep him from serving twenty years or so in a French prison for something he didn't do."

Jim paused. He fancied that he could hear the rustling of skirts in the hallway. Lathrop looked up pleadingly—

"What can they do to me for that?"

"They can give you two years in the Federal prison—same as they did Lannigan. But they probably won't. They did that to Lannigan because he was known as a professional crook. You'll most likely get off with a heavy fine—and it'll clear Tim of that French stuff."

"Are you telling me the truth?"

Teddy Nelson broke in, somewhat explosively—"Hell! Jim Hanvey ain't no liar."

"You can choose," explained Jim easily, "between that and a certain long stretch for this Rawlings affair."

Lathrop looked up piteously. "I'll do it," he said at length. "Tell me what to write."

Hanvey dictated slowly and carefully, and when he was finished he summoned Mary Lannigan to whom he read the confession. Then, with Mary as a witness, Noah Lathrop signed.

The following day Jim accompanied Mary Lannigan to the Pennsylvania Station whence she departed for Atlanta to break the gladsome news to her husband. She was tearfully grateful— "Aw! stow it, Sister—I didn't do a darn thing except have a little fun...."

From the train he went to an unpretentious hotel in the West Fifties where, a few moments later, he found himself alone with Teddy Nelson.

Teddy was very much at ease. He waved his hand airily—"Have a seat, Jim. Make yourself comfortable." Then, defensively—"But leave that nickel-plated cigar case in your pocket. I don't mind talking to a detective but I'm not willing to smell his cigars."

Jim ignored the request. And as the first horrid blast of cigar smoke assailed Teddy, Jim vouchsafed a bit of information—

"I fixed it for you, Teddy. Saw Simpson and Clarke this morning—gave 'em the pearls. They were so tickled it was a cinch getting them to promise to lay off you."

Nelson sighed relievedly. "Great stuff, Jim. I've been hanging on to those things for a year—knowing that I didn't have a chance to get rid of 'em, and hating to heave 'em in the river. Now they're safely gone and I've helped a pal. Gee!" he smiled—"I'll bet Tim is gonna be happy when he hears the news."

"You tell 'em, Teddy. But not near as happy as Mary was when things come out all right. She sure done wonders for Tim—"

"Wonders, me eye. It was you who did it all, Jim. Wasn't it you who came to me in the first place and suggested that I approach Lathrop on this deal? Didn't you wise me up to the whole works and show me how it'd be a better thing for everybody—me included? Mary did her part all right, Jim—but the whole idea of my selling those pearls to Noah Lathrop was yours—any thanks that Tim Lannigan is handing out is due you. And I'm going to tell him so."

Jim regarded him gravely. "You're gonna keep your mouth shut, Teddy. Shut tight. One yawp out of you to either Tim or Mary about that and by gosh! I'll turn you and Lathrop both up. Which might not be so hard on you, Teddy—but would be hell on Lathrop—him owning three automobiles."

The Knight's Gambit

Jim Hanvey posed pridefully before the triple mirrors. He hitched his trousers one notch higher, affectionately patted the lapels of his new coat and carefully adjusted the cerise necktie. Then he faced the covertly grinning clerk and his voice held that beatific nuance with which a small boy calls attention to the magnificence of his first baseball uniform.

"Swell, ain't it?" queried Jim.

The clerk, a dapper little fellow who was garbed according to the dictates of the latest fashion folder, was professionally enthusiastic. "Perfect, Sir. You never looked better in your life." Under his breath he added a fervent: "And that ain't no lie."

Jim delighted himself with a further survey of his mirrored self. And, in truth, whatever the ensemble might have lacked from an esthetic standpoint it more than atoned in brilliancy.

The enormous and pudgy figure of the detective was enfolded in a new and ill-fitting suit of near tweeds. A pink silk shirt was stretched tightly over the upper portion of his anatomy. A collar of inconsequential height but amazing girth encased the vivid tie. Below the trouser cuffs was a brief expanse of white sox which topped a pair of peak-toed russet shoes. Above Jim's collar flopped twin chins which bounded on the south a countenance of bovine heaviness. The whole was topped by a new gray felt hat which seemed in constant danger of tobogganing from the crest of the bulbous head.

Jim Hanvey's tiny, fishlike eyes held a gleam of self-approval. Then, as he inspected himself, they closed slowly, held shut for a moment, and uncurtained with even greater deliberateness. His big hands were elevated idly until the fingers found the elaborate golden toothpick which hung suspended from the heavy chain connecting the upper vest pockets. His chest inflated and a sigh escaped his pursy lips—"I've been wantin' an outfit like this for a mighty long time," he commented. "An' I just never sort of come around to gettin' it."

The clerk discreetly lowered his head to scribble hieroglyphics on a sales pad. "Anything else, Sir?" he interrogated meekly.

"No-o. Don't believe there is....Oh! yes—a silk handkerchief."

That article was purchased and Jim fitted it with meticulous care into the breast pocket of his coat so that the pink edging was displayed to weirdest advantage. "How much does it amount to, Son?"

"Seventy-two, fifty."

Jim whistled. "Gosh! Swell clothes sure do come high." Reluctantly he extracted a battered wallet. "Here y'are. I want my other clothes sent to the hotel." Then, with pitiful eagerness, "I couldn't look no better, could I?"

"No," answered the clerk with perfect candor. "You surely couldn't."

Jim Hanvey departed. He walked with the peculiarly stiff and self-conscious gait inevitably attendant upon the wearing of new clothes. His big shoes creaked with every step. His expression was one of radiant self-satisfaction. For years he had craved an orgy of new-clothes purchasing and now that the exigencies of his profession had furnished an adequate excuse he had done himself exceeding proud.

He entered a suburban street car and sat stiffly in his seat misinterpreting the amusement of the other passengers for envy. It never occurred to Jim that his clothes were in shockingly bad taste or that his appearance was grotesque. He was a simple and lonely soul with the male's innate love of bright colors and flaring finery rampant within him, his desires untempered by the inhibitions of culture. He loved the flagrant and flamboyant in dress and secretly harbored an ambition to carry a cane. He owned two but thus far in his career they had remained cloistered. He had never quite mustered sufficient courage to drag one of them into the street. But some day...

Forty minutes later the street car reached the end of its run and Jim alighted. The suburb silently proclaimed the opulence of its residents. Wide, tree-shaded streets bounded by broad, velvety lawns behind which hugely handsome residences reared their architecturally perfect forms; gardens which paid flowering tribute to landscape experts; sinuously winding driveways, spurting fountains, cleanly clipped hedges. An atmosphere of forbidding and exclusive wealth. Parked by the curbs were limousines of the more expensive makes. Early that morning Jim Hanvey would have felt ill-at-ease in the neighborhood. Now, resplendent in his new regalia, he believed serenely that he fitted comfortably into the picture. His manner was that of the man who belongs. He regretted that he had not bought a cane: a heavy, gold-headed cane. Or, perhaps, a man of his mammoth physical proportions would better carry a malacca stick*—one of the slender, whippy ones....

He sought information from a disdainful chauffeur as to which

---

* A cane made of malacca wood, a species of rattan palm native to Sumatra.

of these estates was the property of Mr. Theodore Weston. But even with the confidence begotten of his magnificent raiment he hesitated briefly before turning up the walkway which led from the street to the massive brownstone mansion nestling far back behind a screen of elms, poplars and shrubbery. There was something about the Weston estate which seemed to elevate it above even its formidable neighbors; a mute announcement of conscious superiority; a formal indifference; an air of casualness such as that affected by the young girl who spends an hour before her mirror carefully arranging her hair in the most attractive way. Jim experienced difficulty in conceiving this palatial place as a home. It wasn't at all Jim's idea of what a home should be. His own tastes inclined to a six-room bungalow set level with the street and perhaps twenty feet back from the sidewalk where a chap could loll of an evening in his shirt sleeves and suspenders with his feet cocked up on the porch railing and the potted geraniums only slightly obstructing his vision.

He moved stiffly up the elm-sentinelled walkway to the broad and imposing veranda which spanned the palace of the industrial king, meticulously scraped a bit of mud from his new shoes, tiptoed to the front door and somewhat timorously pressed the button. Like magic the door swung back and a butler appeared.

"Mr. Weston home?"

The butler's forehead corrugated slightly. His face lost some of the fixed rigidity of expression natural to it. He surveyed the visitor with an admixture of bewilderment and insolence.

"Yes."

Jim fidgeted nervously. The butler maintained an uncompromising silence—which Jim eventually terminated.

"Tell him Jim Hanvey wants to see him."

"Hmm! Your card, please."

Jim fumbled wildly. "Gosh! I left my card in my other suit."

He jerked his thumb in apologetic explanation. "Just tell him it's Jim Hanvey and everything'll be jake."

The butler disappeared in the cavernous recesses of the mansion leaving the monster detective thoroughly ill-at-ease. In a few moments he returned, expression slightly altered. "Right this way, Sir."

Hanvey followed. Their feet were soundless on the rich rugs. Jim was left alone in the dim, lavishly comfortable confines of the library. He seated himself on the lounge, hitched up his trousers at the knees to preserve the crease, and waited.

Less than five minutes later Weston appeared. He was a thin, undersized man with a peculiarly high forehead and deep cavernous eyes. His step was mincing but his manner betokened a wealth of nervous energy. He paused on the threshold and stared with ill-concealed amazement at the unwieldy figure which rose from the lounge to greet him.

It was a case of mutual surprise. Jim Hanvey had been prepared to meet a towering, aggressive, physically powerful individual—a man whose physique was in consonance with his reputation in the industrial world. For Jim knew that Weston was all-powerful: fair but ruthless, a hard fighter and a game one. The little man in the doorway was rather of the lounge-lizard type....

As for Weston he could not believe that this mammoth individual who bulked before him was the person who had been recommended as the best detective in the country. Jim was not at all of the detective type. His new raiment accentuated the flabbiness of the form, intensified the general impression of lethargic indifference and general unfitness. And so the two men stared, each struggling to readjust in a moment his preconceived idea of the other. It was the financier who spoke first, his voice snapping with a peculiar steely timbre not at all in accord with his diminutive size.

"Mr. Hanvey?"

"Yeh....Mr. Weston?"

"I am Mr. Weston."

"Mr. Theodore Weston?"

"Yes."

"Gosh...." Jim paused suddenly. Weston stared intently.

"Say it," he prompted.

"You're a runt," proferred Jim. "I thought I was gonna meet a big feller."

"And you," countered Weston, "look more like a side-show freak than a detective."

"You said it. I never was awful strong on looks an' my figger never caused me to be mistook for no sylph."

They stood facing one another in the subdued light of the library. Jim covertly straightened his tie and patted his new coat. Jim was very well pleased with himself. He wondered whether this man had noticed his new suit—

"Nice suit of clothes you've got on, Mr. Weston."

"Eh?" The smaller man was startled. "Oh! Thank you."

"You're welcome." Jim hesitated. "I'm awful strong for swell clothes, ain't you?"

"I don't notice them much."

Jim sighed disappointedly. "Thought not...."

Weston motioned his visitor to a chair. He extracted from his desk a humidor of fragrant Havana cigars, and as he was doing so, Jim reached for a battered, near-silver cigar case which reposed in the inside pocket of his coat. Each extended his to the other. Jim's were short and fat and very, very black. Weston took one from the case and Jim accepted one from his host. Each sniffed at his gift, each made a poorly concealed wry face and each placed the cigar carefully beside him with the remark—"Smoke it later." Then each man lighted one of his own. As the fierce aroma of Jim's projectile assailed Weston's nostril's, the little man winced. But Jim did not notice. He was inexpressibly content with the strong fumes he generated. And so they smoked on as they chatted idly. Weston finally caused the conversation to veer to the subject.

"You have been recommended to me, Mr. Hanvey, as the one man capable of helping me out of a dilemma. I cannot question the judgment of the men who have bespoken you."

"Fine. That's awful nice of you, Mr. Weston."

"I'll admit—" honestly "—that I am somewhat surprised by your appearance. This is a matter which requires infinite tact and delicacy. It's not—er—what you might call strong-arm work."

"That's good," endorsed the detective. "I'm in awful poor trim."

"It is, in fact, a problem such as detectives seldom meet with; an affair of diplomacy. It involves no particular moral turpitude. Yet the intervention and assistance of friends cannot aid me at all— which is why I have sought outside—and professional—help."

"In other words," summarized Jim slowly, "somebody's tryin' to slip somethin' over on you."

"Precisely. Not in a business way. That would be relatively easy to cope with. In entrusting you with this story I must impress upon you the necessity for strictest secrecy. My confidence must remain inviolate. As a matter of fact, I find myself excessively embarrassed....I—I—scarcely know where to begin."

"Hmm! An' you're doubtful about beginnin' at all, ain't you, Mr. Weston?"

"No. Not exactly. With the endorsement you have received from business associates of mine...."

"You still think I look like such a slob I ain't the man to show no finesse. Ain't that it?"

"You state it rather crudely, Mr. Hanvey, but you have hit the bull's-eye."

"Well," Jim slumped in his chair. His eyes closed with

maddening slowness—remained shut for a second—then opened even more slowly…."I'm willin' to do my best to help you out. But if you want me to enter a beauty contest, I guess we'd better call it off."

"It isn't that, Mr. Hanvey. You see, the primary essential is that you come here as my guest for two or three weeks."

"In this house? Gosh!"

"That will be necessary."

Hanvey deliberated. Once again he gave vent to the ocular yawn which interested—and somewhat exasperated—his host. "I reckon I'll have to put up with it then," he sighed.

Weston smiled slightly. "I don't believe it will be as terrible as you anticipate. The—er—reimbursement in this affair, Mr. Hanvey, will be adequate. More than adequate, should you happen to be successful."

Jim waved a pudgy hand. "Never mind that. I'll take a chance if you will."

Again silence settled between them. Weston sat forward in his chair with his keen eyes glittering across the room. Finally he rose abruptly and stepped mincingly across the library to the window. Jim remained slouched on the lounge, apparently asleep. A miasma of rancid smoke hovered about his Brobdingnagian figure.

The descending sun of early evening bathed the dapper figure of the little industrial giant in a soft, mellow light. He stood by the window staring out—at something—silent, intense, a bit morose. And finally he spoke without turning his head.

"Hanvey?"

"Yeh?"

"Come here."

Jim rose with a grunt and waddled across the room. His enormous bulk completely shadowed that of the smaller man. And now there had come a slight change in the atmosphere. Weston's use of Jim's last name and a sudden pathetic drooping of the narrow shoulders bespoke the fact that he had reconciled himself to his disappointment in Jim's appearance and was willing to place his trust in the big detective. He spoke in a sharp but toneless voice.

"Look yonder," he directed, pointing down the winding, poplar-lined bridle path which twisted toward the house from a rich green valley beyond.

Jim blinked slowly—and looked. His first impression was one of enthusiasm for the pastoral beauty of the scene: a gradual blending of formal gardening into the rich lusciousness of untrammelled nature; a gentle tinting of the gold of early evening; the silver of a brook in the valley below…a wealth of color and of natural beauty.

Then his fishlike eyes discerned two persons on horseback, a man and a woman, who were walking their mounts slowly toward the house. They rode close together and they were conversing with an absorption which made plain that the outside world did not exist for them. The girl had half-turned in her saddle in order that her eyes might feast unrestrainedly upon the man; while he, conscious of his power, was injecting the full wealth of an engaging personality into the task of holding her undivided attention.

They approached slowly, the mounts scarce moving, and as they came closer something in the magnificent stature and military carriage of the man stirred memory in the mind of the obese detective. But before recognition came to him his attention was once more attracted to the girl.

She was young—that much was evident even at the distance separating her from Jim. There was something about the slim, boyish figure; the artless eagerness with which she hung upon the words of her companion, which proclaimed extreme youth.

And, too, the way she sat her horse—carelessly, easily, as though she belonged. The girl wore no hat, her rich brown hair was piled carelessly atop the exquisitely shaped head. Her left hand held the rein loosely, her right hung by her side. It held a riding crop which she twiddled aimlessly. Up through the poplar-lined bridle path they came...the shadows spotting the roadway like the stippling of a pen-and-ink artist.

"My daughter," said Weston simply and without turning. There was affection in his voice—and worry—and abounding pride. Jim responded to the tone with all the sincerity of his emotionful nature.

"Swell-lookin' kid," was his comment.

He turned his attention to the man, now limned in the glow of the late evening sun. He was a perfect foil for the girl; a figure of powerful, dominant masculine maturity offsetting her naïve girlishness. He wore an immaculate riding costume. He rode like a Centaur, swaying to the stride of his horse...oblivious to everything save the girl by his side. He was talking, head inclined toward her. And then Jim recognized the man and he emitted a slow, amazed whistle. Theodore Weston turned.

"You know him?"

"Yes."

"Who is he?"

Jim favored the man with a prolonged scrutiny. It was scarcely possible...but there was certitude in the tone with which he made answer to his host's question.

"That's Whitey Kirk."

"Who is Whitey Kirk?"

"The cleverest con man in the world," was the answer, and there was a ring of professional admiration in his voice. "I didn't know he was a friend of yours—"

"He isn't."

"There ain't anything to be ashamed of if he is. Y'know I'm

awful strong for Whitey—Warren is his real name—because of the fact that he is so good. For ten years that baby has been pullin' jobs, big jobs, wide-open jobs—and they've never fastened a thing on him. He's a wizard, that's what. He's tackled everything from stock swindling to smuggling and he's gotten away with it. I can't help liking a man with his brains and ability. And nerve—Oh! Mamma!"

Weston walked heavily back to the table of black walnut which occupied the middle of the library. Jim followed slowly, and then, seeing that the attention of his host was not upon him, deftly exchanged the two cigars which lay upon the desk—so that his own vicious black one was once more in his possession. "Fair exchange," he told himself, "ain't always robbery."

Absently Weston reached for the rich Havana which had thus been returned to him, lighted it, and puffed meditatively for a few moments. Hanvey slouched opposite in an easy chair, allowed his fat fingers to toy idly with the golden toothpick which hung from his cable-strength watch chain. He contemplated the little man, wondering what was coming, and, without knowing why, feeling a sense of sorrow and of personal responsibility.

"That," said Weston suddenly, waving toward the window which they had just vacated, "is why I sent for you."

"Yeh?"

Silence. From outside came the crunch-crunch of horses' hoofs on the gravel driveway, the sound of a man's voice—and a girl's—then nothing save the soft sighing of the evening breeze through the trees which surrounded the stately home. It was Theodore Weston who punctured the silence—

"What is this man's criminal record?"

"He ain't got none. We know he's crooked, we even know most of what he's done. But we ain't ever been able to get the goods on him."

"He's never been arrested?"

"Nary time."

"That will make it more difficult—very much more difficult. Perhaps too much so." He was silent for a moment, and then—with a sudden intensity which surprised Jim: "The man is a criminal, Mr. Hanvey. It shall be your task to prove it!"

"Hmm!" Jim's glassy orbs closed—then opened—with exasperating leisureliness. "Why?"

"Because—" and Jim liked the directness of Weston's speech, "that man is engaged to marry my daughter."

"Gee!" commented Jim Hanvey. "That's tough."

"It is worse than that—it is horrible. She is not quite eighteen years of age. He is—Oh! about forty I judge—"

"Forty-one."

"They met at Ormond Beach last year. We have a winter place there. My daughter is a golf enthusiast. This man, it seems, was down there playing golf—peculiar pastime for a criminal—"

"Whitey's a gent."

"Madge was injured one day on the links—struck by a golf ball on number ten fairway. She was stunned. Number ten is farthest removed from the clubhouse. This man Kirk was playing right behind her. He is a powerful fellow and he carried her to the clubhouse in his arms. From there she was taken home in a car which he provided. I thanked him and he introduced himself. It never occurred to me that he was not a gentleman. He told me he was a graduate of one of the large universities—"

"He is."

"—And we were all emotionally grateful at the time. We magnified the very simple favor which he had done for us. Certainly it never occurred to us to scrutinize too closely the very natural friendship which rapidly developed between him and my daughter. We didn't take it seriously—somehow a parent finds difficulty in appreciating the maturity of his own child.

"We all liked him. His natural gentility was the only credential we asked. He and Madge were together everywhere: he appeared to be a man of means, culture and leisure. We fancied that he had a paternal interest in her. They golfed together, played tennis, swam, rode—a very delightful winter idyll. And the day Madge told her mother and me that she was engaged to marry this man—well, Mr. Hanvey, unless you're a father—and have received a shock through your child—a shock involving the happiness of that child—you cannot understand."

Jim fidgeted uncomfortably in his chair. The voice of his host rang with fierce bitterness...."You sure are up against it, Weston."

"I investigated him, suddenly realizing that Mrs. Weston and I had been criminally negligent. I was amazed by the fact that I knew nothing whatever of him save that he bore all the earmarks of a gentleman. He vouchsafed no personal information. I brought the family back north—and investigated further. The thing was horrible enough as it was—a seventeen-year-old-girl engaged to a man of forty. She wouldn't listen to reason....I tried to be tactful in my handling of the situation. You see," simply, "I am worth a great many millions of dollars and it was only natural that I should be careful...marrying for money, you know—"

"Yeh—sure. I know."

"As though the situation itself were not sufficiently bad, came the report that the man is a notorious criminal. I told Madge and she went straight to him with it. He laughed—said he had bitter enemies who were trying to injure him. Defied them to prove that he had ever been crooked. Suggested that they produce a prison record. Of course it couldn't be done. You can imagine the effect on an impressionable young girl—in love for the first time. She fancied him a persecuted man—she said flatly that she didn't believe a word of it and intended to stand by him...."

"Good sport," breathed Jim heavily.

"She is. Too good. I talked to him—straight from the shoulder. He gazed at me blandly and said that my accusations were false. I offered him his own price. He didn't even have the grace to get insulted—merely stated that he didn't have a price. Alleged that he was genuinely in love with Madge. I threatened him. He laughed. I ordered him never to see her again. He told me coldly that if I persisted in any such foolish course he'd induce her to elope with him. And finally, because it seemed the wisest thing to do, Mrs. Weston and I sanctioned a secret engagement, hoping against hope that the true nature of the beast would show—and Madge would be awakened.

"It hasn't worked, Hanvey. She is more infatuated than ever. That's why you were recommended to me. They told me that you were the one person who might be of real assistance."

Jim leaned forward in his chair. "Me? How can I help?"

"I have been told that you know crooks better than any other man in the world. That you can work miracles with them—because you understand them. I ask you pointblank, Jim Hanvey—will you undertake the task of saving my daughter from this man?"

Jim lighted a fresh cigar. Through the haze of rancid smoke he stared at the little financier. "I'll undertake it on one condition," he said slowly.

"And that is—?"

"—That I be allowed a free hand. Absolutely."

"Done!"

"Good. Remember, Weston, I'm liable to pull a bone—the chances are that I'll flunk it. Whitey Kirk is the cleverest crook on two continents. He's in soft here—awful soft. He ain't gonna let go easy. But if you're willin' for me to try—I'll try. If I flop—it won't be because I haven't done my damnedest."

The smaller man rose, crossed the room and dropped a hand on Jim's fat shoulders. "You won't fail, Hanvey."

"Why not?"

"Because," replied the other, "it means too much to Madge. If you're what they say you are—you'll put it over."

Jim rose awkwardly. "I'll do my best. I'll have to stick around here for a week or two." He looked down upon his new and shrieking raiment—"Thank goodness I already bought a new suit. I'd hate to look like a bum in a swell joint like this."

Twenty minutes later Jim Hanvey departed for the city in one of Weston's limousines. He lolled against the rich upholstery enjoying to the ultimate the luxury and uniqueness of the experience. At his modest and untidy apartment he swiftly packed a near-leather suitcase with those articles which he fancied would be essential to his new rôle of society butterfly. He left the apartment, entered the limousine for the return trip—then suddenly halted the chauffeur—"Just a minute, Buddy. I forgot something."

He re-entered the building. When he returned to the car a few minutes later he nervously clasped the thing which he had forgotten.

It was his light malacca cane.

He reached the Weston home shortly before the dinner hour and was shown to his rooms; a bedroom, parlor and bath suite on the west wing of the mansion. He gazed apprehensively about and experienced more than a hint of trepidation. A valet arrived to inquire whether he might assist Mr. Hanvey to dress for dinner.

"My Gawd, no!" roared Jim. "You'd make me feel downright bashful."

In the living room he was introduced to Mrs. Weston, a sweet-faced and surprisingly young woman considerably larger than her husband. Mrs. Weston pressed Jim's hands as she wished him well. "Theodore says you'll succeed, Mr. Hanvey...he says he knows you will."

"He's an awful wise guy."

"You don't know what it means to us."

"The heck I don't. Believe me, Mis' Weston—I know a heap about this. An' say—if it ain't impolite to ask—how long is it before we eat?"

It was in the library immediately preceding dinner that the detective met Whitey Kirk. That gentleman, tall and broad and handsomely debonaire in his dinner jacket, strolled into the room puffing on a cigarette. He paused and stared through the semi-gloom toward the large and strange figure in the outrageous clothes. The figure moved forward and, as though from a distance, Whitey heard the voice of his future father-in-law—"...my friend Mr. Hanvey. Mr. Kirk."

Then Jim's limp hand and the well-known voice—"Sure, me an' Whitey Kirk is old friends, ain't we, Whitey?"

"You know one another?" Weston's simulation was very poor indeed.

"I've had the pleasure of Mr. Hanvey's acquaintance for a number of years."

"Yeh—sure he has, Mr. Weston. We've had business dealin's with one another—as you might say."

Kirk had regained his impassivity and by no slightest gesture did he give testimony to the internal seethe nor the swift groping of his keen brain for the answer to this new problem. The presence of Jim Hanvey betokened trouble—great gobs of it—and trouble was the one thing which Whitey Kirk was at that moment most desirous of avoiding. He negotiated Jim into the glare of an electrolier[*] while he

---

[*] A chandelier with electric bulbs—a brand name that first appeared in 1881 and became a generic term for such a fixture.

himself stood in the shadows, but he gained no information from the bovine expression of the triple-chinned detective. Jim sat stolidly, lids curtaining his expressionless, fishy orbs, fingers twiddling the golden toothpick. Theodore Weston gazed interestedly from one to the other. He felt a queer confidence in the ability of the ungainly detective, and didn't understand the feeling. Jim was the apparent personification of the ultimate in human stupidity, but Weston's keen, sparkling eyes had not missed the flash of apprehension which had whitened Kirk's face at the moment of recognition.

And then Madge Weston burst into the room—billowed through the door like a stray zephyr. She called gay greetings and then, girl-like, made directly toward Warren Kirk—pausing abruptly at sight of the stranger. She accepted her father's introduction matter-of-factly and immediately set about the task of making the stranger feel at home. It was plain to her that he was out of the picture—a veritable china-shop bull—and she was more than a little sorry for him. Jim responded eagerly to her advances, and the warmth of his response grew more keen when he noticed that Kirk was highly displeased.

Here was the sort of girl who made an irresistible appeal to Jim—pretty in a fresh, wholesome, sensible and entirely immature way; eager, unspoiled, urgent with life and vitality; far, far removed from the genus flapper—all of whom were anathema to Jim. Flappers frightened the big fellow. They had a manner which he could not fathom, their quick vapid repartee passed over his head, he held the consciousness that he was the butt of their covert ridicule. But not with Madge. She was herself—wholesome and delightful and girlish—By the time they entered the dining room Madge and the big detective were the best of friends.

The dinner commenced as an ordeal for Jim until he realized that he could never solve the fork riddle and devoted his entire attention to enjoyment of the rich and rare food. Mrs. Weston smiled toward her husband—she had the soul of the true hostess, the hostess who enjoys the enjoyment of her guest. True, Madge was a trifle shocked by his lack of table manners, but that was soon borne with—and then forgotten. He *was* having such a good time!

Alone, following the dinner, the three men were silent. Warren Kirk was decidedly ill-at-ease. Finally he rose: "Mighty fine night, Jim."

"Huh?"

"Beautiful night—outside."

"Ain't so worse inside."

"Want to stroll round the grounds?"

"You mean you want to have a talk with me?"

"Not exactly—"

"Sure." Jim, with difficulty, hoisted himself from the chair. "But remember I'm a rotten walker, Whitey."

A shade of annoyance flashed across the man's face. "My name is Warren."

"A'right, Warren. Le's travel."

They descended from the spacious veranda to the moon-drenched garden. The night air was soft and warm and saturated with the odor of lilacs. From far off came the tinkle of a piano and the sensuous strains of a violin—and in the street somewhere children were playing and calling gleefully to one another. Everywhere quietude and beauty and peace. Side by side the two men walked: Jim's big figure waddling on short, fat legs; Whitey's broad shoulders thrown far back, his firm, muscular limbs moving with easy rhythm. And it was the taller man who broke the silence. He spoke without turning and his voice was frigid and direct.

"What's the big idea, Jim?"

"Hmm! Just visitin' my ol' college chump who I ain't seen since we graduated from Harvard together."

"Let's cut out the kidding. What are you here for?"

Jim's voice was mildly reproving. "Don't you know?"

"I can guess."

"A'right. You got my permission. One guess ought to be enough. If you miss I'll give you another."

"You're here—" Whitey's icy voice came slowly, his words close-clipped—"to break up my romance."

"Your what?"

"Romance."

"With that kid?"

"Yes—with that kid."

Jim's heavy head rolled in earnest negation. "Naw, son—you're all wrong. I ain't here to bust up no romance."

"Listen to me, Jim Hanvey—you've got a reputation for telling the truth—"

"I'm telling it now. I ain't here to bust up no romance, Whitey. I'm here to keep you from gettin' away with whatever graft you're planning."

"I'm not planning anything except to marry this girl."

"Well—that's a pretty good graft, ain't it? Good-lookin' kid—young—heiress to about twenty million bucks. Mmm! I'd call it a real swell graft."

"I'm in love with her—"

A harsh note crept into the detective's voice. "That's a lie, Whitey, and you know it. If you was you'd clear out. You know you can't bring her nothin' but misery. Now what I want to find out is this—are you plannin' to go through with this deal an' marry her, or have you got a price?"

"I have no price."

"You can't be bought off?"

"No."

"Well, that makes my job harder. I thought maybe you was lookin' for a soft spot and didn't want to queer things by bargaining with the old man. It'd be worth a heap to him to get rid of you. Not that you ain't a good crook, Whitey—an' in a professional way I ain't got nothin' but respect an' admiration for you. But as a gent, Whitey, you ain't worth a damn."

For a few moments neither spoke. It was Kirk who broke the silence. "You must know already that you can't queer me with the kid."

"Does look like a tough assignment."

"There isn't anything you can do."

"Yes there is."

"What?"

"Well, for one thing, I can make it downright embarrassin' for you—so durned embarrassin' that maybe you'll decide you'd better break it off with the girl and begin to talk dollars and cents."

"Not a chance."

"No?" A pause, and then—"I'm glad you think so, Whitey. But lookin' over that young lady kinder careful it strikes me that if she was ever convinced you was a crook she'd give you the go-by so fast you'd think you was a popboy* at an automobile racetrack. Yep—that gal sure never would stand for no crooks payin' her rent—not if I've got her right."

"Perhaps not," admitted the other, "but you can't hang a thing on me. You know I'm a crook and I know it. But nobody has ever gotten a thing on me. Not a thing. In ten years I haven't slipped once—not a single time."

Jim gazed at him keenly: "That's what you think," he said with peculiar emphasis.

---

* Another indecipherable slang phrase.

They returned to the house; Hanvey expressionless as ever, Kirk struggling to conceal the worry inspired by Jim's air of confidence. Whitey knew that he had never slipped in his decade of criminality—he knew but he wasn't sure. Perhaps, somewhere in that period, there had been an error of judgment, a weakness which he did not suspect. He knew the axiom of the criminal world—a detective may make a thousand mistakes and yet be successful; a criminal cannot err once. Warren Kirk realized that he was only human—and therefore fallible. And if Jim knew something and could prove it...

Later in the evening Kirk persuaded Madge to accompany him to the veranda. Scarcely had they left the room when Jim fired a question at her parents—"Knowing what you do about this guy, why'd you agree to their engagement?"

"Madge is headstrong," was the simple answer. "We thought it best to appear to consent."

"Mmm!" Jim nodded slowly. "It sure is a pleasure to work with folks which uses their heads for somethin' more than havin' a picture taken of."

Meanwhile, on the veranda, Whitey Kirk was talking with low-voiced earnestness to the girl. "It's this way, Madge—Hanvey is a detective and a good one. He is one of the leaders of the police clique which for years has been attempting to hang something on me. Your father has fallen under their influence. He has hinted to you that my past is not all it might have been. He has hired Jim Hanvey to come down here and prove to you that I am crooked." He bent his handsome head close to her wide-open, frightened eyes. "I believe I am a gentleman, little girl. I want you to promise that the minute you lose your trust in me you will let me know— and I shall leave you. But if you're willing to stand by me..." With a little sob she seized his hand and pressed it tightly.

"Don't talk that way, Warren. *Don't!* I can't bear the thought that anyone even thinks you are not all right. And don't suggest that I won't stand by you. I love you, dear...."

He took her in his arms then and kissed her, and even as he did so there was a coldly calculating light in his gray eyes. He was playing this game for big stakes. It was the chance of a lifetime—an opportunity to insure affluence with safety. And Madge was a pretty good sort. He wasn't in love with her, of course, but on the other hand he might do worse in the selection of a life partner. Nice, clean kid—and sensible...."Gee! it'd sure bust things higher than a kite if Jim could ever prove to her..."

And so after the silence of midnight had fallen over the house, Whitey Kirk sat staring from the window of his room. Beside him was an ash tray filled with cigarette stumps.

Jim had him worried. Whitey knew—none better the ability of the ponderous detective, knew that he would not be absolutely safe until he was actually married to the girl. It wasn't that Jim had discovered proof of any past transgression so much as there was danger that Jim might frame him.

Whitey knew well the romantic strain rampant in the soul of the ponderous visitor, realized that Jim believed he must save the girl. And he realized that, all other methods failing, there was every likelihood that Jim would frame a robbery or a bit of crookedness in such a manner that he would appear guilty. "He might even plant a jewel robbery," reflected Kirk, "and plant the loot in my room. Then, if they caught me..."

Early the following morning he went riding with Madge and forewarned her of that possibility. Madge was horrified and indignant, but there was in her eyes a queer, questioning light which had been absent the previous night. Madge was seeing a great deal of smoke and instinctively she found herself wondering whether, after all, there might not be a bit of fire. She cast aside the idea as unworthy—but it persisted subtly and she was downcast and constrained for the last hour of their time together.

But she was blessed with a strain of sterling loyalty and active fighting qualities. Immediately upon her return home, she sought an interview with her father. It was brief, surfeited with mutual pain, and very much to the point. Father and daughter were honest with one another.

"Why are you opposed to my engagement, Dad?"

"The disparity in age, for one thing."

"What else?"

"I don't like Kirk."

"You believe he is not—all that he might be?"

"Yes, Dear."

"Why?"

"I have had him investigated."

"Yet you never heard of a man who was as evil as they say Warren is who has never been caught, have you?"

"No."

"Then why persecute him? Why not play fair? Why make me unhappy?"

"Believing what I do, Madge—"

"The police are down on him—for no reason. They've been persecuting him for years. If what they say were true, Dad—" and her voice crescendoed bitterly—"they'd have proved something. But it's not true, and I want you to know that I shall stand by him in spite of you and Mother and this fat Mr. Hanvey and all the rest of the world."

Weston crossed the room and took her face between his hands. "I like you to talk that way, Daughter. I like my little girl to be a good sportsman. I'm not trying to persecute Warren Kirk: I'm trying to get at the truth. You have no objections to that, have you?"

She thought it over for a moment—"And if you discover that these allegations are untrue?"

"Then you may marry him whenever you wish."

She walked slowly from the room. She and her father had always been pals. He was fair to a fault—and honest. She responded to the fairness of his present attitude. She loved the Warren Kirk she thought she knew. If he was not that man…If, beneath the polished exterior, there was blackness…She went quietly to her room to ponder.…

When she came downstairs shortly before the luncheon hour Jim Hanvey was waiting for her. His huge figure overflowed a chair in the reception hall and he lumbered to his feet at her descent. Somehow, despite the nature of his mission, she could not find it in her heart to dislike him. There was something infinitely pathetic and appealing about the man—a vague, elusive quality which excited the maternal instinct in her breast. The cheap, ready-made clothes which flapped so grotesquely about the ill-shapen figure were not funny…she liked Jim Hanvey and she admitted it frankly. He bowed now with elephantine lack of grace.

"Good mornin', Miss Madge."

"Good morning."

Jim glanced around apprehensively. "I've been sittin' here waitin' for you. I wonder if you'd talk to me for a minute?"

She arched her brows in surprise. "Certainly."

"Let's go where no one can hear us."

They repaired to the library. Jim hitched his chair very close to hers. "I want you to understand just one thing, Miss Madge—I'm a friend of your'n." He cleared his throat. "I want to come clean with you—if you'll let me."

"Please do."

"Well, first off I want to tell you why I'm here. I'm here—" his fishy eyes closed slowly, opened even more slowly and then fixed glassily and compellingly on hers—"I'm here to break off this match between you an' Whitey."

Her lips parted and she leaned forward. "Why?" she cried. "Do you, too, believe that he is—a—a—not what he should be?"

Jim Hanvey's ponderous head rolled from side to side.

"No ma'am!" he said explosively, "I don't!"

"What?" Her voice rang with incredulous amazement.

"Whitey ain't no crook—and that's what I wanted to tell you. He's on the level, that kid is. They've been out to get him for the last ten years and they've not succeeded. Why? The reason is because he's straight. But they've had it in for him. If he'd ever slipped—even an inch—they'd have got him. That's what I wanted to tell you—that I'm here as your friend. Of course I think he's pretty old for you—but that's your business and his. Your father thinks I'm gonna try to hang somethin' on Whitey. I'm not. But it's better for a friend of his to stick around than to tell the old man how I really stand and have him hire some one who has it in for Whitey. He wouldn't have a chance then. They'd frame him. And I just wanted to explain this to you so you'd know you can trust me."

Impulsively she clasped his big right hand in both of hers. Her eyes were shining: "I don't know how to thank you. And I *do* trust you—Oh! so much! It's horrible, what they're saying about Warren—and I know it isn't so. I—well, do you mind if I tell Warren that you're here to help him—to help us?"

"No," returned Jim dryly, "I don't mind. Tell him. He'll be awful interested."

And Whitey was interested when she told him the following morning. He was more than that, and the amazement which was writ large upon his features was reflected in the fury which surcharged his voice.

"It's a damned lie—" He did not catch the startled, hurt glance which she bestowed upon him. "Jim believes I'm crooked. He's here to prove it to you. And when he says he's our friend, he lies."

She cringed slightly. The intensity of the man troubled her. It was something which her immaturity could not understand; a new vision of this hitherto soft-spoken, gentle, thoughtful man. A tremor of doubt assailed her. Girl-like, she could not comprehend the bitterness which seemed so unnecessary. For the moment Whitey Kirk had stepped out of character.

Later she told Jim that Kirk was distrustful and Hanvey insisted that the three of them meet for a chat. Kirk violently opposed the suggestion. Things which he could not fathom were happening too swiftly for his comfort. He was afraid of Jim and did not know how to combat this new tack—this brummagem friendliness. It was Madge who insisted that the trio talk things over, and Madge who made evasion impossible. Lowering* and sullen he greeted the impassive Jim who puffed placidly upon one of his murderous cigars and appeared happily oblivious to the rancor in the other's manner. But Madge was noticing—and she was vaguely uncomfortable for Jim.

"What's your game, Jim?" Whitey Kirk came straight to the point.

"Game? Who said I was playin' a game?"

"You know perfectly well that when you told Miss Weston you were here in the rôle of friend, you lied."

"Mph! You don't care who you call a liar, do you?"

"No I don't, and——"

"Well——" softly—"I'm too much your friend to get sore at you about doin' it. Ain't that the sensible thing, Miss Madge?"

"It is." She clipped her words short with a mannerism keenly remindful of her father. "And I must say, Warren, that you seem unnecessarily severe."

---

* Scowling (pronounced "low" as in "allow").

He swung wrathfully upon her. "I tell you that your father has employed this man to destroy our happiness—to break off our engagement—"

"He told me so himself," she answered with some asperity.

"He did?"

"Certainly. And he said he was remaining here because he is our friend and because if he resigned any other man who assumed the task would be our enemy. Isn't that simple?"

"Yeh," chimed in Jim, "ain't it?"

Kirk gazed at him through half-closed eyes. "I still don't get the drift—"

"It's just this," explained Hanvey. "Everybody says you're a crook—but you ain't—are you?"

"No."

"Folks just think you are. They're terrible unjust to you. You're really a gent and you're engaged to a swell young girl. All you want is a chance to marry her. Well, I'm here to see that you get that chance."

"That isn't true!" snapped Kirk bluntly.

"Why not?"

"Because you know good and well——" He pulled himself up sharply, suddenly remembering that his fiancée was an auditor "—that you think I'm not on the level."

"Aw, Son, you're doin' yourself an awful injustice. I never knew a straighter, nicer feller than you in my life. I've always been your friend. I've always told these other dicks who've been after you that it wasn't no use—that they'd never get the goods on you so they might as well quit tryin'. Honest, I have."

Kirk turned away. "One warning, Madge," he flung harshly over his shoulder, "this man isn't to be trusted."

She stared after his retreating figure, her own countenance aflame with embarrassment. Jim Hanvey, alone of the trio, seemed unperturbed. His attitude of disinterestedness was superb, and when she would have apologized for Kirk he cut her short. "That's all right, Miss Madge. I don't hold it against poor Whitey. They've been houndin' him for so long he's just naturally suspicious of everybody. Don't you go lettin' this little scene worry you. Just remember that I'm your friend. Real—sure-enough friend."

· She left him there and scarcely had she disappeared within the house when Kirk returned. His face was pallid and the gray eyes were blazing beneath the thinly pencilled brows. Jim greeted him with a broad grin. "Back again, Whitey?"

"Yes. What I want to know——"

"I'll tell you one thing you *ought* to know—that is you pulled an awful bone just now. The way you acted you almost convinced me I was wrong and that you really are a crook."

"Come off that, Jim. What are you driving at?"

"Just trying to help you out. You an' Miss Madge. Terrible swell kid. I'm strong for her."

"You can't hang anything on me."

Hanvey met his eyes squarely. Then the detective's lids closed with interminable slowness. At the termination of the protracted ocular yawn he gave vent to a single comment. "Nobody in this world ever batted a thousand," he said.

That night the three principals in the little drama gave themselves over to intensive thought. Jim speculated least of all. He was more than merely satisfied with the results of his preliminary work, although he was yet somewhat appalled by the difficulty of the task he had undertaken—and with the urgency of success. He shuddered in his big, simple heart at the thought of the girl's future should his efforts meet with failure. Whitey was all right in his own sphere—but this girl did not belong there and he knew that Whitey could never fit himself into her world.

As for Whitey Kirk, that gentleman was victim to a severe and obsessing worry. He had been apprehensive from the moment of Jim's arrival on the scene and had already laid a predicate of defense against any possible move of the detective. But the first move had caught him unprepared—it had come from an unexpected quarter and he found himself off guard. Jim's expressed friendship was the one thing with which he did not know how to cope. He realized that he had pulled a strategic blunder that afternoon—all through the evening Madge had been cool and unlike her naturally effusive and effervescent self. Madge was thinking—and Whitey didn't want Madge to think. Her nimble brain contained too much of her father's powers of logical deduction.

Kirk could not vision the goal toward which Jim was heading. That Jim had a definite objective, he did not doubt. He knew that the protestations of friendly interest were untrue—but he could not prove they were untrue. The very fact that Hanvey's strategy was unintelligible to him caused additional worry. He could face a definite attack. This one, subtle and evasive, bewildered and rendered him horribly vulnerable.

Madge sat at her window, staring seriously across the silhouette of hills. In her eyes was a brooding reflective light which was at once doubting and speculative. Instinct informed her that Jim Hanvey was her friend. She could not help but trust him. And she had that day made the startling discovery that there was something to Warren Kirk beside suave gentility. She had glimpsed beneath the surface and had seen there a hardness and a grimness which she—eighteen and in love—had never suspected.

There was little sleep for her that night and she did not come down the following morning until long after breakfast. She had forgotten an engagement to ride with Kirk and learned with an inexplicable measure of relief that he had gone alone. In the morning room she found Jim Hanvey smoking one of his vile cigars and worrying himself over the proper place to drop the ashes. She settled herself for a chat—and so, eager and friendly, Whitey Kirk found her when he returned from his ride. He remonstrated with her, and, as she had discovered a granite something in him the previous day, so he now learned that there was a strain of firmness in her which did not brook opposition.

"I think you're unjust and unreasonable, Warren."

"I know what I'm talking about."

"Has Mr. Hanvey ever harmed you?"

"It isn't his fault that he hasn't. He has tried."

"How do you know?"

Kirk's face flushed. That was a question which was embarrassing to answer. He knew well enough, but—"I know—that's all."

"That isn't sufficient for me, Warren. I like Mr. Hanvey and I believe he's our friend."

Kirk's face hardened unpleasantly. "He may be yours, Madge; but he isn't mine."

They had walked down the rosepath together and now she left him abruptly and returned to Hanvey. He gave no slightest indication of interest in their conversation. He stared stolidly at nothing at all and allowed her ample time to recover her mental equilibrium.

Kirk again tried to solve the riddle. Jim was proceeding with a smug complacency which worried him. Mentally, he checked over the list of his criminal exploits. He was positive that each had been excellently covered but he wasn't sure. Now. He had been sure until Jim appeared on the scene. But nothing could explain Jim's air of confidence save the certainty that he had uncovered some supposedly closed trail of Kirk's. But if Jim Hanvey was planning to discredit Kirk in the eyes of the girl, his actions gave no hint of that fact. It was the following morning, after a hearty tiff between Whitey and Madge, that he found her crying in an arbor and slumped down beside her consolingly——

"Aw! c'mon, Kid—that ain't no way to carry on. Whitey didn't mean nothin' by what he said."

She faced him squarely. There were tears in her eyes but no suggestion of weakness in the firm line of her jaw. "It isn't what he said, Mr. Hanvey—it's what he didn't say."

"Well then—he didn't mean nothin' by what he didn't say. Whitey's a swell feller, Madge. A nawful swell feller. Best in the world. He's got his faults—we've all of us got them. But I'm strong for Whitey an' I'd give anything in the world if he'd believe that."

"So would I," she said. "I trust you, Mr. Hanvey. I don't know why—but I do. Perhaps it's because I like you so much."

Jim blushed like a schoolgirl. "Gee! them words is music to my ears. There ain't many folks have said that to me, Miss Madge. Y'know—it seems that when folks meet up with a fat man they think all they got to do to prove they're good fellers is to give him a razzin'. Goshamighty, a fat feller likes friends as much as a skinny one. More, I'll say. He needs 'em more." He breathed heavily with the exertion of prolonged declamation. "That's why I wisht Whitey would like me an' trust me like you do. Matter of fact I've just been achin' to solve his problem, but he wouldn't let me get within firin' distance—you'd think I was gonna eat him."

"You've been aching to solve what problem, Mr. Hanvey?"

"His an' yourn."

"How?"

Jim looked away. "I don't exactly like to tell you. If Whitey was to suspect I was hornin' in on his affairs he'd get plumb peeved. Reckon I'd better wait. But it *is* a terrible good solution."

"What is it?"

Her interrogation fairly crackled. Jim grinned. "Anybody listenin' to that would know you was your father's daughter, Sis."

"What have you in mind?"

"Nothin' special—just an easy way out. Somethin' Whitey would of thought of long ago if he'd been twenty years younger." He stared reflectively at the sky—"Elopement!"

The color receded from her cheeks. For a moment she sat motionless, then leaned forward earnestly. "Would he?"

"Elope? Goodness goshness! yes! Feller who wouldn't elope with you would be a wooden indian.* 'Course I suppose he's figured that it'd get you in dutch with your folks, but I've been studyin' them out, an' I know they're so nuts about you they'd forgive you right away. Ain't it so?"

"Yes....Mr. Hanvey, I've been hoping that Warren would suggest that. I have, really. I know it sounds unmaidenly to say it—but I've been so worried and so uncertain. And recently Warren has acted so peculiarly—since you came here, that is....I wish it was over and done with."

"That's the way to talk, Sis. And I want you to know I'm here to help you all I can."

"You will?"

"Positively. But—" ruminatingly "—I wouldn't mention that fact to Whitey if I was you."

She nodded agreement. "Perhaps I had better not. But I'll count on you just the same."

It was that night that she walked through the gardens with Kirk and broached her plan. She did it simply and naïvely—she was worried, she said, recent developments had mitigated the perfection of their happiness. He had become morose and she worried. It was better not to go on this way. If he really loved her, he wouldn't wait—he'd just carry her off....

Whitey Kirk scarce believed the evidence of his senses. He

---

* That is, a wooden figure of a Native American, usually in a headdress, as often decorated the outside of tobacconists—hence, an unfeeling person.

was amazed and exultant. Ever since the moment of Jim's arrival on the scene he had longed to suggest an elopement, but he was afraid. Jim would find out some way, and then there'd be thunder to pay. He had feared it would be a tactical blunder, might arouse her suspicions of over-anxiety on his part.

His agreement was instant and enthusiastic—sufficiently enthusiastic even for her girlish, romance-loving heart. Within an hour their plans were laid: they were to announce after dinner the following night that they were going for a ride. At about eight o'clock they'd leave the grounds in her own high-powered sport roadster into which their suitcases would previously have been put. Then across country to the next town—and marriage. Whitey was whistling gleefully when they returned to the spacious veranda, but Madge was victim to a strange admixture of emotions. On the one hand was the thrill of active romance—on the other a feeling that she was doing wrong, that she wasn't playing fair with her parents; that, perhaps, after all was said and done, Whitey wasn't exactly the man for her.

Some of her doubts she expressed to Jim the following morning. He laughed away her fears. He had advised it, he said, because it was the simplest way out of a serious difficulty. A problem, he explained, was only a problem until it attained solution. It became then, a status. Those were not Jim's words, but that was the sense of them. She was only half-convinced and told him so.

"But I trust you, Jim Hanvey. I'm taking your advice. I'll do what you say."

"You really love Whitey?"

"Y-yes."

"Then elope with him tonight."

All through the long afternoon she was distraught. Her suitcase was packed and ready. Immediately following a peculiarly strained dinner Whitey Kirk disappeared. He returned in a few minutes having, in the interim, placed his suitcase in the girl's car. The world was a very bright and rosy place for Whitey just then. He glanced contemptuously toward the slothful, hulking figure of the detective. Not the least item of the prospective triumph would be Jim's discomfiture.

For her part, Madge was uncertain and unhappy. Only her immaturity and her fear of that youthful bugbear known as "backing down" prevented an eleventh-hour retreat. But, starry-eyed and firm-jawed, she set herself to go through with it. She had said she'd do it and she would—come what might. But she experienced none of the happiness which she had fancied would be hers upon her nuptial night. There was only a vague, formless terror…time and again she turned to Jim Hanvey for comfort. Jim knew—she could talk to him. He tried cumbersomely to reassure her, and succeeded partially. That evening he was to her both mother and father…they were very close to one another; the big, ungainly detective and the bewildered, emotion-driven child of a millionaire father.

At 7:30 o'clock Whitey Kirk called Madge aside.

"Your suitcase in the car, dear?"

"Yes," she answered softly.

"You put it there yourself?"

"Yes…." Then she hesitated and bit her lip. Madge had never been taught to lie. "Well, not exactly myself."

"What do you mean: Not exactly?"

"Nothing."

"What do you mean, Madge?"

"Well, somebody put it there for me."

"Who?"

"I don't see what difference that makes, Warren."

He quizzed her with an intensity which he himself did not understand. "Who was it?"

Her head was flung back defiantly.

"Mr. Hanvey!"

His jaw dropped slowly. Then his fingers tightened on her arm. "Jim Hanvey?"

"Yes."

"Then—" He was striving to adjust himself to this queer development—"Then Jim Hanvey knows about this elopement?"

"Yes."

"You told him?"

"No. That is—not exactly."

"Good God! Madge, can't you realize what you've done? You've spoiled the whole thing. If Jim Hanvey knows of this we may as well call it off. We'll never get away with it. I told you from the first that he was here to prevent our marriage. And now that you've told him—"

Her voice was level and firm in defense of the detective.

"And I've told you *you* were wrong, Warren. Jim is my friend and yours. He won't stop our elopement."

"What makes you think that?" His voice contained a sneer.

"Because," she announced calmly, "the idea of this elopement originated with Jim Hanvey!"

His grip on her arm relaxed. He gazed at her in incredulous astoundment. His brain seemed momentarily atrophied. Of all possible disclosures this was the most disturbing. It had been sufficiently alarming to learn that Jim was aware of the proposed elopement but to be informed that the idea had originated with the portly detective was a stunning blow.

He questioned the girl dazedly, choosing his words with care, holding himself in leash that he might betray none of the violent emotion which seethed within him. He might have suspected… might have known that Jim was not entirely inactive. And all the time, while the girl was explaining, his own brain groped for an answer to the puzzle. What was Jim planning? What *could* he be planning? As from a great distance he heard her words—

"And so you see I was right and Jim is your friend."

An uncontrollable fury shook him. The words were out of their own volition—"He's a damned sneak! Butting in on my affairs!"

She recoiled. The viciousness of the man's attitude, his venomous speech....He saw his error quickly and for the next ten minutes devoted himself and his expert talents to the task of making amends. She was only half convinced...."We'll go through with it," he said grimly. "Jim will double-cross you—you'll see. But we'll go through."

She went to her room. The farewell to her dainty little sanctuary was not easy. She dabbed at her eyes with a tiny lace handkerchief and prayed for the moral courage to renege at this eleventh hour. But that courage did not come—she was too young and her philosophy was builded about a tenet of gameness. She had said she'd elope with Warren Kirk and elope she would despite the instinct which cried to her in warning.

She pulled herself together with an effort, set her lips in a straight, determined line, and—with shoulders thrown back and head held high—descended the stairway. Her eyes roved questioningly about and she felt more than a hint of regret at failing to discern the hulking figure of Jim Hanvey. Nor did she see Kirk. She inquired his whereabouts of her father.

"I'm sure I don't know," answered Weston. "I saw Kirk strolling about with Jim Hanvey but I don't know where they went. Weren't you going riding with Warren?"

She nodded in dumb misery. As they reached the veranda Kirk appeared from the dusk. He seemed nervous and, in the light which streamed through the doorway, his face possessed a marked pallor. He addressed the girl: "All ready, Dear?"

"Yes." She turned to her father. "Where is Johnson? I want him to get the roadster."

Weston answered. "Johnson has gone to town in the big car, Dear. I'll get the other out for you."

"No." Her manner denoted anxiety. "I'll back it out myself. You talk to Warren."

There was no eagerness in her manner as she progressed slowly toward the garage in the rear of the big house. A premonition of disaster was with her, the irrevocability of the thing was depressing. Game as she was, there was considerable trepidation at the thought that she was thus wilfully abandoning the placidity of her existence for a future unknown and with a man whom she had just come to realize she scarcely knew.

She climbed thoughtfully into the roadster, assured herself that her suitcase and Whitey's were there, and then started the motor. Its rhythmic hum brought no elation this night. Just before slipping into gear, she reached to the dashboard and switched on her headlights. As by magic the interior of the garage was illumined by the brilliant glare. And then, as the significance of the sight disclosed by the sudden illumination penetrated her consciousness, she capitulated to her overwrought nerves. She screamed.

"Dad! O-oh! Dad!"

She sat motionless, gripped by a horrid fear, until her father stood beside the car, and as she alighted uncertainly her eyes discerned the figure of Warren Kirk farther back in the shadows. He hovered there uncertainly. Her father held her arm anxiously and then, as he saw her distended eyes, he followed their direction and a startled exclamation escaped from between his lips. For, in the very corner of the garage was a bundle of flashy, vivid clothes—a bundle bound securely by ropes and rendered mute by a gag.

"He's dead!" The girl's eyes flashed accusingly upon Kirk, and then back to the pitiful figure of Jim Hanvey in the corner. Jim was slumped grotesquely, his chin hung forward on the massive breast, a thin trickle of blood coursed down his fat cheeks and lost itself in the fat recesses of the ample chins.

How long she stood there she didn't know. She remembered her father leaping across the garage, whipping out a gold pen-knife as he did so. And she knew vaguely that Kirk was beside her, his hand on her elbow. She shook his hand off and he moved away as though she had struck him. Weston administered first aid to the stricken man from a silver pocket flask and not until the fishy eyes wavered open did the girl move, and then it was to dart across the garage and drop to her knees by the side of the ungainly figure. She pillowed his head on her breast and soft, crooning mother-sounds came from between her lips. She wiped away the thin stream of blood with the hem of her skirt. Jim rousing himself with an effort, blinked dazedly into the glare of the auto lamps and shook his head. His voice came lugubriously—

"Gosh! I sure feel like Friday the thirteenth."

As Jim, with the aid of Theodore Weston, struggled to his feet, Whitey Kirk moved slowly into the circle of light. His finely chiselled face exhibited great concern. He voiced a question— "What happened, Jim?"

It was Madge Weston who answered. She, too, had risen, and a new maturity seemed to have enveloped her. With a quietly dramatic gesture she removed from the fourth finger of her left hand the ring which Kirk had given her. She extended it to him.

"You know what happened to him, Warren."

"I don't...." His denial was fervent. "I'll swear to you, Madge—"

"Take this, Warren. I'd rather not discuss the matter."

His eyes held hers. And the man saw there a light of finality which was beyond question or argument. With that revealing glance he knew that he had lost. Madge turned to her father and gave a calm, quiet, womanly explanation—

"I was about to elope with Warren. He was afraid that Mr. Hanvey might try to stop us. And so he committed this—this cowardly act—"

"I didn't!" It was Kirk defending himself passionately. "I give you my word. Jim, you know I didn't do this. Tell them—"

"It doesn't matter what Mr. Hanvey says," retorted the girl sadly. "He has always been your friend and he's your friend now. He'd probably say you didn't do it, wouldn't you, Mr. Hanvey?"

"Yeh." Jim's big head nodded slowly. "I prob'ly would. I ain't aimin' to git Whitey into no trouble."

"You see, Warren, he's standing by you to the end. For it is the end, Warren. The very end. I've learned a good deal in the last few days. Somehow, I marvel that I didn't know before."

"But I didn't do it, Madge. Tell her that I didn't do it, Jim."

Jim met his eyes levelly. "I ain't accused you of nothin', have I, Whitey?"

Kirk stood rigid, staring from one to the other. From father and daughter he received stares of unveiled hostility. From Jim Hanvey only a mild, blinking reproof. Kirk's big figure shook with fury and he smashed one fist into the palm of the other hand.

"It's all a damned lie!" he shouted. "I had nothing to do with this and Jim Hanvey knows it."

"Well," came the quiet retort from the detective, "I ain't said you did, have I?"

It was Madge Weston who interposed. "It doesn't matter what either of you might say," she remarked coldly. "And now, Dad, I think we'd better help Mr. Hanvey into the house."

They supported the big figure between them. Whitey Kirk stood aside as they passed him. Later, after Weston and Madge had bandaged Jim's slight scalp wound, Kirk dispatched a note to Madge protesting his innocence and begging for an audience. She returned a curt refusal and the following morning, without again having seen the girl, Whitey Kirk abruptly departed the Weston home.

That afternoon Jim Hanvey and Theodore Weston faced each other across the polished surface of the walnut desk in the library. Jim was puffing peacefully upon one of his favorite black cigars and his host was struggling manfully with its mate. But however horrible the cigar might have been, it was not sufficiently malevolent to negative entirely the unalloyed exaltation which Weston was experiencing.

"You accomplished the impossible, Jim. I'll never forget it. I didn't believe it would work——"

"I wasn't so dog-goned sure of it myself," answered the big detective slowly. Then he grinned ruefully as he tenderly rubbed the bruise on his head. "I'll hand you one thing, Mr. Weston. Your bindin' an' gaggin' wasn't such a fine job—but believe me that sure was one awful wallop you hit me. I don't wonder Miss Madge was so sure that Whitey done it. She never would believe her Dad was that cruel."

Weston was deeply apologetic. "You insisted that I hit you hard."

"Sure I did," chuckled Jim. "I'm just remarkin' that you certainly took me at my word."

Pink Bait

THERE was nothing about Mr. Thomas Matlock Braden to mark him as being other than a perfect gentleman. From the moment of his unostentatious arrival he blended perfectly into the tinsel background of the fashionable Indiana resort hotel and while he regretted that the other guests were not aware that he possessed eleven new tailored suits he found contentment in the fact that they were equally ignorant of his eleven aliases.

Tommy Braden was old enough to appreciate the benefits which accrue to one who treads the path of rectitude, and, by the same token, he had attained to a philosophy which was based upon the theory that there was no transgression provided one is undiscovered. He was slightly more than forty-five years of age, tall and lean and quietly purposeful. His black hair was graying at the temples: he presented a picture which impelled passers-by to turn and murmur: "What a distinguished looking gentleman."

In cultivating this external aspect of severe probity, Tommy assumed a virtue which he had not. Morally, Tommy was a total loss. He was courteous and suave and cosmopolitan. And unscrupulous. He feared nothing save detection and ordered his existence upon the hypothesis that the legally constituted authorities are, on the whole, a stupid lot who have mastered the fundamentals of criminology and care nothing and know less about the finer points of the science.

He had long since graduated from the ranks of ordinary crooks. He now handled only tasks which required extraordinary finesse, infinite patience and an all-embracing knowledge of human nature. He selected his clients with as great care as he chose his victims and the former, at least, had small cause to protest his treatment. Certainly Mr. Michael Donley fancied himself extremely fortunate in having secured the cooperation of so eminent a personage in the criminal world.

The deal between Messrs. Donley and Braden had been consummated in a few moments.

"You know them Vanduyn poils, Tommy?"

"Yes."

"I got 'em."

"I know it."

"How'dja get wise?"

Mr. Braden's thin, ascetic lips expanded into a tolerant smile. "You bungled that job horribly, Mickey. Every dick in the country knows who pulled that job. They'll nab you the first time you turn around."

Mr. Donley made a rueful grimace. "You said it, bo. There ain't a fence will touch 'em. That's why I come to you."

"Yes?"

"How about sellin' 'em for me?"

"I might consider it."

"I'll split fifty-fifty."

Tommy Braden laughed lightly. "You amuse me, Mickey; truly you do."

"An even split—"

"I won't do business with you in that way, Mickey. You're a

common crook and I don't care to enter into a co-partnership with you. However, I'll buy the pearls from you for five thousand dollars cash."

"Aw! Tommy."

"Very well." Mr. Braden waved insouciantly. "Sell them elsewhere. I'm rather busy these days."

Mr. Donley knew that he was caught and he knew that Tommy Braden knew it. It was impossible for Mickey to dispose of the gems; in fact, there was a strong likelihood that even Tommy Braden would find it an impossible task. Certainly there was little doubt that it would tax his capacities to the utmost.

Mickey studied closely the inscrutable countenance of his companion. In it he read a subtle enjoyment of the situation. Mickey was annoyed—chiefly because he was helpless.

"Awright Tommy. Where's the five grand?"

"Where are the pearls, Mickey?"

"They're cache'd. Didn't dare bring 'em here. The bulls've got me shadowed. It's a shame the way they hound a poor crook."

"It is, Mickey; it certainly is. But it proves that you're wise to sell them to me. They don't care anything for your carcass; they can pick you up any minute they choose. What they're after is the jewels. Pretty nice reward they're offering, isn't it?"

Mr. Donley shook his bullet head sorrowfully. "Ten thousand berries. Gosh....But the point is—where'll we meet?"

Mr. Braden did some careful thinking. "Let's say tomorrow afternoon at two o'clock at the corner of Boulevard and Thirty-second street, Bayonne. And be sure they don't trail you."

Mickey laughed shortly. "The dick that follies me there is going to have went all over Joisey."

They met as per schedule. Tommy Braden at the wheel of a borrowed sedan. Together they rolled slowly down the Hudson County Boulevard toward Bergen Point. Mr. Donley produced a chamois sack and from it poured forth a stream of pink glory. "Gawd! ain't they beauts?"

Tommy's eyes glittered with the appreciation of a connoisseur. "Very fine, Mickey. A rope of matched pearls...hmm! I should say they're worth a hundred thousand dollars."

"Ev'ry dime of that. Say, listen—how 'bout raising the ante a grand or two?"

"Don't be silly, Mickey. Here's your five thousand. Give me the pearls."

Mr. Donley left the sedan at Eighth Street and returned to New York via the Jersey Central. The route chosen by Mr. Thomas Matlock Braden was considerably more circuitous. He crossed the Kill von Kull to Port Richmond and traversed Staten Island to St. George where he boarded the New York ferry. He reached his apartment, concealed the pearls carefully and four days later departed for Indiana.

Braden's mind was agile, and before his departure he had carefully planned every move of the delicate game. For one thing he had obtained several magazines which contained pictures of a certain Mr. Jared Mallory. Mr. Braden had always been interested in Mr. Mallory. The interest had been aroused once by the casual comment of a detective friend that they were not dissimilar in appearance. Mr. Mallory was a trifle older, true, but he had the same lean, sinewy figure; the same easy grace of bearing; the same appearance of gentility and the same touches of gray at the temples. Of course no person who knew Mr. Mallory could ever confound the twain, but a person who had never seen Mr. Mallory (and few had beyond his limited circle) could very readily believe that Tommy Braden was he, provided that belief was suggested.

Tommy Braden was a great admirer of Mallory's. The latter was all that Tommy would have liked to be. He was immeasurably wealthy, he did not work, he existed in a little world of his own and looked with fine and distant disdain upon the senseless turmoil of a commercial world. If he dabbled at all in the marts of commerce it was with a magnificent aloofness which kept his name clear of financial news. One could imagine him as a person whose fortune was invested exclusively in government bonds. But the greatest link between Messrs. Braden and Mallory lay in the fact that the latter was by way of being a jewel collector.

Tommy, too, collected jewelry, although in a rather more informal way. A gem to Mr. Mallory was a thing of beauty and of glory; something to be treasured and gazed upon and studied. Mr. Braden, being rather grossly material, saw in a jewel only its intrinsic worth and its marketable value where the method of its coming into his possession had been a bit questionable. But he loved jewelry none the less…the viewpoint of the two men was basically the same although diametrically opposite in the working-out; Braden saw jewels in terms of cash; Mallory saw dollars in terms of gems.

Jared Mallory was known to the masses in a vague way, such as a king is known. He was a person without a public personality. He shunned publicity and human contact outside his own little personal circle. He was a living definition of the word exclusive in its sociological application…and so it was that very few persons were aware of the fact that Mr. Mallory had but recently sailed for France. Tommy Braden knew it, but that was only because Tommy happened to have an interest in Mr. Mallory. And now Tommy planned to cash in on his observation of the millionaire jewel collector.

Tommy's decision to visit the famous Indiana resort was the result of careful deliberation. He knew that this was the last place in the world that Mr. Mallory would ever visit, and it was logical to presume that Mr. Mallory's intimates would also shun it. They were to be found on private estates situated in Florida or along the Carolina coast…anywhere but at a blatant resort hotel.

Nor was Mr. Braden wrong in his conjecture. Of the thousands of guests who thronged the hotel lobby, the golf course, the casino—there was not one who had ever personally seen the famous Mr. Mallory although there were several whose bank balances contained as many figures as that of the gem collector. Which did not mean that Mr. Braden's fellow-guests were socially doubtful but rather that Mr. Mallory's status was such that the hotel would have considered he was paying it an inestimable compliment by deigning to visit.

Tommy arrived at the hotel late one evening. He knew that one or two guests commented upon his distinguished appearance as he crossed the lobby. Such comment always pleased Tommy. It was a tribute to something which was innate. He liked to tell himself that he was not a snob…he intended fully that the reputation of Mr. Mallory should not suffer by reason of any misapprehension which might be more or less deliberately engendered in the minds of his fellow-guests.

He registered in a cramped scrawl which bore a startling similarity to the labored chirography of Jared Mallory. But Tommy was nothing if not honest. The clerk whirled the register and glimpsed the signature——

THOMAS M. BRADEN—New York

"I wired for a suite…." Tommy's voice was rather indifferent, his manner bored.

"Yes sir. Certainly sir." The gong. "Front. Show Mr. Braden up to Suite F."

The dinner hour approached. Mr. Braden bathed and dressed with scrupulous care in an ultra-conservative dinner jacket. There was about his rather statuesque figure an air of stateliness which harmonized with the conventional simplicity of his garb. His dress was so unobtrusive as to command instant attention. He descended to the lobby, crossed to the dining room and slipped a crisp and ample bill into the willing hand of the headwaiter by way of assuring himself the proper respect.

He knew that more than one person commented upon him during the course of the meal. For the most part he kept his eyes down, but when they did chance to focus upon some person, that individual experienced the unpleasant sensation of being looked through. More than one consulted the clerk after dinner for information as to the identity of the stranger who had now retired to a corner of the lobby and was puffing lightly upon a monogrammed cigarette.

Among those who had particularly noticed Tommy was a couple from the Middle West: a rather wizened gentleman of some fifty-five years and his unduly ample wife. Mr. and Mrs. Edgar H. Morse had, for the past five years, been frantically attempting to create the impression which Mr. Braden was now registering so profoundly. Wealth had come to them in an unexpected flood. They were not crude persons but they did lack the background which is essential to true culture and, as earnestly as they had struggled for financial success during years which were rather more lean than fat, so they set about adjusting themselves to the social demands of their miraculously acquired millions.

They were rather pathetic as they hung on the fringe of things and sought to absorb in a few years the social ease which must be born in one. They were not aggressive in their wealth—as a matter of fact they scarcely understood it; had not yet fathomed its meaning. And their tastes were those of the contest-answerers who send in to the editor lengthy replies to the prize query: "What would you do if you suddenly inherited a million dollars?"

Mr. and Mrs. Morse strolled over to the desk and made inquiry of the clerk.

"Oh! him? That's Thomas M. Braden."

His manner indicated that anyone who was anyone would certainly know Mr. Thomas M. Braden. Mr. Morse caught the nuance and uttered an enlightening—"A-a-ah! So it is."

"He's a wonderful looking man," commented Mrs. Morse. "So distinguished."

They managed to seat themselves near Tommy. He appraised them scientifically. There was no mistaking their new and complete wealth—"Woman—no taste—but nice. Swellest modiste in New York—make me the grandest gown you got. He's a bird that ain't sure yet whether he ought to wear plain or patent oxfords with his dinner jacket. They look soft."

He was apparently oblivious to their proximity until Mr. Morse apologetically borrowed a match. He did so apprehensively and was put instantly at ease by Tommy's manner. But Mr. Braden immediately appeared to lose interest in them. He was gazing out across the lobby—in but not of the crowd. And just when the Morses had become discouraged Tommy turned to them with a question—"How far is the golf links from the hotel?"

Edgar H. Morse expanded instantly. He orated jerkily upon the nearness of the first tee, the condition of the course, the scenic beauties of the place—and wound up with the inevitable question of all golfers: "What do you shoot?"

Tommy shrugged, "I'm not very good. When I break a hundred I'm satisfied."

"Just my game. I did a 98 today and I'm tickled pink. Of course I hole every putt and most of 'em don't. You booked up for a game in the morning?"

Tommy Braden bestowed upon his companion a stare in which there was the faintest hint of disapproval; a stare such as he fancied Jared Mallory might confer. Morse felt a sensation of faintness.

"No-o," answered Tommy, "I'm not."

There was an awkward pause. Edgar Morse desired to invite this regal gentleman to play with him but he dreaded a rebuff. And just when the subject was about to expire naturally, Tommy ventured a polite "Why?"

"Why—er—a—I just sort of thought....That is, if you weren't——"

"That we might play a round?"

"Yes. Yes." Eagerly. "If you would—that is, if you'd care to."

"Delighted. What hour shall we tee off?"

"Don't know—course crowded—have to get starting time." He rose excitedly. "'Scuse me minute. I'm in strong with the starter—give 'im cigars—and—er—things. See if I can't fix it...." He darted away, leaving Tommy with Mrs. Morse. She favored him with a wistful little smile.

"That's real nice of you," she said. "Eddie just dotes on golf."

"I'm sure I shall enjoy it."

"Oh! sure you will. As soon as you get to know Eddie real well—that is, if you should—you'll like him tremendously. He's been awful lonesome here...."

Edgar H. Morse returned, flushed and triumphant. "Fixed him. Ain't hard when you know how. We're off at nine-fifteen. Say, I'm all pepped up."

Tommy took a cigarette from a platinum case. He extended the case to his new-found friend. Edgar Morse took one and glanced at the monogram. He wanted to note the brand of cigarette this gentleman used that he might unostentatiously duplicate it at the earliest possible moment.

His eye focused upon a simple monogram. Private brand... but no: the initials were distinctly not T. M. B. He inspected more closely, then lighted the thing and inhaled deeply. "Fine cigarette. What make?"

"My own," answered Tommy Braden suavely.

They chatted amiably for a few moments and then Tommy rose, expressed polite regrets and moved away. "T'morrow morning, remember," the little man flung after him. "We'll have a great round. Er—a—that is, I hope we will."

Tommy smiled his best Mallory smile, indicating the ultra-correct degree of mild enthusiasm. And when he had taken hat and stick and disappeared Mr. Edgar H. Morse did a very peculiar thing. He reached eagerly into the ash tray and rescued there from two frayed cigarette stubs. Mrs. Morse was duly horrified.

"Eddie! What in the world!"

But Edgar did not hear. He was frowning slightly and his gaze was fixed intently upon the monogram of Tommy's privately made cigarettes.

"Listen, Ella—you heard him say they were his private cigarettes?"

"Yes. But a good many gentlemen——"

"Sure. Sure. I'm not saying they don't. But there's something peculiar about this chap. See this monogram here—it ain't T. M. B. at all. The initials are J. M."

From the deepest shadows of the spacious veranda, Tommy Braden was a witness to the little scene. A slow smile of satisfaction creased his thin, patrician lips. "So much for him," he murmured. "That Mallory monogram was a great idea. Our trade mark—once seen, never forgotten."

The game of golf was enjoyed by both men. They played a nip and tuck contest which atoned in competitive value what it undoubtedly lacked in skill. It was not until the seventeenth green when an impossibly long putt caromed off a match stick and clicked into the cup that victory finally perched upon the Morse banner. The little man was jumpy with excitement.

"Great game—wonderful. Ain't often I meet a guy I like to play as much as I do you. Besides, most of the chaps I know can beat me—beat the tar out of me. I'm an awful dub. Say—we got to do this again—a—that is, I hope we got to."

"We shall," smiled Tommy. "I've enjoyed the morning immensely."

From the eighteenth green they strolled to the clubhouse where they indulged in long, tall lemonades which appeared to inspire Mr. Morse with no particular enthusiasm. "Got something in my room.* C'mon and sample it. That is—a—if you care to."

Mr. Braden was delighted—far more than he cared to admit. One glance at the suite occupied by the Morses and he was well satisfied that he had picked his victim competently. He knew just about what this suite was costing and his keen eye missed no detail of the many which shrieked new and amazing wealth.

Mrs. Morse inquired interestedly as to the details of the match—a frequently interrupted and garbled account which had to do with lucky breaks, horrible kicks, phenomenal putts.... "We're gonna play again in the morning," finished Edgar. "That is—er—Mr. Braden says he wants to. 'Course I'm not blaming him for kicking. That last putt of mine didn't have any right going down. I always did believe that putting was too all-fired important in this game...."

The fraternity of golf engendered a friendliness which would have been long in developing else. It was decided that they should dine together that night, and about five o'clock in the afternoon Tommy visited the florist shop in the hotel where he ordered a corsage bouquet sent up to Mrs. Morse. "Right here," he reflected,

---

* This was during Prohibition, it will be recalled: Mr. Morse invites Braden to have an alcoholic drink in private.

"is where the old dame gets hooked right. And at the same time I exterminate another bird."

"Shly write the card?" inquired the obtrusively blonde young lady at the counter.

"No-o." Tommy produced a card which he flipped across the counter. She glanced at it indifferently.

"Cash?" she inquired, "or shly charge it to y'r room, Mr. Mallory?"

He started visibly. "What's that?"

"Shly charge it to your room or juh wanna pay cash?"

"I mean—what was it you called me?'"

She glanced at the card. "Mallory. That's what the card here says, an'——"

He snatched it brusquely from her hand. "Wrong card," he snapped making an effort to appear as though he were making an effort to appear unembarrassed. "Here's my card. You may charge it to Suite F."

He whirled and moved away, his manner denoting extreme irritation. The rather fullblown young lady stared after him. "Now ain't he the pussy's ankle?" she murmured reflectively. "Gets sore because he slips me the wrong card. That ain't nothin' to get peeved about." An assistant manager drifted toward her counter. "Say, Gus—who's the flossy bird with the gray thatch which just rambled away from here?"

The young gentleman shrugged. "I got worries of my own, Susie. What's the matter—he been trying to date you up?"

"No. But he ordered a corsage sent up to some female an' he slipped me the wrong card. I looks on the card an' reads the name an' I says 'Shly charge it to your room, Mr. Mallory?' an' with that he like to of bit my head off. He just about gives me the bum's rush gettin' that pasteboard which he tears up right away. Then he slips me this one—Mr. Thomas Matlock Braden—I don't see nothing to get excited about just because he slips me the wrong pasteboard, d'you? What difference does it make to me if his name's Thomas Braden or Jared Mallory or what it is. I reckon neither of them handles is gonna start no war—Say! Gus—for the love of Mike, what's eatin' you? If you feel like that you'd ought to see a Doc."

The ninth assistant manager put out a delicately restraining hand. "Jared Mallory?" he said half to himself.

Susie was annoyed. "Now listen at me, Gus—"

"I thought Braden wasn't his name. Jared Mallory! Holy Suffering Catfish! Say, you ain't sure about that, are you, Susie?"

"No. Of course I ain't. I only know it, that's all. If you think my lamps have went bad you can assort them card which he flang on the floor."

It took the young man but a few seconds to recover the torn bits of pasteboard and arrange them in proper order. "Well I'll be darned—Jared Mallory is right. Say, lemme tell the Chief."

Susie restrained him briefly. "Who is this bird Mallory—that you should get all het up over him? Who did he ever kill?"

"Jared Mallory," explained the excited young man, "is one of the richest nuts in the United States: that's all. He's got a bankroll so big you'd have to have four eyes to see it all."

"Then why the alias?" she queried practically.

"This joint ain't Mallory's size. He's the kind of guy who thinks he's slumming when he visits a hotel like this. Is that clear now?"

"Sure—sure it is, Gus. Clear as mud."

It required just five minutes of the young man's time to transmit his enthusiasm to the manager. "Of course," counselled that dignitary, "you shall do nothing to embarrass Mr. Mallory. If he desires to visit us incognito—"

And within ten minutes the manager had informed two of his particular friends that Jared Mallory, the millionaire, was registered at the hotel under the name of Thomas Matlock Braden. By dinnertime that night a dozen persons knew it and before morning Tommy was a marked man—at which Tommy merely smiled a thoroughly satisfied smile. "When Mr. Barnum spoke his famous words," he soliloquized, "he must have been timing things with a slow watch."*

It was fully forty-eight hours before the rumor of Braden's identity reached the ears of Mrs. Edgar H. Morse. At receipt of the tidings she almost collapsed. "That's right—I knew all the time he was somebody tremendous." And she proceeded to recount the incident of the monogrammed cigarettes.

But it was in the privacy of the Morse suite that the knowledge received a most thorough threshing out. "Golly!" breathed Edgar. "Think of me bumming around with Jared Mallory. Honeybunch! we're sure sliding up the social ladder now, we are. I thought there was something funny about those cigarettes. And he's a gentleman right—he is; so much of a one he don't have to be watching his step all the time. Funny he should like me—er—a—that is, if he really does."

Thus far Mallory was merely a name to Edgar Morse and Edgar Morse was only a name to Tommy Braden. Each set in motion inquiries as to the other. Tommy's task proved the easier.

Within five days he was in possession of full information regarding the financial and social standing of his prospective victim. He knew that Mr. Morse had been a ten-thousand-a-year man with an aptitude for saving until a certain wild venture in war babies† had catapulted him into the multi-millionaire class; so suddenly, in fact, that neither the excitable little man nor his

---

* Braden apparently refers to the slogan (probably incorrectly) attributed to American showman P. T. Barnum: "There's a sucker born every minute."

† Not actual children, rather, bonds or other securities sold during World War I or which increased in value because of the war.

wife had yet adjusted themselves to their new position in life. Tommy rather liked them; they weren't the offensive type of *nouveau riche*—there was nothing aggressive or vulgar about either. And Tommy was convinced that he would not be doing them an injury by selling to them the Vanduyn pearls. According to Tommy's way of figuring the detectives would never suspect that handsome jewels in the possession of Edgar H. Morse had been come by illicitly, so that, under the deal he contemplated no one would be the loser. "No one except Vanduyn," he mused, "and that baby is stung anyway."

Information regarding Jared Mallory came less readily to Mr. Morse. Mr. Mallory was not among those present in the Dun and Bradstreet reports;[*] but now that the great hotel was agog with knowledge of Tommy's supposedly true identity, scraps of information were working into a comprehensive—and rather flattering—whole. As a matter of fact the actual presence of Jared Mallory would not have excited the curiosity caused by Tommy's incognito. There was something irresistibly intriguing about a man who sought to conceal his eminence—something of greater allure than the eminence itself. Mr. Mallory—so general comment had it—possessed the wealth of Crœsus,[†] the family tree of a Plantagenet[‡] and he was inclined to be more or less of what the public expressively if inelegantly terms a nut.

Within a week all doubt which may have existed as to his being Jared Mallory had been removed. The manager had personally made occasion to visit Tommy's room when Tommy was absent. He found a half hundred cigarettes monogrammed J. M., one or

---

[*] Dun and Bradstreet have marketed independent analyses of the financial condition of companies and individuals since their founding in 1841.

[†] The legendary king of Lydia (596–547 BCE), said to be phenomenally wealthy.

[‡] The Plantagenets were the royal family of England from 1154 to 1485; their dynasty ended with the death of Richard III. They were succeeded by the Tudors.

two handkerchiefs with the same embroidered initials and an ancient letter addressed to Jared Mallory's New York address.

But even at that Tommy was not entirely satisfied. He closeted himself one day with the manager and explained to him that a telegram might possibly come to the hotel addressed to Mr. Mallory; in which event it was to be delivered to him. No such telegram ever arrived, but whatever doubt may have remained to the manager was promptly and effectively set at rest. Nor did that personage maintain the secrecy which had been demanded of him. True, he passed the information only to certain intimate friends who, in turn, conveyed it to their own intimates—until the positive knowledge was the property of the entire guest personnel.

There was, of course, an avalanche of attention showered upon the supposed Jared Mallory to all of which he was magnificently indifferent. He was courteous and frostily impersonal. He accepted one or two invitations with an air of bespeaking condescension, and through it all he vouchsafed his intimacy only to the Morses.

But even with them he maintained a reserve. Edgar Morse, prideful of his recent success, told Tommy of it, thereby bringing no agony of soul to Mr. Braden; but of himself Tommy never spoke. He did mention casually an acquaintanceship extending from Cape Town to Bombay and from New York to Sydney; he spoke feelingly and with passionate intensity whenever the subject of jewels was mentioned and he openly admired an unusually handsome emerald which Mrs. Morse possessed. But not once was he other than Thomas Matlock Braden—even on the memorable evening when Mrs. Morse, carried away by her interest in the conversation, addressed him as Mr. Mallory.

Tommy's forehead corrugated in a frown of annoyance. "What's that?" he inquired with frigid politeness.

She flushed scarlet. "Why—er—you see, folks around the hotel say you are Jared Mallory of New York."

There was no doubting his anger. His voice came in crisp and incisive negation: "I am afraid I am not responsible for gossip. I am not Jared Mallory."

Ella Morse was flustered and her husband came eagerly to her rescue. "Now don't you go blaming Ella, Mr. Braden. She's been hearing so much about you being Mr. Mallory and all the folks in the hotel wanting to know if you really were, that she—I—that is, we—we've sort of called you Mr. Mallory to ourselves and the name kind of slipped out. It ain't any business of ours who you are—and we didn't go to cause you any embarrassment...." He paused and spluttered. Tommy stared coldly.

"I understand, Mr. Morse. And I am sure that Mr. Mallory would not be at all flattered."

"No—of course he wouldn't. He'd prob'ly be awful sore. That is—er—a—not because folks thought you were him—of course you're as good as he is any day in the week, including Sundays—but on account of his feeling—well you know what I mean."

"Yes. I'm sure I do. But let's don't discuss it further. I prefer to remain Thomas M. Braden."

"'Sall right with me, Mr. Braden. You can be Willie Jones if you want to and it don't make any difference to us, does it, Ella?"

But after Tommy had parted from them that evening after a session at the casino, Edgar swung on his wife. "Goshamighty, Ella—wasn't he sore when he found out folks knew who he was?"

She nodded. "Can you blame him, Eddie? Here he's taken all this trouble to make folks believe he ain't Jared Mallory...I reckon he's terribly put out. But there isn't a doubt in the world that he's him. If he wasn't Mr. Mallory he wouldn't get peeved about folks thinking he was."

The friendship between Tommy Braden and the Morses

flourished after that little verbal clash. If unpleasant memory of it rankled in Tommy's mind, he gave no indication and his suavity and friendliness put them completely in his power. They drove together—in Morse's car—and Edgar and Tommy played golf daily. He shunned the society of the other guests, rigidly maintaining his attitude of impregnable exclusiveness. And it was after a fortnight of this that the subject of jewelry again came up: neither Edgar nor his wife suspecting that Tommy had introduced the subject.

He appeared to become inspired. He thrilled them with romances of famous gems. The history of renowned jewels he had at his finger-tips. They were seated in the parlor of his suite, the air filled with the fragrance of excellent cigars...."But after all," declaimed Mr. Braden, "there is only one jewel which is worthy the name."

"And that is?"

"The pearl."

They were in enthusiastic agreement. Tommy launched into an expansive account of the pearl fisheries which he claimed to have seen, he explained to them the mysteries of great pearls and enthralled them with his enthusiasm. And then——

"I'm passionately fond of them," he confessed boyishly. "And I have something here—if you'd like to see it."

A significant glance flashed between the others. The jewel collector had been humanized by his hobby....He opened one of his trunks and a few seconds later returned with a battered leather case of sizeable dimensions. They gathered near him at the table, and then, very slowly and worshipfully, he flung back the lid.

The Vanduyn pearls smiled up at them in pink perfection. Mrs. Morse gasped with delight.

"Oh-oh! How glorious!"

Tommy caught up the rope of gems and ran them caressingly

through his fingers. "They are among the most perfect pearls in the world—each one a match for every other one. Each has its history, its romance. It has taken me years to collect them."

They were mesmerized by the magnificence of the jewels. And, while they stared under the spell, Tommy talked softly and well about them. He described the long stretches of sandy beach, the atolls and palm stretches of the somnolent South Seas—the slumbering coral reefs, the mahogany-skinned Kanakas.* His voice trembled as he described the pearl fishing operations; the shark menace; the dangers faced by the pearl producers. He was a natural actor and he held the little manufacturer and his wife in the hollow of his hand. And then, just when it seemed as though they could no longer endure the glory of the thing he showed them—he snapped the case shut and turned away.

In a second he had dropped back into his customary manner: scrupulously polite, a trifle distant, unutterably exclusive. But the Morses were no longer with him in spirit. They were dazed. It was Edgar Morse who sounded the words which brought a lilt of triumph to the heart of Tommy Braden.

"I'm rather sorry you showed us those, Mr. Braden."

"Sorry?"

"Yes. I want them."

Tommy smiled good-humouredly. "Then I, too, am sorry. I'm afraid there are no other pearls precisely like these."

Tommy Braden knew he had builded well. He deliberately shunted the conversation from the subject of jewelry, knowing that the little man and his sweet-faced wife would discuss the pearls once they were alone again. Nor was he wrong. They were

---

* Originally the Hawaiian word for "people" and thus the name given to native Hawaiians. By this time, it referred to the Melanesian peoples spread across the South Pacific, many of whom worked in Australia on sugar plantations or cattle stations or as servants in towns; they were often treated horribly and reduced to near-slave status.

captivated by the sheer beauty of the things; and their suddenly aroused passion had nothing whatever to do with the intrinsic worth of that which they had come to covet.

"If he would only sell them," she said wistfully. "They would cost a fortune, but——"

"It isn't the money," he answered. "Mr. Mallory doesn't care for money and he does care for his pearls: that's all. I'm sure he'd never sell them—er—that is, I don't think he would."

"We could ask him."

"I'm afraid we couldn't. We might hint around...that is, kind of test him out."

But, somehow, they found that assignment unreasonably difficult. Their mention of the pearls the night following excited no response from him, but on the night after that he consented to again display the magnificent rope. He told them off, jewel by jewel...but his manner forbade the mention of a sale. Talk of dollars and cents in connection with their flawless beauty would have been a sacrilege.

Morse did essay one valiant attempt—"We'd be awfully appreciative, Mr. Braden, if you could help us get some pearls exactly like those—er—a—that is, if there are any."

The other man shrugged. "I'm afraid there are not," he retorted briefly.

Tommy was playing an ultra-careful game. He was making progress slowly but surely; casting himself in the rôle of quarry. And he might have continued in just that way had not something occurred on the ensuing day which caused him considerable apprehension.

At first he did not see the Gargantuan figure which hulked at the desk and wrestled with the register. It was not until the stranger turned and surveyed the lobby through glassy, fishlike eyes that a premonition of danger smote him. His face hardened and he whistled sharply through his teeth.

The person at the desk was not one to inspire any emotion other than the most intense amusement. He was a man of overflowing girth and lumbering manner. His clothes were grotesquely misfit; the coat flapped loosely about the protuberant torso and the material of the suit glistened with a sheen begotten of arduous wear. Beneath the pants-cuffs shone a brief expanse of cheap, lavender sox topping aggressive russet shoes, the toes of which rose to points. From the top of the vest there was exhibited a small area of lavender silk shirt, a purple polka-dotted necktie and a collar of insignificant height but amazing circumference.

But it was the face which inevitably engaged the attention— engaged it and held it even more than the absurdly powerful gold chain which spanned the vest and held dangling from it a golden toothpick with which the big man toyed absently as he gazed about the lobby. The face was a fitting final touch to the ensemble. It was an enormous face; a pudgy, expressionless face; a face flanked by loose, pendulous jowls ruddily complexioned; a face like a great pudding set with two glass marbles.

A casual observer might have believed that those eyes were sightless as they stared stonily across the lobby. Once or twice the man blinked—the process consuming an interminably long time. He yawned with his eyes, but it did not seem to matter whether they were open or closed. And at length he heeded the irritable summons of an excessively peeved bellhop and turned to follow that person into an elevator.

Tommy Braden stood flatfooted staring as though at an apparition. But once the cage door closed, Braden crossed the lobby swiftly and glanced at the register.

JIM HANVEY—New York

He turned away. He strolled out upon the spacious veranda where he lighted a cigar and puffed reflectively. Eddie Morse and his wife, Ella, would not have known their friend at that moment. Tommy's face was hard and bitter and there was fear delineated in it. He put his thoughts into unspoken words—

"What the hell is Jim Hanvey doing here? Why should a detective like him come to a joint like this?"

Tommy Braden, by dint of hard and untiring work, had risen gradually to the very top of his profession. The road had been neither easy nor undangerous. He had faced disappointment and reversal with a bravely smiling face—and now he had come to the point where he felt entitled to reap the fruits of his endeavor. Tommy had been the despair of detectives. He operated with an easy suavity and a level-headed cunning which sent them running up blind alleys in the futile search for evidence to convict, so that thus far Tommy had avoided the inconveniences of jail—save in the case of a single slip in the early days of his career.

That single jail sentence rankled in Tommy's breast, and it had inspired in him a wholesome fear of state boarding houses. In jail one was deprived of one's individuality and individuality was Tommy's greatest stock in trade. He intensely disliked swapping his name for a number and his exquisitely tailored clothes for a uniform. It seemed a great pity that the state had no more judgment than to fail to differentiate between crude, lumbering crooks and gentlemen of the profession who operated with delicacy and finesse. But, after all, Tommy Braden feared only one man in the detective world, which was why he was so visibly disturbed at finding himself a fellow-guest of that one man.

The following morning he played golf with Edgar Morse. He unbent more than ever before and dazzled the little business man so thoroughly that Morse's mind was not on the game and he lowered his course record seven strokes. "By Golly!" reflected Mr. Morse, "there ain't a doubt that this Braden or Mallory, or whoever he is, really likes me."

Tommy was annoyed. He had been enjoying the cat-and-mouse contest and Jim's advent forced him to greater speed than he had planned. They walked in from the eighteenth green together, consumed large drinks of iced sarsaparilla which Mr. Morse insisted was excellent for the blood, and then Tommy made his way to the hotel while Mr. Morse selected his favorite putter and a half dozen balls for a session of utterly useless practice on the clock course.

Tommy saw the hulking figure of the mammoth detective too late to avoid a meeting. He was perturbed but at the same time thankful that his introduction to Jim at this particular time should come while he was unaccompanied. And realizing the inevitability of a talk with Jim, it was he who spoke first.

"Well, well, well—if it isn't my fat friend."

Jim looked up. Heavy eyelids closed over glassy orbs with maddening slowness, held shut for a moment, then uncurtained with even more annoying deliberateness. There was no doubting the sincerity of the surprise which was reflected upon the pudgy countenance.

"Well I'm a sonovagun! Tommy Braden!" Their hands met in a clasp of sincere cordiality. "It is Braden now, ain't it, Tommy?"

Tommy smiled with rare good-humor. "Surest thing you know, Jim. Thomas Matlock Braden."

"The whole works, huh? What's it feel like to be masqueradin' under your right name?"

"Pretty good, Jim; pretty good. I've retired on my income."

"Quit the game?"

"Entirely."

"That's fine, Tommy—fine. I'm tickled pink to know it. I

always like to see a crook with sense enough to know when he's got plenty. There ain't nothin' like honesty, my boy, when you've made all the money you need."

"That's what I figured, Jim. There wasn't any use for me to continue running risks....Of course I'm not what you'd call a rich man, but then I'm pretty well fixed. And not being tied up with a frail, it don't cost me much....You know how it is."

"Sure, Tommy—I know." Jim blinked with friendly approval upon the other. "Dog-gone if you don't look like a million dollars ready money, Son. Silk shirt, trick pants an' everything. Say, what is there to this golf thing that makes sensible men dress funny thataway?"

"Ever played?"

"Naw! Imagine an elephant like me chasin' a dinky little ball over the meadows."

"Better men than you have fallen for it."

"Sure; I know that. But it's my figger, Son. The links wouldn't stand for it."

Jim turned and walked with Braden toward the hotel. Tommy was ill-at-ease despite the apparent ease of his manner. Jim's face bore an expression of bovine contentment; he looked like a child—or a simpleton. Tommy knew that he was not a good man to have around, and yet he was afraid to protest too fervently that he was now treading the path of rectitude. Yet his curiosity shrieked for appeasement.

"Funny to see you here, Jim."

"Me? I reckon it is. I've been some awful funny places, Tommy."

"Vacation?"

"Uh-huh. An' I just naturally got sick of lowbrow joints. Besides, a lot of the big boys in your line of work drift by here during the season, and so I thought I'd try this seven-forks-dinner stuff for a while. Guy never gets too old to learn, you know. Of course I ain't like you—you're a gent an' you fit. I'll bet you wear a movie screen shirt* for dinner, eh?"

"Yes. Everybody does here."

"But one. Say: 'jever see me in evenin' duds? No? Honest, I look like next week's wash hangin' out."

"Doesn't exactly fit your style of beauty?"

"No. I reckon when the good Lord gimme a knack of rememberin' faces an' understanding human nature, He figgered His part was done. If faces was fortunes I'd be bankrupt."

They attained the ornate lobby where, at the desk, Tommy secured the key to his suite. "Come up, Jim?"

"Uh-uh. Got to stroll around: exercise, the Doc says. Gosh! how I hate it. See you later, Tommy. Awful glad you've turned straight."

"Nothing like it, Jim. I never thought I could run across you like this and feel safe."

"Shuh! I wouldn't bother you none."

But despite outward appearances, Tommy Braden was uneasy. It wasn't that he was in any way connected with Jim's visit to this particular resort but rather that Jim's proximity was unhealthy for any gentleman who was upon transgression bent.

Certainly there was no safety in continued procrastination. He had the Morses just about where he wanted them and he figured that the best thing he could do was to sell them the pearls and make his get-away. He knew there'd be no particular trouble—

There wasn't. They dined with him that night, only Tommy being aware of the hulking lonely figure which munched by itself in a secluded corner of the dining room. Edgar Morse was radiant: he was exuberant over his record-breaking golf score and as the dinner progressed he went over for the dozenth time every

---

* He means a stiffly starched white shirt, very much like the material used for movie screens of the day.

shot from the first tee to the eighteenth cup. Tommy warmed up considerably. He even unbent so far as to say that Edgar was the first genuinely congenial person he had met in years. He hoped that their acquaintanceship might not perish when they parted, and—Oh! yes, he was leaving in a few days. He wished that there was something he might do to indicate to Mr. and Mrs. Morse the depth of his appreciation for the pleasure their society had afforded.

He correctly interpreted the eager glance which passed between husband and wife. "There is," burst out Edgar, then bit his lip in embarrassment: "Er—a—that is, I was just thinking— I'm kind of crazy, I guess, and——"

"What is it, Morse? Anything in my power...You see, I have few real friends. I am more or less well fixed in a financial way, and in such a position one becomes distrustful of persons who protest friendship....Tell me what you were thinking."

"I can't—really. 'Tisn't possible."

"Indeed it is."

"No. Can't."

Tommy beamed upon Ella Morse. "What is it, Mrs. Morse? Certainly we are sufficiently intimate to permit frankness."

She flushed. "Not to that extent."

"Pshaw! If there's any favor—"

"Well, it's this," exploded Morse. "If you wouldn't get sore— that is, if you understood—but of course I can't ask you because they mean more to you than just what they mean and—that is, it isn't like you just had them, and—Oh! damn it! I've got myself all balled up!"

Tommy frowned slightly. "I judge you have reference to my pearls?"

"No! No! Certainly not. That is, I didn't go to pull a bone, and—"

Mrs. Morse leaned across the table. "Yes, Mr. Braden, he does mean your pearls. He's embarrassed because we both realize that it is utterly out of the question to even suggest that you part with them, and——"

Tommy lay back in his chair. He had an infectious laugh and he now injected the full radiance of a pleasing personality in the laughter and good-humored glance he bestowed upon them. "So that's it, eh? Well, well, well! You folks certainly are funny. What in the world should cause you embarrassment about wanting to buy my pearls? Of course you want to own them. I'd be rather hurt if they didn't impress you with a desire for ownership. Why man! man! I'm complimented."

Morse was beaming. "Dog-gone if you're not the finest fellow I ever met. You see, pearls like those are something that can't be bought from a jeweler…and we both love 'em. We're not strong for diamonds and platinum and stuff like that. Pearls—they're classy and rich—and all such as that. And of course from the first minute we saw them we got to thinking how swell it would be if Ella could own them…that is, some just like 'em."

"There aren't any just like them."

"Sure! We know that. Gosh! as if we didn't! Now if you were broke or something I'd have offered to buy them—but money doesn't mean anything to you, and—"

Tommy's face had grown serious. He spoke with a rich tremolo effect. "You really want them that much?"

"Want them! Holy smokes! man, you don't know!"

"Very well. I hope you'll permit me to present them to Mrs. Morse."

For a moment there was silence. Morse and his wife stared aghast at this man who offered as a gift a priceless rope of matched pearls.

"Give 'em——"

"Mr. Braden! I couldn't!"

"Certainly you could, Mrs. Morse. You and your husband have afforded me an extremely delightful vacation. It would be a pleasure to present those pearls to you. After all, their intrinsic worth is not to be measured against friendship."

They were dumbfounded. And at length Edgar Morse started to argue. He was overwhelmed by his friend's generosity, but of course it was out of the question for him to accept such a gift. On the other hand if his friend was willing to part with them at all, he would do both an inestimable favor by permitting him to pay for them—any price which Mr. Braden chose to ask; any price at all.

"I'd rather give them to you, Mr. Morse."

"Can't be done—impossible. Entirely impossible. But if you'd only let me pay you...."

"You positively will not accept them as a gift?"

"Positively."

"I'm sorry. Very sorry. But if you put it that way, I agree to sell them to you. You may have them for just what they cost me—seventy-five thousand dollars."

Morse's voice trembled with emotion. "That's wonderful of you, Mr. Braden—wonderful. And I realize that we shall remain indebted to you beyond words. The trouble you've taken...the love you have for them...."

"Let's don't talk about them any more, Morse. I shall get the pearls from the safe tomorrow and give them to you." He smiled slightly. "And if you should change your mind during the night and be willing to accept them as a gift, I hope you will let me know."

But they did not change their minds. Instead they talked until far into the morning hours of this Genie...this gentleman who, for reasons quite his own, masqueraded under the name of Thomas Matlock Braden.

Nor did Tommy Braden immediately drop off into slumber. He donned dressing gown and slippers and sat by an open window staring out into the night. Tommy was exceedingly well pleased with himself. He had operated adroitly…certainly there was no hint of suspicion in the minds of his victims. There was a profit of seventy thousand dollars in the transaction, no mean addition to his bank account.

The presence of Jim Hanvey in the hotel was less disturbing now. Tommy smiled at the prospect of some day telling Jim of the deal which had been consummated under his very nose…he knew Jim intimately and realized that he would see the humor of the situation. There was something irresistibly funny in the thought that this profit should have been turned within a hundred feet of the one detective in the world for whom Braden held a wholesome respect.

Tommy was up early the next morning. The nearness of his triumph begot a shakiness of nerves which was not unnatural. Matters had moved along like well-oiled machinery from the outset. There had been no single hitch to beget doubt or worriment.

"Hey! Tommy!"

Braden stopped short to gaze into the expressionless countenance of Jim Hanvey. The elephantine detective was smiling vacuously.

"'Lo Jim. Taking a beauty stroll?"

"Uh-huh. Pretty country around here, ain't it?"

"Beautiful."

"Walkin' my way, Tommy?"

Braden's eyes narrowed. He wasn't, but—"Yes," he said and they moved off together; Braden tall and slender and handsome, Hanvey short and thickset and shapeless; a human pudding in a serge sack. It was the detective who spoke first and his tone was mildly reproving.

"Thought you told me you wasn't up to nothing around here, Tommy."

"I'm not." With simulated indignation.

"Then how does it happen that everybody in the hotel thinks you are Jared Mallory?"

Braden threw back his head and gave an excellent imitation of carefree laughter. "That's the funniest thing that's ever happened to me, Jim. You know I don't look unlike Mallory—"

"No-o, you don't. But on the other hand you and him ain't no twins."

"Exactly. But the first or second day I was here somebody started the rumor that I was Mallory and there wasn't any stopping the thing."

"You ain't been trying very hard to, have you?"

"No. Frankly. It amused me to be mistaken for him."

"No—er—reason?"

"Certainly not, Jim. No one has told you that I ever admitted being Mallory, have they?"

"No-o. They haven't—that's right, Tommy."

"Well, then——" virtuously. "What more could you ask? I'm registered as Thomas Matlock Braden and you know that is my true name. To folks who have quizzed me on this Mallory stuff I've insisted that Braden is my name. My baggage is marked with the initials T. M. B. which couldn't possibly be twisted to stand for Jared Mallory. It certainly isn't my fault, Jim, if a lot of fool people choose to believe I'm someone I'm not, is it?"

"No. I reckon it ain't, Tommy. Of course you can't blame me for thinking it funny—when I heard folks saying that you was Mallory. It looked kind of queer."

Tommy dropped an affectionate hand on Jim's shoulder. "You can't help being suspicious of everybody, can you, Jim? Why, dog-gone your time, I've been running straight for so long it's a habit. That's why I didn't even use an alias down here. Goodness knows a fellow can't come any cleaner than to drop a dozen other names and use his own, can he?"

Jim nodded heavily and blinked with interminable slowness. "I feel a heap relieved, Tommy. I sure would hate to see you try to pull something—and I'm glad we had this little talky-talk. Hope you ain't sore at me for thinking maybe there was something queer."

"Not at all, Jim; not in the least. Wouldn't have been natural if you hadn't."

Braden moved away, his last impression of Jim Hanvey was of an abnormally heavy man staring at him through glassy eyes. Against the background of rusty serge he saw a set of fat fingers toying idly with a gleaming gold toothpick.…"Poor Jim. He's a hound once they give him the scent but he is so anxious to believe that every crook is honest.…"

In his room again, Braden telephoned the Morses. Edgar Morse answered and made an appointment for three o'clock that afternoon. The pearls were mentioned: Tommy repeated his offer to present them to his friend. Morse was grateful, but yet found it impossible to accept so valuable a gift. He assured Braden once more that there would be no less an obligation despite the payment of a sizeable sum of money. Tommy was relieved.

The morning dragged endlessly. Braden took his driver, mid-iron and a dozen balls and went to the practice tee where for an hour he slashed out clean, straight shots averaging more than two hundred yards in length. Golfer though he was, he experienced no thrill from the direct, cleaving flight of the balls: he was sufficiently a golfer to know that if his mind were not elsewhere the golfing results would be less satisfactory.

His lunch was tasteless. His eye quested through the huge dining room for a glimpse of Edgar Morse and his wife. They were nowhere to be seen. He knew that they were either lunching in the grill or out driving. The hands of his watch progressed with exasperating slowness. He feared that something might go wrong at the eleventh hour…occasionally he touched the leather case in the inside pocket of his coat.…

But he did not permit his impatience to cause a tactical blunder. It was fully ten minutes past the hour of his appointment when he rapped upon the door of the Morses' suite. Edgar answered in person. The eyes of the little man were a-gleam with eagerness. One glance at Morse and Mrs. Morse convinced Tommy that all was well. They were effusive; couldn't thank him enough for his generous offer of the previous evening and they hoped that he hadn't changed his mind—and that he wouldn't later regret having sold the pearls.

A paen of triumph sang in Braden's heart. He extracted the pearls from his pocket and snapped the case open. Mrs. Morse gasped. He lifted the rope of pearls and personally fastened them about her throat. She was almost tearful with excitement.

Edgar Morse produced a pocket check book. "And now if you will permit me, Mr. Braden—I—er—believe seventy-five thousand is the amount you mentioned."

Tommy nodded. "Yes. That is exactly what they cost me."

Edgar Morse held his pen poised. Rich color flooded his cheeks. He hemmed and hawed for a moment and then—

"I hope you'll pardon me, sir—but how shall I make this check out?"

Tommy frowned. "What's that?"

"How shall I make it out—that is, er—to whose order?"

"I'm afraid I don't understand."

"Well, I mean—you know there's the idea around the hotel— that is, about Jared Mallory, and—"

Tommy's voice was crisp. "Just make the check out to Thomas M. Braden."

Morse nodded and wrote swiftly. He extended to Tommy a check for seventy-five thousand dollars payable to Thomas M. Braden and drawn upon the Loop National Bank of Chicago. "I didn't mean to give any offense, Braden. Of course you understand what I thought—that is, other folks were saying—"

"Quite all right, Morse; that's perfectly all right. I have really been exceedingly annoyed by this silly idea that Braden is not my name." He folded the check and slipped it casually in his pocket. "By the way, are we golfing in the morning? I was hitting them mighty cleanly in practice today."

Alone in his room again Tommy inspected the check. Veteran though he was, his heart was pounding. He had played cunningly for big stakes and had won a well-deserved victory. There remained nothing for him to do but pack up and get away; then to convert Morse's check into cash and disappear. He decided upon a European trip; Paris had not known him for several years and he longed for the sensuous pleasures of the Boulevards.... He ripped open the drawers of his dresser and the doors of his chifforobe:* the task of packing promised to make up in speed what it may have lacked in neatness.

Of course he knew that he must manage his going away carefully. Morse must not know that he was hastening his departure... he'd carry one suitcase and send back for the trunks the next day, or else eliminate them from his scheme of things. The important task was to place a maximum of distance between himself and his victims in a minimum of time. He worked feverishly at his packing, pausing occasionally to glance at the check which had recently been handed him. He was a trifle sorry for the Morses, but, he figured that they could well afford to lose the money... nor would it prove a loss unless by some mischance the pearls

---

* A portmanteau of "chiffonier" and "wardrobe," first marketed by Sears in 1908—a combination of a bureau with drawers and a compartment in which to hang garments.

should be recognized and there seemed little likelihood of that. Certainly the Morses did not move on a social plane where they were likely to meet persons familiar with the Vanduyn pearls. They might, of course, boast that they had purchased the pearls from Jared Mallory and news of this might reach that gentleman which, in all probability, would start something. But, in so far as Tommy could figure, no one was suffering through the transaction. What injury had been inflicted upon the Vanduyns had been done long ago.

It was a pleasing philosophy and Tommy Braden felt quite virtuous. He scarcely heard the light rap on the door. Only when the rapping became insistent did he open.

Jim Hanvey waddled into the room. He wore a suit which he fancied was a tweed. It hung loosely about his ungainly figure. The golden toothpick was very much in evidence. Jim blinked slowly—"Gosh! Tommy, you ain't going away, are you?"

Mr. Braden was flustered. He had a premonition of disaster. If only he could hold Jim off for a brief span of time...."Just running up to Chicago for a few days, Jim. Coming right back. Merely carrying one bag."

"Awful swell diggings, Tommy. How much do they sting you for this soot?"

"Plenty, Jim, plenty. Say, how about trotting up to Chi with me for a day or so?"

"Naw! Can't stir, Son. I've got to stick around here another day or so if it kills me. How long you planning to be gone?"

"Oh! two or three days at the most."

"No special business or nothing like that, is there, Tommy?"

Tommy flushed. He had a disturbing presentiment that there was a menace cloaked beneath Jim's words. "Nothing wrong, if that's what you mean, Jim."

"Good boy. It wouldn't be wise for a guy that's as well fixed as you to take another flyer. Of course I know there's plenty of temptation and all that—but the game ain't worth the electric flashlight,* Son—not by a durn sight."

Braden was ill-at-ease. "Wish you'd come along with me, Jim. I hate to travel alone."

"Sorry, Tommy."

"You'll be here when I get back, won't you?"

Jim shook his head ponderously. "Nope. Don't reckon I will. Got to hike back to N'Yawk and turn in a report. I've been right lucky recently, Son; right lucky."

Braden was relieved. "Landed your man?"

"No-o. Not exactly. I wasn't particularly interested in that. It was an insurance company that sent me down here and all they wanted was the stuff. Interesting case, Tommy; awful interesting."

"I'll wager it was." He crammed two suits of pajamas in the traveling bag.

"You know," Jim's voice was easily conversational, "we'd almost given up hope of ever getting them Vanduyn pearls back."

Tommy Braden sat down very suddenly. "The—the what?"

"The Vanduyn pearls. Remember the case? Mickey Donley pulled it."

Braden leaned forward. "I don't quite make you, Jim. Do you mean to tell me that you've recovered the Vanduyn pearls?"

"Surest thing you know. We knew Mickey couldn't get rid of 'em so we watched the boys he was calling on. Trailed 'em thataway, see? And the poor sucker that bought 'em off Mickey found a goat and sold 'em—and I got 'em that way. I'm right lucky about things like that."

Mr. Thomas Matlock Braden was dazed. He knew that Jim

---

* A joke—a play on the old saying "the game isn't worth the candle," a phrase that meant the game (the entertainment) was so worthless that the cost of burning a candle was more than it merited.

Hanvey was speaking the truth. And yet—He gave ear to the even monotone of the detective.

"And say, Tommy; next time we meet I'll take you on in a golf match. I'm getting my first lesson this afternoon. I run across a swell feller last night. Guy named Morse: Edgar H. Morse. Know him?"

Tommy stared. He moistened dry lips with his tongue. "Go ahead, Jim."

"Well, Eddie Morse is taking me out on the links this afternoon. He says it ain't so hard if a guy is willing to practice for fifteen or twenty years. Think of me swinging a golf club. I'll feel like a sap. But anyway I like this bird Morse. Feel like I and he was buddies even though I never met him until late last night." Jim blinked slowly as he toyed with the gold toothpick which rested against his vest. "He's interested in joolry, too, Tommy. Me and him had a long talk about pearls and things. He knew all about the Vanduyn robbery; remembered the whole thing the minute I reminded him of it. Uh-huh, me and Eddie Morse got along fine together."

Tommy Braden sought to readjust his battered scheme of things. Above everything, he was a game loser. A thin, twisted smile appeared on his lips.

"I'm a fool, Jim."

"How so, Son?"

"For thinking that you are the idiot you appear to be."

"Gosh! I couldn't be that, could I?"

"Hardly. I take it, Jim, that you knew the person to whom Mickey Donley sold the Vanduyn pearls. You located him at this place and followed him here. You discovered that there was considerable mystery about him and also that Edgar Morse was his only intimate acquaintance. You presumed, of course, that Morse was the goat—and so you went straight to that gentleman and warned him against buying any pearls which might be offered. Is that correct?"

Jim grinned in pleased surprise. "Golly! Son, you're clever. How'd you know all that?"

"Just guessing, Jim." He rose heavily. "I'd better travel along, I suppose. I'm mighty glad you're not going to nab the poor fish who tried to pull the deal. You're a white man, Jim Hanvey."

"Shuh! We don't care nothing for that feller. It was just a bit of a business deal with him. Hmm! So you're running up to Chicago, eh?"

"Yes." And then—"Why?"

"Oh! nothin' special. Except that if you should happen to be thinking of cashing a check which somebody might have given you on—well, say the Loop National Bank; I think you'd better change your mind. You see, the feller which gave you that check happens to be a friend of mine and just to avoid embarrassment I suggested to him last night that he should make out the check on a bank where he hasn't got any money. And he kind of seemed to think it was a good idea."

Tommy Braden had the grace to laugh. He clasped Jim Hanvey's hand—

"Thanks for the tip, Jim. You're surely a thoughtful chap. And one of these days we'll try some golf; what do you say?"

"We sure will, Tommy—unless it turns out that I ain't got sense enough to learn the darn game."

THE END

READING GROUP GUIDE

1. Do you like Jim Hanvey as a character?

2. Have you ever been conned? Did you find yourself thinking that you might have been taken in by some of the con men and women in these stories?

3. Do you think that Hanvey cultivated his image as unsophisticated or unpolished?

4. Do you find Cohen's dialogue natural and believable? Do you think that is important to your response to the stories?

5. What appealed to you most about these stories? What bothered you?

6. Does knowing about Cohen's "Florian Slappey" series affect your enjoyment of these stories (see "About the Author," page 229)?

FURTHER READING

JIM HANVEY SHORT STORIES:

"Buyer's Risk," *Detective Magazine*, May 9, 1924.

"Detective Hanvey Pays a Midnight Call," *American Magazine*, May 1926.

"Free and Easy," *Red Book Magazine*, April 1926. Collected in *Detours* (Boston: Little, Brown, 1927).

"The Frame-Up," *American Magazine*, June 1928.

"As the Twig Is Bent," *American Magazine*, November 1928.

"Jim Hanvey Intervenes," *American Magazine*, February 1930.

"The Hollywood Bridal-Night Murder," *Illustrated Detective Magazine*, September 1931.

"A Gentleman for a Night," *American Magazine*, October 1931.

"A Diamond Setting," *American Magazine*, January 1932.

"Cold Cash," *American Magazine*, March 1932.

"High Seize," *American Magazine*, February 1934.

Untitled story, *Scrambled Yeggs*, New York: Appleton-Century, 1934.

"Double Jeopardy," *The Saint*, December 1957.

JIM HANVEY NOVELS:

The May Day Mystery. New York: D. Appleton, 1929.
The Backstage Mystery. New York: D. Appleton, 1930.
Star of Earth. New York: D. Appleton, 1932.

FLORIAN SLAPPEY COLLECTIONS:

Florian Slappey Goes Abroad. Boston: Little, Brown, 1928.
Florian Slappey. New York: Appleton-Century, 1938.

ABOUT THE AUTHOR

Octavus Roy Cohen (1891–1959), little remembered today, was a prolific writer of more than sixty books, hundreds of short stories, five plays, and the scripts for thirty movies. Born in Charleston, South Carolina, he was a cousin of the mystery writer Rodrigues Ottolengui (see *Final Proof* in this series) and, like him, born to Jewish parents. He attended Clemson College (later Clemson University), graduating in 1911, and in 1913 he gave up a brief career as a newspaperman when he was admitted to the bar in South Carolina.* He practiced for only two years and took up writing fiction.

Cohen began writing for magazines, such as *Snappy Stories* and *All-Around Magazine*, and soon became a popular contributor to the *Saturday Evening Post*. His first stories appeared there in 1919, and his work was featured regularly in the *Post* until the 1940s.† While he wrote fiction of all sorts, his first love was apparently

---

* Cohen married the following year and had a son, Octavus Roy Cohen, Jr.

† According to the FictionMags Index, Cohen wrote 164 short stories, three novelettes, and two articles for the *Post*. William G. Contento and Phil Stephensen-Payne, eds., FictionMags Index, updated August 25, 2019, http://www.philsp.com/homeville /fmi/0start.htm#TOC.

the mystery genre. His first series sleuth was David Carroll, created in 1918 and described by mystery critic Jon Breen as "small, energetic, and relatively colorless."* His second creation, Florian Slappey, was one of the earliest Black detectives in crime fiction and made Cohen's reputation. Cohen drew on his upbringing in South Carolina to depict his version of the Southern experience and wrote more than 250 stories set there. Slappey was a comic stereotype of Black Americans, a sometime-detective first operating in "Bumminham" and then in Harlem.† Even when Slappey moved to New York, Cohen continued to write about the "African Negroes of the South," as he put it in a 1925 interview in the *New York Times*: "The cultured Negro is quite right when he says my stories do not portray his feeling. The more subtle Negro who goes to college…is a different individual altogether… I have never pretended to write about the whole Negro race."‡

In the 1920s and 1930s, the Slappey stories appeared nearly weekly in the *Saturday Evening Post*.§ "They belonged to an era now past," wrote the *New York Times* in Cohen's obituary, "the era of the 'blackface' comedian, when the Negro appeared in fiction as a caricature rather than a reality."¶ William L. DeAndrea, in his *Encyclopedia Mysteriosa*, describes Slappey as a "decent,

---

* Jon Breen, "A Note on Octavus Roy Cohen," *Mystery*File 46 (November 2004), http://www.mysteryfile.com/cohen/breen.html. Cohen actually created several other series characters: Eric Peters, a railway porter, and two police officers, Lt. Max Gold and Lt. Marty Walsh. Breen's note also includes a fine bibliography of Cohen's mystery fiction compiled by Steve Lewis, listing thirty-eight books of Cohen's that have some crime fiction content.

† Slappey was clearly a prototype of the stereotypical Black characters of the popular radio show *Amos 'n' Andy*, for which Cohen wrote.

‡ Quoted in Cohen's obituary, "Octavus Roy Cohen Dead at 67; Known for Stories of the South," *New York Times*, January 7, 1959. Cohen died on January 6 in Los Angeles.

§ In 1920, Cohen's play *Come Seven*, starring Earle Foxe as Slappey, ran for seventy-two performances on Broadway.

¶ "Octavus Roy Cohen Dead at 67."

if bumbling detective, and his cases are often well enough con-
structed to stand up, if the reader can overlook the prejudices of
an earlier age."* The Slappey stories were collected in two books
and a wide range of magazines. Kevin Burton Smith, editor of
the influential *Thrilling Detective Web Site*, noted, "The Florian
stories, unfortunately, while arguably even more popular in their
day than those featuring [Jim] Hanvey, are now more famous for
their unflattering and offensive portrayal of African Americans
than their historical significance."[†]

Cohen's career might be only a footnote in the history of crime
fiction, a reminder of the shameful history of depictions of the
Black experience in America by white writers, if it were not for
his third significant creation, the detective Jim Hanvey. Hanvey
too reflects Cohen's Southern upbringing, not in his race or even
his dialect, but in his small-town ordinariness. Hanvey is also
infused with Cohen's sense of comedy. Deliberately uncouth and
without any veneer of sophistication or polish, Hanvey feels real
and likable in a way that Cohen's other characters do not.

"Later in his career, Cohen finally did change with the times,"
observed Bruce F. Murphy, in his *Encyclopedia of Murder and
Mystery*.[‡] In the 1940s and 1950s, Cohen wrote crime fiction in
a more contemporary style, such as *Romance in the First Degree*
(1944), about a war veteran who investigates a murder in the
upper classes of New York, and *The Intruder* (1955), about a
police detective caught up in the murder of a playboy. At the time
of his death in 1959, Cohen's literary career merited a half-page

---

* William L. DeAndrea, ed., *Encyclopedia Mysteriosa: A Comprehensive Guide to the
Art of Detection in Print, Film, Radio, and Television* (New York: Prentice Hall General
Reference, 1994), 68.

† Kevin Burton Smith, "Jim Hanvey," *Thrilling Detective Web Site*, accessed November 2,
2020, http://www.thrillingdetective.com/hanvey.html.

‡ New York: St. Martin's Minotaur, 1999, 104.

obituary in the *New York Times*: "Octavus Roy Cohen Dead at 67; Known for Stories of the South. Wrote Dialect Series about Negroes—Also Author of Novels, Mysteries, Films."

THE DEAD LETTER

An undelivered letter with a cryptic message
holds the key to an unsolved murder

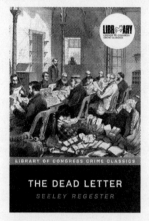

When Henry Moreland is found dead on a lonely New York road after a violent storm, it seems he died of natural causes while walking to the home of his betrothed, Eleanor Argyll. An examination of the corpse reveals, however, that he was killed by a single, powerful stab wound. His wallet was untouched, eliminating robbery as the motive—but who would want to murder the well-liked and respected man?

Richard Redfield, an old family friend who harbors a secret love for Eleanor, vows to bring Henry's killer to justice. Richard soon finds himself out of his element. Together with a legendary detective named Mr. Burton, he embarks on an unsuccessful mission to find the murderer. When suspicion turns to Richard himself, he leaves the family behind and goes to work in the "Dead Letter" office in Washington. Then a mysterious letter from the past turns up, and a new hunt begins...

This twisting tale is the first full-length American detective novel, written under a pseudonym by Metta Victor in the 1860s. It revived American crime fiction, which had languished after Edgar Allan Poe's short stories of the 1840s. Combining elements of Wilkie Collins's *The Moonstone* and the "sensation" novels popular in England, it opened the doors for generations of American crime writers to follow.

For more Library of Congress Crime Classics, visit:
sourcebooks.com